-BOOK ONE-

Filter

THE VON STRASSENBERG SAGA

by

Gwenn Wright

© 2010

For my husband, Matt, whom I love;
     Always have, always will.
For my sons who teach me something new every day.
For my parents, Dan and Brenda,
  whose love and generosity have kept us afloat
        in more ways than one..
For my Father who makes all things new.
                              ~gw

Time present and time past,
Are both perhaps contained in time future,
And time future contained in time past.
~T.S. Eliot
Burnt Norton

Prologue

Vienna, Austria
1866

"That monk is a doddering fool."
He remained bent over the microscope, speaking more to his Petri dish than the imbecile who had come to question him.
"Yes Doctor, but what you're working on..."
"Will ensure Austria's power for eternity."
The man scoffed. He had heard of the scientist's maniacal zeal. His mother had warned him that being intelligent was admirable and, if utilized properly, profitable but there came a point when it was nothing but a detriment. Genius was often followed by madness, she had said. Looking at the frenzied younger man, Dr. Rochenstein fully appreciated the wise woman his mother had been.
"The University," he continued. *"Needs more assurance of the potential success of your work."*
A bitter laugh resonated within the form hunched over the microscope. *"You mean they would like to know when my work will begin repaying their generosity."*

It was not a question.

Everyone knew of the lavish expenses of the professor, but no one was certain of what the money was being spent on. There was gossip and speculation that perhaps he was building some great invention, but this was circulated only among those who did not know his particular field was biology.

Kevin looks at me and I know he isn't seeing the little girl I used to be, all pigtails and gangly limbs. He isn't seeing my mother's daughter or even my mother anymore. As his eyes linger over me, stopping here and there in the most uncomfortable places, I know he isn't really even seeing me as I am. The bloodshot eyes staring out of the alcohol-flushed face are seeing a girl, nearly of age, who owes him a tremendous debt of gratitude.

He has had no shortage of women over the years. He kept them from me at first, being careful of what I saw and, disturbingly, heard. But, as I grew older, and he saw that I was not growing into a refined young lady but that the poverty and desperation of our lives has made me something harder, coarser, he stopped caring. There were one-night stands and those who didn't bother staying more than a few hours; those who got what they wanted, just as he had, who used him just as he used them, and left promptly after. Occasionally one might last a few weeks, but rarely. They didn't want a man with responsibilities.

I.e. me.

A man with responsibilities and no car and an

address that changed at least every fifth month depending on the compassion of our landlord at the time. I was the only unchanging factor in his life and knew he blamed me for his lack of constants. If he hadn't done the right thing, if he hadn't been so good to me and true to the promise he had made to my mother then his life would be different.

But he had been true to my mother's wish.

She had been obviously pregnant when he had taken her in. And when she had asked him to care for me, he had agreed.

They had pulled me from the hemorrhaging, dying body of my mother and turned me over to the care of the man who was not my father. He had taken me home to their tiny apartment above the old hardware store and done what little he knew to take care of me.

It took less than six weeks for him to realize his mistake. Maybe even less than six hours, but he never abandoned me. He clung to me as though I was the last remnant of some great and powerful love.

And that gave me hope that maybe my mother was really something else and not just some girl who got knocked up by a guy whose name she didn't even know. She was something special, someone worthy of a man's loyalty and devotion.

Saint Louis, Missouri 1877

"Do not be so upset Katherine. It's just a silly little dinner party. There will be other chances to meet the young man."

"I am more interested in meeting the Count, mother."

"No doubt." With graceful, nimble fingers Mrs. Demure tied the lace at her daughter's throat.

"Oh but mother, you have heard the rumors and you must let me at least have a peek."

"Indeed I shall not!" Banished or not, the Count was not a man whom Mrs. Demure wanted to fall out of favor with, particularly in regard to her two daughters. The man was worth more money than the Queen of England it was said and was building the finest home this side of the Mississippi. A home of such proportions and grandeur meant only one thing: the Count intended to stay. This would not bring such a stirring of hope to all the mothers in town if not for the most fortunate fact that Count von Strassenberg had a son. He was reportedly a boy of about eighteen and had no siblings. The Demure girls stood a *fairer chance than any in town of securing the affections of the boy.*

But not tonight.

At least not for Katherine, the younger of the two. Katherine was considered a great beauty, greater even than her sister, but she was born tired and frail. Most of her time was passed with reading. She was therefore fortunate in having an ambitious lawyer for a father, a man who himself was widely read and boasted wherever he went of the great personal library he possessed.

"When this spell passes Katherine, your father will introduce you, if we do indeed not find the Count to be altogether evil," she whispered with mock foreboding, "but for now, you must rest and wait."

With that, Henrietta flitted into the room. At eighteen she was just a year older than Katherine, but possessed the beauty and poise of a much older girl, a woman rather than a silly flighty girl. Katherine hated her most of the time.

"I hear the father is a bit of a dark lord," Henrietta giggled. "Oh well," she said dipping down to check her reflection in the vanity's glass. "I suppose the boy and I can establish ourselves in Europe and leave daddy back here in his dark, brooding castle." She dotted her nose with powder and adjusted her bosom.

Mrs. Demure gasped, but only slightly. Henrietta had been forward and proud since she had realized there was a difference between boys and girls. This had given Mrs. Demure sufficient time to grow accustomed to her oldest daughter's wanton behavior.

Katherine swung her legs over the side of the bed. "O mother, it isn't fair that she gets to go down. She will completely humiliate you and father! Look at her! She

---

12

looks like a tart!"

"Katherine!"

"O mother, you know it's true. I may be broken and sickly but at least I have some dignity." Henrietta leaned over her sister, her barely concealed cleavage poignantly displayed. "Dignity is not what counts or their sons are after." With a swish and a wave of obnoxious perfume, Henrietta left the room. "I am sorry Katherine, but unfortunately," and here Mrs. Demure sighed, knowing the unfairness and stupidity of it all, "Your sister is right. You know it pains me to say it is so." Katherine slumped back. Mrs. Demure kissed her daughter's brow. "I will tell you all about it in the morning. Now get some rest." With a more graceful swish of her own skirts Mrs. Demure was gone, leaving Katherine to plan her escape. She would not be waiting for this pain to pass. She would meet the Count tonight.

Three

My life is hard. No one would rob me of that. The clothes I am wearing came out of a knotted up black plastic trash bag from a resale shop downtown. And not the downtown where shiny cars wink at you in the sunlight. If a car winks at you in this area it's being driven by a person you would be best to avoid.

My side of downtown is crumbling and skirted by chain link fences.

Kevin's out of work again. Staying sober for eight hours out of the day was too much for him.

It always is.

So I work here, at Dobson's Market, fifteen hours a week during the school year. That's my Friday, Saturday, Sunday job.

Since Dobson doesn't want to get in trouble for overworking a minor we worked it out with his younger brother that I would work the rest of the week at the family restaurant. Fifteen hours here. Fifteen hours there. No benefits anywhere and crap pay everywhere.

But for now, it's holding us. We've been in the same place for three months now. I've opened my own bank account, that Kevin knows nothing about, and I'm paying the bills as they roll in.

And we're finally making it.

Eventually, though, he'll come out of his stupor and

realize things are getting comfortable and he'll want to know where the money is.

But maybe by then I'll be gone.

four

"Go on now, Miss." Josephine, the Demure's only maid, tried to shuffle Katherine from her hiding place behind a tapestry that hung just outside the dining room. "Go on now, they're almost done with their soup. And your father and the Count are just talking business. Don't wear yourself out standing here spying for such boredom as that." Katherine peeked at her from behind the tapestry. "But Josephine, the son is lame." Josephine was obviously a little taken aback by the excitement Katherine found in this. "Not lame so much, Miss, more like he's tormented. Poor boy."

"Tormented by the sun! How lovely!"

"I never did understand you Miss Katherine. But if the boy is anywhere near as handsome as his father, the shock may nearly kill your sister."

Katherine stifled a giggle, "Indeed."

Josephine shook her head and started back toward the kitchen. "You are too much in those books, Miss Katherine." She shuffled only three feet away before jumping, rattling the china, at the sound of the knocker. A vase nearly fell to the floor as Josephine quickly turned and struggled to unload her tray onto a hall table. "O

Miss Katherine," she hissed. "He will certainly see you. Silly girl!" Chairs were being pushed back from the table in the adjoining room.

Josephine, already at the door, righted her curls and glanced furtively back to make sure Katherine was hidden. Satisfied, she flung the door open.

The back of Josephine's neck flushed crimson at the sight of their visitor. Katherine was barely able to suppress the giggle. "Viktor, son of Count von Strassenberg of Austria," announced Josephine, rather a bit too grandly. The young man stepped inside. Katherine cursed silently. Josephine had moved, blocking her view, all she could see of the stranger was perfectly coiffed, raven-black hair and a pale forehead. Josephine, choking on her words, dipped in a curtsey and stepped aside. Katherine ducked behind the tapestry. While she wanted to see, she most certainly did not want to be seen. She heard long strides across the wooden floor. Just in front of the dining room door, they stopped. A cacophony of overdone greetings rose as the dinner party met the new arrival. Katherine dared a peek.

"Have you finished it yet?"

Charlene slams her tray down beside me, not because she's mad but because Charlene overdoes everything. It's not like it's out of a need to be dramatic, she just came naturally that way. Passionate. Exuberant. Uncontrolled and unrefined. That's Charlene. And she's almost as poor as me and Kevin, almost. Her dad is sober but disabled. Some kind of freak accident when he was working as a mechanic at the only reputable car dealership this side of town.

I finish chewing the rubbery substance the cafeteria ladies refer to as "pizza." I thought maybe I was mistaken as to its classification because the stuff at the restaurant isn't so...chewy, but the menu says this is pizza. "Did I finish what?"

Charlene squeezes her plump bottom between mine and the freshman next to me, not asking her to move.

"Duh, the new *Evening Shade*."

When we were younger Charlene and I were considered complete morons and geeks because we wore third -hand clothes and spent all of our free time reading. It's this thing literate people do, but apparently it wasn't cool. And then in ninth grade this new series came out and it's all the rage and the popular girls think it's wicked cool. They've made movies out of the series and there are t-shirts and posters and every other marketable thing imaginable. Candies even. So now reading is acceptable. Charlene and I consider ourselves to be the only true fans of *Evening Shade* because we were reading them before the marketing blitz.

The rich girls can buy their own copies. For everyone else it's a tooth-and-claw fight at the library over their one copy of each book in the series. Mrs. Henderson, the librarian, loves me. Before I started working and before earning money became a fascination of mine, we became well acquainted. The library was quieter and cozier than my ever-changing address. And, as it turned out, Mrs. Henderson is a huge fan of teenage paranormal romances. We were thick as thieves. And that's how Charlene, Mrs. Henderson and I became friends.

Some people have clubhouses or the mall to run away to. Charlene and I had Mrs. Henderson and the library.

"No, I've been working on that stupid paper for Roberts."

"That is a stupid paper." Charlene pops open her chocolate milk and takes an enthusiast gulp, finishing half of the inadequate box. "Well hurry up with it will you? Or it'll be overdue and you can't renew it because Posey Jenkins has reserved it and so has Ophelia What's-Her-Face."

I crunch my last bit of salad from my free-or-reduced lunch. "I'll try to finish it tonight on break."

"What time do you get off? Can you drop it off on the way home?"

Would I risk my life and my purity for Charlene's obsessive reading habits? Yes. For her and no one else. Because I know she would walk the dark back streets of Nashville for me. And, in the six years of our friendship, no one has ever bothered us before. Many, many times I have slinked out my bedroom window when one of Kevin's more vocal guests had joined us and I slipped

19

through the shadows of side streets, to make my way to the quietness of Charlene's mundane home.

So tonight wouldn't be any different.

He stood there, towering over Josephine, as though waiting. Why they had paused in the doorway, Katherine did not know, but then just before they continued into the dining room, Viktor's eyes drifted toward the floor, to where the tapestry brushed the wood, and he smiled. As though he could see through the heavy fabric, his eyes roamed toward hers and locked. With a silent, conspiratorial laugh he allowed Mr. Demure to lead him into the dining room.

Katherine welcomed the noise of the continued greetings. It would cover her footsteps as she fled. She was halfway up the staircase, clutching the rail and her skirts, imploring her weakened limbs to carry her faster, when she heard her mother's gasp.

"Katherine!"

She was too smart and too shocked at being caught in her nightdress to quit her ascent. Clumsily, feebly she pulled herself more desperately up the seemingly endless steps.

"My apologies," she heard her mother saying. "She was to be resting in bed. Just a curious child," Mrs. Demure prattled on nervously.

The stairs were simply too high, too finely polished and her skirts treacherously long for legs that could no longer bear to straighten. Her foot caught and wet palms gave way and everything came down, plundering her mother's dreams of a successful marriage for one of her girls. Katherine saw Henrietta's face, which was not at all shocked by her sister's tumbling form, merely infuriated by it, as she rolled heel over head. Mrs. Demure and Josephine screamed. Three men were rushing the steps. Their black jacketed arms looking like the flapping wings of crows as she caught glimpse after tumbling glimpse of them. Why were there so many stairs? She continued down, no longer scrabbling to grab a baluster but surrendering to the pull of gravity and her own clumsiness, knowing at some point she would reach the bottom. She closed her eyes as the flapping birds closed in on her.

Her mother and Josephine had stopped screaming.

The men were all asking questions of her. It was all spinning and thundering, the blood rushing through her brain in a torrent. She looked down at her mother, white and leaning on Josephine, and at Henrietta's annoyance.

She stopped tumbling before reaching the floor. Her father was over her, his face floating above her. "Katherine. Katherine can you hear me?"

What was he talking about?

"Katherine are you all right?" *Mr. Demure awkwardly reached forward to brush the hair from her eyes.*

"Viktor carefully lift her and carry her to her room," *the stranger's voice said. Viktor? She knew no Viktor. Her father was edging away, shifting her weight into the arms of an unseen force. He was pointing now in the* direction of her room and she was rising in strong arms. Uncertain if it would faithfully respond, Katherine urged her trembling hand to brush the last strands of chestnut hair from her eyes. And froze.

They were his strong arms. It was his careful grace. It was his tender, firm grasp that carried her toward her room. She dared not look up, beyond his square jaw or the tip of his sharp nose. She did not want to see what his eyes might be saying about this silly little girl who had ruined a perfectly fine dinner party to hide behind a curtain. There was pain, somewhere in her body, but the torment in her mind was distracting her from realizing it. Her mother must be mortified.

But Henrietta...Henrietta would be what? Jealous most likely. This was the perfect sort of scenario she was always plotting against Caleb McDonelly, the handsomest boy in town. And Katherine had pulled it off effortlessly in front of the most captivating and mysterious young man she had ever beheld.

Mr. Demure hurried forward, ushering them into Katherine and Henrietta's room. "Here, son, place her here."

It was unavoidable as he lowered her to the soft mattress. She could not help but to look up into his icy eyes, like the faintest of blue struggling through the clouds before a snow. Were they gray or blue? She gave herself no time for observation, jerking her eyes away from his before they could mock her and her childishness.

"Doctor, would you please?" Mr. Demure stepped aside, but Katherine did not see the Count/Doctor approach. She stared intensely at a sketch pinned to her wall. There was shuffling and cold hands and prodding fingers. Katherine endured the doctor's silent inquiries *without protesting, waiting for the lean shadow at the end of her bed to vanish.*

Why would he not just leave?

The man with the accent stepped away. "She is fortunate. There appear to be no injuries." Would her pride count? Her mother's shattered hopes?

Mr. Demure leaned in and kissed his daughter's forehead and gently spread a blanket across her. "I have always warned her that her curiosity would be the death of her. That or her clumsiness."

She heard the men laughing as they drifted out of the room.

The shadow stayed.

She wished he would go. The burning tears ached to be set free. She couldn't restrain them much longer. With a trembling, unwilling hand she rubbed her throbbing forehead and exhaled deeply.

For a moment she believed he had left, but as she shifted away from the wall she sensed him there beside the bed. He was very close.

Wretched curiosity!

But she would fight it and not look.

"Katherine," he whispered, his breath rolling in a warm wave across her cheek. A traitor tear spilled out, the humiliation was too much to contain. Gently, a finger dabbed the wetness from her skin. He said it again, softly, as though it pleased him just to say it, "Katherine."

"Viktor!" the accented voice bellowed from below. And then the shadow was gone.

Darkness overwhelmed her then and carried her away to a land of crows and mocking strangers.

Seven

"You want a ride home Rocky?"

"No thanks, Mr. Dobson," I tell him, not because I wouldn't really like to not walk home through the constant drizzle and darkened streets, but because the man weirds me out a bit. Being alone in a car with him...that just isn't going to happen. Not that I think he'd ever lay a hand on me, but just the same, I don't like the way his eyes slowly roll over me. I don't think he realizes it's so ridiculously obvious to everyone around, but it is. Everyone knows the boss is always checking me out and it's embarrassing.

I don't get it.

My body isn't fantastic. But, living in an area where men aren't raised to be gentlemen, I have learned that it doesn't take much to entice a man. I've never understood the other girls at school who try so hard. They plump their limps and push their cleavage up to their chins, but none of that's really necessary. The men are going to look anyway.

Kevin has always said I'm a natural beauty like my mom and that I would have to try real hard to be ugly. I used to think he was crazy, just muttering things to make an awkward little poor girl feel better about her unfair growth spurts (going up, not out). Now, though, as more eyes begin to follow me, I think maybe Kevin was actually right about something.

And I don't like it.

I try to pull myself into a hunched ball and keep my hair in my face so they can't see me. When they look, they're looking for something I'm not willing to give and I want them to know that.

As I walk down the street now, and I mean straight down the middle, I sweep both sides with paranoid eyes. It isn't the worst neighborhood, but it isn't exactly the kind of place you want to let your guard down. The houses and businesses here are packed tightly together, a mishmash of shapes and angles and sizes; like a swollen shantytown. Most of the houses are rented out, the original owners having moved on to brighter pastures on the newer side of town. Kevin and I have been living in a house that we suppose was actually painted white but looks more gray now, the owners never considering it worth their trouble to paint a house that would only be occupied for a few months at a time.

But we've had it for three months and it's starting to feel like home. It's starting to feel dangerous, like something I would miss if we had to move. It's a feeling I don't welcome as I probably should, because I know it won't last. Kevin won't let it.

All these thoughts swirl through my head, crowding out any normal teenager thoughts. There are no boys floating around, no dreams of college or a better life, just the plan to make it through the next day. And to make it without going insane.

Headlights appear over the hill and I move over to the cracked and uneven sidewalk. I try to make myself look confident and strong and unbothered by their approach without looking like a hooker, but boys this side of town aren't geniuses at reading signals. They wouldn't read the instructions anyway. They would make up their own rules to the game.

It's a commercial/residential area, speed limit 25, but whoever this is drives like it's a traffic accident at rush hour.

A lot of people think it's the speeders that are the troublemakers, the bad boys. I say it's the guy going ten in a thirty. He's taking his time to look for trouble, for a deal or a girl.

This is a bad boy car and it's slowing down for me.

It feels like my blood is pulled from my head and feet and hands and takes up residence in my gut, leaving my nerves exposed and raw and my skin tingling with exposure to them. I pluck my baggy shirt out, away from my slender form and insist that my shoulders ignore their burning desire to curl in. I have to look strong. Look strong and they won't think they can have you so easily.

"Won't you tell it again?"

Katherine covered her head with the pillow, trying to block out her sister's endless requests. "No Henrietta, I will not."

"But you tell it so splendidly."

Henrietta jumped back as her sister sprang out from behind the defensive wall of pillows. "Of course I do, Henrietta! I was the one falling down the blasted staircase."

Mixed in with Henrietta's pride was a sudden hint of victory. "Tell me again Katherine or I will tell mother you swore."

"I did not swear," she growled. "And even if I had I would just tell mother it was something I had heard my big sister say and I had no idea it was such horrible slang. Now leave me alone." Grabbing her pillow, Katherine flopped back over, intent on ignoring any further requests.

"Katherine..."

"Shut up, Henrietta!"

This time she was on her feet, wobbling furiously in front of her shocked sister. "Do you not understand, you selfish twit? It was humiliating! I fell down the stairs, unintentionally!" She sank into the bed. "It does not matter anyway. I do not find him favorable. He is...odd and so...tall."

"Taller than any man I have ever seen and handsome and rich, you idiot. What does it matter if he's odd?"

It was not a battle to be won. "Just leave me be, Henrietta. If you want him, throw yourself down a staircase, he can rescue you and you can be happily wed to the son of the banished, dark lord."

Just then a loud banging resounded through the home. Henrietta glanced at the darkening sky outside her window. "Who on earth?"

"Oh," Katherine moaned, retreating beneath her pillow. "It is most likely your great love come in the mysterious twilight hour. Go to him, for he waits for you."

"You really are insufferable Katherine." But Henrietta was already up, checking her reflection and readjusting her unprepared bosom.

"Indeed I am."

She heard a frenzy of slippered steps and swooshing skirts and then the barely restrained flight down the staircase. Voices. Josephine and Henrietta and one too low to make out.

"Oh hang it all," Katherine groaned, throwing the pillow off again and going to the glass to check her own reflection. Her father was most likely right. One day her curiosity would be the death of her.

Henrietta was at the door, edging Josephine out of her way.

"I was just telling Master Viktor here that Mr. Demure is still at the office and we are not expecting him back until *late this evening and that Mrs. Demure is not yet returned from calling on the Marshes, Miss."*

Henrietta tried to wave the plump little maid away. "It's all right, Josephine. I am more than happy to receive Mister von Strassenberg."

Bright red splotches bloomed across Josephine's modest cheeks. "Begging your pardon, miss," she interjected, stepping between the ravenous Henrietta and her prey. "It would be improper. Mrs. Demure would not forgive me."

Henrietta never turned from Viktor, who stood patiently in the doorway, looking amused. "Oh hang your proprieties and modesties Josephine. After the show Katherine put on the other night, ruining everything," she smiled pointedly at him. "Mister von Strassenberg deserves a chance to see that his neighbors are not crazed lunatics. At least, not all of them. Pray Mister von Strassenberg, what is it that brings you?"

Uncertain but unwilling to tangle with Henrietta, Josephine scuttled away.

Viktor surveyed the flushed young woman before him, who imagined herself to be stunning in all her presumptuous glory. He seemed to be allowing a time of suspense in which to grow her aching desires. Her breath caught, swelling her already swollen bosom. Katherine cringed, knowing this was a practiced ploy, which her sister believed men found seductive. Katherine mostly thought it was ridiculous.

Without a word, Viktor's stormy eyes skewed away from Henrietta and, sensing that her chances of being caught were rising dramatically, Katherine backed into the shadows.

"I came to inquire," he began slowly and Henrietta's

breath caught again, heaving her ridiculous bosom. "After your sister, Miss Katherine."

Without the intent, or even any practice, Katherine's own breath caught in a sharp little gasp. The horrid man! Did he mean to prolong her humiliation! Henrietta's head cocked slowly in the direction of the betraying gasp, her frame rigid with instant jealousy. Viktor took this all in and, upon translating it, his eyes once again found Katherine in the shadows.

Wrapping her robes closely around her, she attempted to tuck herself away. Henrietta openly followed Viktor's gaze to the alcove just beyond the staircase. There was no hiding.

Viktor boldly stepped around Henrietta, his eyes locked on Katherine's shadowy hiding place. He addressed the darkness. "Miss Katherine, my father asked that I call on you, to inquire as to your well being."

A sigh of relief from Henrietta, "Your father asked you."

Viktor ignored her. "Miss Katherine?" He waited for her to step forward. She accepted that she would have to move out of hiding at some point or he would never leave. Pretentious, stubborn thing that he was.

Her heart began a chaotic rhythm within her chest and she cursed him silently for it. She didn't want him; this arrogant, unconventional young man who couldn't see past his own needs to save her further embarrassment. And here she was again in her robes, her hair undone and flowing down her back in a tumult of unkempt waves. She would have to humiliate herself and her mother again just to appease this spoiled young man.

But why was her heart fluttering and why were her hands beginning to tremble?

31

Henrietta's face was dark with envy but she would not give up so easily. As Viktor stepped in front of her she began adjusting her cleavage and pinching her cheeks and biting her lips.

Katherine stepped from the shadows. As they rolled off her, revealing her pale skin and chestnut hair, Viktor moved closer to the staircase. Katherine approached the balustrade, saving him from having to come any farther.

"Are you well?" he asked.

"Yes sir, very well, thank you. And thank your father for his kindness." His face did not alter. He merely stood there, staring at her, making her wretchedly uncomfortable. Henrietta moved forward, encroaching upon the awkwardness of the moment. "There, you see," she said, taking his side. "She is perfectly well, as lame and sickly as ever. No change." She smiled as though this little joke at her sister's expense would please him and he would find her very clever.

He continued to study Katherine's down-turned face. Slowly his eyes shifted to Henrietta. "She does not look sickly to me." Katherine dared to glance up, just enough to witness Henrietta's shock and immediate smoothing-over. Perhaps this infuriating young man did have some better qualities. Anyone who could torment Henrietta could not be so horribly vile.

"O she has always been sickly. Tired and fragile."

"I have suffered greatly most of my life as well."

Henrietta laughed lightly at this trifling fact. "But you do not look it as she does. Indeed sir, you look positively robust."

"The move has been favorable for me. I find myself," he inadvertently moved closer to the steps. "Strengthened in this strange, new land."

Henrietta tinkled with laughter again but Katherine saw the searching thoughts and knew her sister had come up with no smart reply. Viktor placed a foot on the first step.

"My father sent a gift for you."

Henrietta's jaw gaped.

"And, if you agree, I would say it would be safer for me to bring it to you," he laughed softly. "Than it would be for you to come down and retrieve it." Henrietta was quickly in front of him, blocking his path. "I will take it to her. It is improper, you know, she is in her robes." Annoyance flicked across Viktor's fine features. "Perhaps we should hang your *proprieties and modesties as well?"*

Fury.

Henrietta was furious, her bosom and her cheeks grew scarlet with ugly blotches of embarrassment and rage. "I see," she said in a low growl and then she was gone, off to scream at Josephine for some imagined incompetence.

Katherine clutched the balustrade as she watched her sister fly from the room. She was perfectly alone with him. Again. Her heart thudded wildly. The trembling in her hands increased and she felt that she would fall in a mortified lump right there at the top of the stairs.

Don't, she told herself, or he will have to save you again and you shall never recover from the humiliation.

She had been too distracted by her own flutterings to notice that he was approaching. "Sir," she whispered, eyes locked on her whitening knuckles. "It really is not necessary."

And then he was beside her. He was surprisingly quick and graceful and she loathed him for it. It made it harder to runaway. She had always imagined moments like these, placing herself in the same situations so many of the heroines in her novels found themselves in. But in life it was different, more humiliating. Why was he so calm and suave and she was such a mess?

He was watching her but she would not turn to him.

Viktor reached into his jacket pocket and withdrew a small box. "My father feels somewhat responsible for what happened."

"That is ridiculous," Katherine retorted, quickly biting her lip. "It could not be further from the truth, is what I mean."

"Yes well, my father has not had a reason to buy a gift for a young lady for quite some time. He is glad for the opportunity, as imaginary as it may be." He held the box out, waiting patiently for her to turn and receive it.

It seemed centuries before she could reach out and take the box, afraid she would look up and catch his eye, or, worse, brush his hand as she accepted the gift.

"Please," he whispered. "I shall be disowned if you do not take it and gush profusely with surprise and gratitude."

She had always imagined herself with some dark, brooding stranger and yet, now that he was in front of her she found that his lack of normalcy affronted her. He was not like any boy she had ever met. There was something piercing and searching in his gaze, almost intrusive. It unnerved her. She felt completely out of control near him and that, in her mind, was unforgivable.

As it seemed to be the safest way to exchange the box, Katherine held her hand out, palm flat, and waited.

He paused.

Why was he always pausing? Why could this man not be rushed? She would not look up but she could sense his amusement, the way he held the box between them. He knew this waiting infuriated her and he was purposefully prolonging it. O she despised him! Standing there in her robes and her undone hair and he couldn't be bothered to quit the game and hurry a bit.

And then it occurred to her that he was waiting and not just to increase her frustration. He was waiting for her to meet his eyes.

Just do it, she prodded herself, and then this nonsense, sheer and utter nonsense, will be done with.

With a long, slow breath Katherine steadied herself and lifted her gaze, and the anger swelled within her. "O you insufferable man!" She hissed, snatching the box. "Why does this amuse you? This is not at all amusing!"

With barely checked frustration she glared into his laughing eyes. This was all a game to him and he was playing with her, playing with the invalid. Was he that heartless? Did he like to tug the heartstrings of unfortunate girls just to watch their torment?

"Open it," he ordered, laughter in his voice.

She growled back, her fingers prying at the lid of the small velvet box, "As you wish. Gladly."

But she could not manage to open the box. Over and over she turned it, but could find no solution. He waited with insufferable patience through what seemed many minutes until at last he reached his long fingers out to assist her. The coolness of his skin brushed against her fingertips and she recoiled at the warmth that spread through her hand. It seemed the heat from his cool touch spread rapidly to her heart, throwing the rhythm into a frenzy once more. "There is a small lock," he was saying, nimbly pushing a tiny latch she had not seen. The lid sprang back. "There." He lifted her small hand in his own and she thought her knees would give way. It was maddening. He seemed to know the effect he was having on her, an effect she did not welcome and could not control, sensible as she imagined herself to be. With a withering glance at his smiling face she dropped her eyes down to the box.

"Oh!" she gasped. "Well that is...I cannot accept this."

"That's not exactly the reaction I believe my father was looking for."

"Indeed," she whispered, lifting the ring from the velvet cushion.

"He hoped that it would fit."

She was trembling inside, the beauty of the gift overwhelming her. The ring, a wide yet tiny band of gold was overlaid with sparkling diamonds and intricate scrollwork. In the center was a large pale blue diamond.

"I have only read of such beautiful things," she humbly whispered. "I cannot accept it."

"Ah," he said, taking the ring from her, skin brushing skin. "But you must. May I?" Before she could offer any protest, he was holding her hand and sliding the ring on to her finger. He sighed, "A perfect fit."

She gathered herself, "I cannot accept this. It's..."

"Impossible for you to refuse," he finished for her. "Take comfort, Miss Katherine, it cost him no expense. It is from his personal collection. I believe it belonged to my great-grandmother or great-aunt or someone such as that."

Katherine began tugging at the ring, "Well then I certainly cannot accept it. I cannot possibly take a family heirloom over such a trifling matter for which your father was not even at fault." The ring was sliding over her *knuckle when he grasped her hand firmly. "Then accept it for my sake, Miss Katherine." He slid the ring back down. "I chose it for you. It seems to suit you."*

"To suit me?" She withdrew, the anger rising again. "How would you know what suits me? You are all presumption. You do not know me and cannot guess my character. I am not some sickly, frail thing that falls down the stairs whenever rich, handsome men come to call."

"Although it would seem so," he smiled.

Frustrated and embarrassed, Katherine stomped her slippered foot. "Oh you are insufferable beyond all men! Have you no sympathy? I believe you have mistaken me sir, for some soft little creature in need of your saving! I am not in need of a tormented man's gallantry! And as for this gift..."

He stepped forward, interrupting her crescendo. "You will keep it."

Surprising herself, Katherine came toward him, seething, "Oh indeed I will. If only to frustrate my ridiculous sister."

At this he grinned but she could find no humor. "You can show yourself out, I assume?" Before he could confirm, Katherine spun on her heel and hurried back to her room, collapsing onto her bed. Her heart was racing. She could not begin to understand herself or her violent reactions toward this young man.

Eddie's Bar is two blocks away. Short enough blocks, I hope. The car slows as it gets closer to me and I'm trying to figure out if I should bolt now or wait until they proposition me. Maybe they're just trying to scare me. I don't want to give them too much satisfaction by running now if all they really want is a chance to laugh at a silly little girl. The engine purrs contentedly beneath its shiny, perfect hood. Dealers. Or Rich-boy Moneybags looking for a good time.

I keep walking, faster now, and despite my good intentions, my shoulders hunch defensively.

Please just be idiots. Stupid, harmless idiots.

I'm ready to cross the side street. Eddie's is so close and most of them know me there. They may be friends of Kevin's but it's gotta be fractionally safer with them than with this shiny out-of-place car.

The darkened window slowly rolls down. I don't want to look. Don't give them the time of day. Just cross to the next block and keep going. Get to Eddie's. Kevin might even be there. He's not much of a social drinker, but he might be, tonight.

My foot hovers over the gutter. It's time to run.

"Miss!"

I nearly trip over the affluence and authority in the

voice. "Miss we're looking for Dobson's Market, do you know where it is?" The question has stopped the frantic pacing of my mind, but my foot is still ready to take flight. I stand like a stork on the corner of Fifth and Washington. "I said, `We're looking for Dobson's Market, do you know where it is?'"

"Maybe she's strung out," the suited young man in the driver's seat offers.

"Maybe she can hear you," I snap. His stupidity makes me angry. This is not what someone who is strung out looks like. He's probably some kind of high-power, daddy's coattails exec who never had to slug it out it in the slums before scoring his shiny, winking car. "And maybe she was taught not to talk to strangers. In particular, strangers who are crawlin' around in fancy cars where they don't belong."

The *Matrix* twins exchange glances, seeming somewhat amused and altogether ready to be done with their assignment.

"Dobson's is closed anyway. But so you know," my foot lands in the gutter. "It's three blocks down, on your right." I start across the narrow street. They creep alongside me.

"How old are you miss?"

Keep walking, don't look. "Not old enough."

He ignores me. "We're looking for someone."

"I thought you were looking for Dobson's." Back on the sidewalk and Eddie's isn't far. "We're looking for some-one who works at Dobson's."

Charlene.

She just started there last week.

What kind of crazy mess has that girl gotten herself into this time?

I stop and look at them. Maybe I can throw them off long enough to get Charlene a warning, give her time to run. "Who?"

"A girl, about your age."

"Most of the cashiers are my age. Name?"

The passenger seems to be weighing something mentally. He looks at me in a scientific sort of way that is almost more unnerving than the way I am used to being looked at by men and consults the contents of a manila folder. After a long moment of flipping and scanning pages, he closes the folder and eyes me again. The less reasonable side of me registers that he is easy on the eyes, but I ignore it.

"Maria Josepha Raquel Demure von Strassenberg."

The blood rushing into my ears sounds more like silence than even the quietest silence I have ever heard. It's the sound of my thoughts being sucked into a black hole, the sound of a numbed and shocked mind.

He looks at the folder again, "Evans. This girl would have been given the last name of Evans."

Kevin Evans.

His parents had been as cruel as my mother. My dying mother had actually asked two things of Kevin Evans as she slipped away. The first and most obvious was that he care for me and keep me out of foster homes and orphanages. Which may actually have been better, but that's neither here nor there. The second, which was more of a demand, and one I wish he had waffled on, was my name. "Name her after me," she had said. And just as he had been the only person alive who had known her full name, so he was the only person ever privileged with knowing my name. And that's just because he gave it to me, tacking his on at the end for the sake of practicality. Maria Josepha Raquel Demure von Strassenberg Evans.

But everyone calls me Rocky.

Rocky Evans.

Except Mrs. Cornwallis of eleventh grade English. She calls me Raquel.

I want to deny it but my thoughts haven't had time to reorder themselves for the purpose of lying and it's too late anyway. I think they heard the blood whisking my brain cells into protective hiding.

Ten

His fist came crashing down on the desk with such force that pens jumped from their stillness, spilling their ink and blotching his research notes. "Get it back!"

Viktor leaned against the frame of the massive door, unwilling to cross the threshold into his father's study. "Father you can hardly expect me to ask for her to return it. It was a gift."

Klaus von Strassenberg's face shifted violently through each possible shade of red and purple and every combination in between. "It was not yours to give! Do you understand the importance of that ring?"

"It is so important that it has remained locked in its little box for what? A century now?"

"Stupid boy!"

"I cannot possibly take it back Father. I imagine Mr. and Mrs. Demure would take it as a bit of an insult and it is doubtful that such unfavorable opinions would be helpful to your... endeavors?"

The old man settled back in his chair. "You must have inherited your impertinence and your stupidity from your mother." He watched as the brief anger played across his son's face. "She was not the most intelligent woman, your mother."

"So you have told me. All that speaks to is your own shallow desires; that you would marry a woman for her beauty or her money and not her companionship, much less love."

His father snorted.

"Unintelligent, but tall," Viktor motioned toward his own towering form. "Because that certainly did not come from you, I believe you are not even as tall as the average man, are you father? That must be so humiliating, to be so great in mind and yet so small in stature."

The Count waved him off, popping a peppermint into his wrinkled mouth. "My height matters not, son. My mind more than makes up for what my physical form lacks."

"Does it?" Viktor laughed. "And that is why the women flock to you?"

Unruffled, the Count took up his pen. "I have no need of feeble-minded companions. And the woman that can match her brilliance to mine is rare, if nonexistent."

"Perhaps what you lack in stature you make up for with arrogance? Then what of my mother? If she was so unintelligent, why did you bother?"

The Count mulled this over. "Necessity."

"Because you needed an heir? What a disappointment I must be, Father. Your only son and with the intelligence of a rock."

"Do not flatter yourself son. A rock would be an improvement. Leave me now and go get that ring or your inheritance goes with it." The Count hunched back over his notes. Viktor turned his back on the shelves and shadows of his father's study and did not stop as the *gravely voice took up its warning, "And you cannot get the ring back by marrying the girl. I will not give you my blessing." Viktor drew the heavy door closed and heard it click. His father bellowed, "I will not allow you to breed with an invalid after all we have done for you!"*

The chill of the corridor seemed more pronounced after the stuffy warmth of the study. Viktor buried his hands beneath his arms, pausing in the forced darkness of the house. Outside the sun shone in all its glory, beating a fierce heat down upon the fortress that was his home, but there was none of its warmth here in the shadows.

Eleven

"Will you come with us?"

"Would you stop acting like a moron?" The *Matrix* twin, I can tell, is not used to be spoken to like the jerk he is. On his side of town his money buys respect. On these streets, it only buys trouble. The driver, in his fine suit, leans across his color-changing friend. "Miss Evans, we're only trying to help."

"Trying to help who? Because I don't remember asking for anyone's help." And I hadn't. Ever. I was getting by just fine without anyone's help. Not even Kevin's. One good thing about living beneath the poverty line: it teaches you how to get by, how to manage without some fancy-car-driving schmuck coming along and shaking things up. Kevin says my pride needs a room of its own. I tell him, maybe he'd be better off if he had some for himself. The *Matrix* driver is more patient than his friend. He tries again. "We're attorneys."

I can't stop the snort that escapes me. "And you're here to help?" He waits for me to finish laughing. It takes a couple minutes before the giggle fit subsides. His snotty friend has snapped his briefcase shut. He's as done with me as I am with him.

"Miss Evans, do you really think, with a name like that, you don't have family somewhere?"

44

Giggles gone.

Dead gone.

Family, he says?

"Do you have access to the Internet," *Matrix* Number 2 asks.

"Are you crazy?" My mouth is still smart, but the insides of me have gone numb with shock.

"Why don't you Google yourself?"

No. I'm out of sass. It's just gone.

Family?

"And when you do..." he leans across the other *Matrix* twin, who eyes me with a kind of mocking condescension. "Call us. We need to talk. We've been looking for you," this he pauses to consider, shooting for accuracy. "Since before you were born."

He doesn't wait for a reply. The car rolls past my deaf, mute and dumb form. I stand on the corner, the music and raucous voices of Eddie's drift down the street toward me, but I don't hear them.

Twelve

"Miss Demure, may I have the pleasure of your hand in the next dance?"

It had been a month since he had seen her, though it had not been a month since he had tried.

Many evenings, as shadows filled the lanes and twilight nestled over the town, Viktor had come to call on Miss Katherine Demure. Not once had he been able to see her.

She was frightfully ill.

With what, they would not say at first, and Viktor suspected they were playing him for a fool. One day, however, just as he was lifting his hand to knock, the door swung open. A surprised Josephine begged his pardon and continued to show Doctor Craig out before welcoming Viktor in. "Is it Miss Demure," he had pressed, not giving Josephine time to greet him properly. "Yes, sir," she had whispered covertly. "She is very ill, sir, very ill indeed."
Viktor had left then, choosing not to bother the family with his lingering presence as he had on the other nights.

It seemed, however, that they had all been mistaken in his intentions over the course of the last month.

Josephine had not told them that upon his arrivals he had always inquired first after Katherine. Henrietta never even considered this, but fawned over him, a sight that Mrs. Demure was too happy to behold. Knowing it wouldn't be proper to call on the younger sister before the elder was married, Viktor kept his intentions to himself. What those intentions were, even Viktor was not certain. What he was certain of was that he longed to see Katherine again, in all her fire and stubbornness. He was desperate for those accusatory, raging eyes...so unlike the plotting, preening eyes of her sister and so many other girls.

"My apologies, sir," Katherine responded a bit too quickly, her eyes locked on his proffered hand. "I am afraid I am still too weak to dance."

"Ah, but I am not! I shall suffer to take my sister's place!" Henrietta, appearing from nowhere, laughed gleefully as though this had been Viktor's plan all along. She took his arm, though he had not offered it.

There was no patience for her silliness left in him. Viktor disengaged himself. "It would seem improper to leave your sister to herself while everyone else enjoys the dance."

Henrietta scoffed. "Oh piff! She cares nothing for dancing or fun. Only her books interest her. Your charms would be perfectly wasted on the silly little thing!"

Katherine hated Henrietta to the very core of her shallow being, but simply said, "Unfortunately my sister is right. I do not dance well even when I am in good health. I am neither witty nor intriguing. I am simply," Katherine shrugged, bored by her own boringness. "I am simply dull."

Viktor would not take his eyes from her, not even when Henrietta reclaimed his arm and began lightly

47

tugging at him. Katherine wanted to look away but the deep, icy seas of his eyes drew her in. With flecks of gold and pale blue they reminded her of lightening and storms on a summer day. Unworldly, she whispered in her thoughts as though he might be able to hear her.

Noticing that her sister and Viktor were gazing a bit too long at each other, Henrietta slapped Viktor's arm with her fan. "Silly boy, we must hurry! They have begun without us!" As he unwillingly left her side, a deep breath rolled into Katherine. She had stopped breathing as she stared into the stormy depths. What had he been pondering that had caused him to look at her in such a way? With hope and pain and puzzlement?

Mrs. Demure swooped over, curiosity burning brilliantly in her eyes. Katherine slid across the seat to allow room for her mother. Subtly, Mrs. Demure leaned in close to Katherine's ear.

"How do they get on?"

For a moment Katherine debated whether or not she should tell her mother that Viktor regarded Henrietta with as much affection as he would a buzzing fly, but thought better of it. Her mother would only think her jealous and childish. Instead she said, "I did not notice. He seems to me very odd." Mrs. Demure tinkled with laughter. "Yes my dear, but one day men will not be such a mystery. They are rather simple creatures and rather easily pleased."

Color rose high in her mother's cheeks, for what reason Katherine did not know, but her mother seemed to have said more than intended.

To distract her Katherine offered, "Aside from that, Mother. I mean, he is very odd indeed. Always staring and brooding. Is that what people in castles do all day? Sit around brooding and imagining how to make the little people around them feel insignificant with the force of one pretentious stare?"

To Katherine's dismay, her mother bubbled with laughter again. Why were people forever laughing at her when she wasn't trying to be funny? She would never understand people. "Oh Katherine," *trilled Mrs. Demure.* "You are a treasure. Such a bright wit." *To her daughter's relief she then planted a light kiss on Katherine's cheek and stepped back into the crowd.*

With a bothered sigh, Katherine stood, stretching out the stiffening muscles of her body. A wave of dizziness blurred the edges of her vision. She tried not to call attention to it, standing very still and waiting for it to pass as it always did. Heaven forbid, *she thought,* that I fall again and have him lift me up in front of all these people. The only redeeming consequence of such a scene would be Henrietta's red, angry face. Yes, *thought Katherine,* that would be worth it!

The haze was taking longer to clear than usual and she swayed slightly, clutching the high arm of the sofa. People were clapping as the music ended, as the room was grew dimmer around her. She was not worried, it was a nearly daily occurrence in her life. It was just that she was usually afforded the luxury of fainting in private. "Oh no," *she whispered aloud, her knees beginning to go soft. Blessedly as she began to sink, there was suddenly, unexpected pressure under her arm guiding her back to standing.*

"I will not be carrying you tonight," *he whispered in her ear.* "I am not available to play the role of the shining knight this evening." *Suave though it was, sarcasm dripped from each word.*

How infuriating he was!

Katherine tried to jerk away but he held her firmly, standing at an angle so the others wouldn't notice he was gripping her elbow. Considerate, *she conceded,* but infuriating just the same. *He continued, "I sent your sister for punch, but, perhaps you are in need of fresh air? And a strong arm to lean on?"*

"Have you no morals?" Katherine snapped, but spotting the top of Henrietta's curls across the swaying crowd, she gathered her skirts and took his proffered arm. Moving with him through the clustered groups of gossipers, trying not to lean upon him too openly, Katherine began to question herself. Why was she allowing him to lead her outside? Whatever could he want? There certainly was no a shortage of fine young ladies to keep him amused.

She thought of the rumors.

The Count had supposedly fled to America after being banished from Austria for dark deeds unknown. The tales had spread all through Europe and everywhere they went his reputation preceded them. Katherine burned to know what could be so horrid that mere rumors of it could chase a count not only from his country but also from an entire continent and across a three thousand mile stretch of ocean. And why had he chosen here? Missouri was halfway across the United States. Though Saint Louis was growing in importance it could not rival the cities of the East. Why here?

She wondered all these things as the cool night air seeped into her lungs. She was grateful for it.

A chill breeze blew across the patio, rustling the leaves of the abundant ivy and a powerful shiver seized her. Katherine drew her arms tightly around herself. Before she could protest, before she could even register

---

the very nearness of him, Viktor was close, drawing her shawl around her shoulders. Despite her greatest efforts Katherine found herself looking up again. He was watching her, as ever, waiting for her reaction.

This time, she found herself uncertain of what to do next. She could turn and go back in, saying it was too cold. Or she could walk across the balcony to survey the grounds below. Or she could do the only thing that seemed possible at the moment. She could simply stand there, accepting his unwavering gaze and wait.

She could not look away. And as she cursed herself for her silliness, she found that she was not breathing even though she felt she was surely hyperventilating.

What was this madness?

He was not the first boy to gaze at her or play the part of the chivalrous knight. There had been a time when the boys in town had considered her a bit of a conquest, a fair damsel to be saved. They had carried her packages and held her umbrella and escorted her home. It did not take long, however, for them to grow tired of her illnesses. The reality of her fragility was too much for them to bear and they had moved on to the tireless energy of Henrietta. And, Katherine had to admit, no young man likes being second fiddle to the brave and handsome men of her novels. She sighed, knowing that no such man truly existed and she would be forced to reconcile her longings for a mundane life.

"What troubles you?" The sigh, she realized and blushed, had been audible. "Are you not well," the concern rose in his voice, the Austrian accent he made efforts to hide becoming thicker.

"No sir," she turned away from his gaze. "Only..." she trailed off. She could not tell him her silly problems.

It was really not a problem at all. Her discontentment was a product of her overly educated mind. So this, *she thought,* is why they do not want women to read. For then we shall know what dreadful bores we have attached ourselves to! And we shall be forever depressed following the revelation. *She cursed her father and his blasted library.*

She looked away, never doubting that he would detect the lie in her eyes. "It is nothing."

A distraction was needed but she found herself unwilling to go back into the crowd. Instead she approached the balustrade. In the absence of the moon, there was nothing but darkness below. Silently, he moved to her side. "Are you tired," *he spoke softly, yet not as to a child. Perhaps that, beyond his uncommonly good looks and polished manners, was what set him apart. Never, even as she had fallen from the staircase, had he treated her as a child. No. He mocked her and challenged her, and all without condescension. She had watched him, all those evenings as he had approached the Demure's home on his gallant black steed. She had watched as he eagerly strode to the door and she had even dared to sneak glances as Josephine welcomed him in and escorted him to her father's study. Time after time he had come, and every time he had seemed just as ardent as the time before. It was the last evening he had come that had awakened a foreign curiosity inside her. She had always imagined Viktor was coming to visit for the sake of Henrietta. His inquiries after her own health she wrote off as part of his chivalrous nature. But that last evening as he trotted away, shoulders slumped a bit, he had stopped and turned his horse. For a moment he had sat there, staring up at the tightly drawn shades of her window. She had dared* not move lest he spy her jewel-green eyes gazing out at him. He had shaken his head and turned back toward home, driving his steed at a breakneck pace.

As he stood there beside her now with the amber glow of the dance hall spilling into the moonless night, Katherine began to tremble...yet not from cold or illness. "I am afraid," her words tumbled into the heavy silence. "That my father has allowed me too much familiarity with his novels." He allowed her pause to fill the air between them. "You see, I am sinfully discontent and there is nothing to be done about it. I am too weak and too ill to go off on any adventures. And let us not forget that I am a lady anyway. And men are all insufferable bores."

A spontaneous bark of laughter erupted from Viktor, making her jump. Katherine gazed sharply across the lawn, keeping her indignant eyes to herself. She was beginning to feel that she could no longer sustain her anger if she met his eyes. "There's no need to laugh!" She fumed, "I shall not speak openly with you if you insist on mocking me."

"Oh dear, Katherine," he laughed gently, wiping at the corner of his eye. "You are a treat."

Exploding with a huff, she turned on her heel and began to make her escape. With the same gentle firmness he always seemed to be using with her, Viktor grabbed her wrist. He did not pull her back and yet he would not let her go. "Do not go, Katherine," his words were but a breath. "Or I shall die of boredom."

He could see, before it even reached her eyes, the retort that was welling inside of her.

"Oh do I amuse you so," she hissed. "Cute little Katherine and her pretty little tantrums?" With a wrenching jerk she tried to escape. His grasp tightened as *he pulled her closer and she winced at the pain.*

"Behave yourself, you little minx, or I shall toss you off this balcony and be done with it."

Her breaths came quick and fast. She had never stood quite so close to a boy. And he was the most handsome and infuriating boy she had ever met. More man than boy. A man like those in her novels.

"You speak of men being insufferable bores, but have you ever turned that judgmental eye upon your own gender?" Viktor turned his gaze away from her and she imagined he was seeing the fine courts of Vienna and Paris. "I have met the finest," an ironic laugh slipped out as he continued, "of your species, so they tell me. They are all the same. They want a man with wealth and property. They want a man who will care for their lavish expenses and otherwise leave them be. They speak of fashions and spend their every waking moment gossiping and plotting romances and weddings. But not you Katherine. I have never met another girl who would hide behind a tapestry in her robes to get a glimpse of a mysterious stranger." His thumb gently stroked her wrist.

Feeling the danger in the moment, Katherine shook herself, tears rising to her emerald eyes. Should she be angry or shocked or insulted that he was so forward?

But she felt none of these things.

Inside, her family and neighbors continued in their gaiety, ignorant of the wealth of gossip occurring just feet away. She could see Henrietta's curls twirling across the floor and knew her sister's eyes would be angrily scanning the room for her escaped suitor.

But outside, in the stillness of the night, neither Viktor nor Katherine moved. Neither did they look at one another. They had reached a point where neither wanted the moment to end and yet, they were not certain how to continue.

In their uncertainty, they chose silence.

Katherine turned back to the darkness of the grounds, leaning against the balustrade for support. Viktor slowly released his grip on her and stood stoically beside her, gazing at nothing, studying his own bewildered thoughts. Inside the song ended and the crowd clapped in appreciation of the musicians and the dancers. Grappling with his fears and anxieties, Viktor gripped the stone railing and spoke into the darkness.

"May I call on you Miss Katherine Demure?"

It was improper and she knew it. Because of her illnesses her father and mother had never presented her to society. She was not well enough and besides, Henrietta was yet unwed. And the Von Strassenbergs were strangers with unknown and rumored pasts.

"You should not ask me for such a thing." Katherine swallowed with difficulty, attempting to force down the impending tears. "You do not even know me."

An elegant finger reached out and dared to turn her chin toward him, "But I am dying to know you, Katherine Demure." She could see his chest rising and falling with the anxiety of the moment. "All those nights I rode out to see you, just a glimpse of you. I would come a thousand nights more, if you will just please, allow me to call on you."

"You must ask my father, it is only proper." Mr. Demure would never hear of such a thing and Katherine knew it all too well. A tear slipped down her night-cooled cheek. Viktor withdrew a handkerchief to wipe away the glistening trail that coursed down her cheek to her trembling lips.

She knew there was music being played inside and people laughing and carrying on but she could no longer hear them. Viktor leaned in closer, his words barely above a whisper, "I am asking you, Katherine, may I call on you?"

What could she say? She turned away from his pleading eyes.

"Only you and I need know."

She tried to think of some sharp remark or some reason why they should not risk it, but nothing came. Finally, feeling the world shift beneath her, Katherine turned to those eyes sparkling with their own summer storms, and nodded.

Thirteen

Saturday is never a busy day at the library. And really, the only reason people tend to come in on the other days is for the free Internet and in the summer, the free AC. It's 7:59 and I'm waiting for Mrs. Henderson to unlock the doors. The thought of busting in last night did cross my mind and knowing that Mrs. Henderson would forgive me once she realized my motives, well that only made the desire stronger. Somehow I resisted and now I'm sitting on the sidewalk, watching outdated Fords and Chevies roll by. A rattling startles me back to the world outside my thoughts. Mrs. Henderson, fabulous Mrs. Henderson, is at the door with her blessed set of keys. As the door opens her laughter spills into the late spring air.

"Child what are you doin'? You know the next *Evening Shade* isn't due out for another five months."

"I know, Mrs. Henderson," I say, stepping around her, careful not to bulldoze the old lady. My nerves are getting the best of me. "But I need on the Internet and fast."

I sit in one of the creaky old chairs and power up the ancient computer, flicking on the monitor and agitating the mouse in my impatience. Other people would be expected to fill out forms and show their library card.

Not me. Mrs. Henderson lets me reign here.

"Child, what on earth?"

"I don't know yet, but as soon as I find out, you'll be the first to know."

It seems like hours before the computer boots up. Why are these infernal computers so ancient? Stupid hick library.

I navigate away from the library's homepage to the search engine's site. What the library is lacking in hardware it makes up for with its high-speed Internet connection. Google my name. *Maria Josepha Raquel Demure von Strassenberg,* leave off the Evans.

Over a million hits and none of them exact.

Maria Josepha...Archduchess...blah blah....so?

Next.

August Demure....attorney...Saint Louis.....1865...

What? Nothing recent? No rich, old granny?

Twenty minutes pass and I find nothing within the last one hundred years. The *Matrix* twins have bothered me, gotten my hopes up and dashed them

without even being present. So maybe some of my people came from Austria. And so maybe my great-something granddaddy was a lawyer. Well at least someone in the family had brains and did something worthwhile....

Von Strassenberg, Klaus...biologist...yadda yadda... Austria.... Washington University, St. Louis...

Well that's two for Austria and two for St. Louis.

All right, one more and then the Matrix twins are getting a nasty call.

St. Louis. Newspaper. *Archives..1877.... Attorney Demure Continues Search for Missing Daughter.* Missing daughter?

Well that certainly sounds like it has some kind of possibility.

Fourteen

She had become accustomed to his odd hours.

Only when the sun slipped behind the towering oaks and sycamores would he casually trot his steed past the Demure home. Her breath would stop and her heart would clench just for a moment as she caught sight of him slipping back into the shadows of the forest.

It was just like in her books, but better, amplified, because it was her heart and her breath and it was real. And he wanted her. Frail and breakable and obstinate as she was, he wanted her.

Not that he had professed his love just yet.

But every evening there he was, skirting the pools of darkness, weaving in and out of the trees until he was certain she had seen him. Katherine had caught herself waiting for him to appear sometimes an hour before she knew was possible. Her thoughts simply couldn't right themselves and she was useless for anything other than thinking about him.

At the sight of him, she would blow out the candle in her window and hurry out through the servants' door in the back of the house. Never did she cross the grounds in the direction she had last seen him. Sometimes she would tarry down the lane and he would eventually catch up with her and whisk her away to the moonlit edge of the river.

Beyond being imprisoned by the sunshine, Viktor also had his studies and lessons during the day. His hours tucked behind their thick draperies were spent fencing and reading heavy tomes in languages she had not yet encountered.

Yet, *her soul breathed with a sigh of anticipation. One day, she knew, he would take her to Europe and show her all the grand things of the world beyond this bustling river town with its endless stream of steamboats and barges.*

Viktor was a different man when he was away from the oppressive airs of his father. And when he was here, in the dim twilight with the hard lines of his face softened by the graying shades of evening, she thought he might be someone else entirely. Away from the structures of society and the demands of protocol, he was warm and open, unrestrained. Except, *she thought,* except for what? *There was still some unattainable part of him.*

He would never speak of his life as a member of the royal society. There were no tales of the Austrian countryside or of gallivanting through Europe. How she longed to hear the stories of their escape from their persecutors. But she would never ask.

Instead he told her of the voyage to New York and how they came to be in St. Louis. And yet, even then he seemed to clamp down on his words, never quite explaining why the Count had chosen to build his new little kingdom halfway across the new country. She gazed at Viktor. His jacket lay beside her, across a large skeleton of driftwood. With studied grace he flung a smooth stone across the swiftly moving current. She imagined, with his sleeves rolled up to the elbows and his hair falling out of place across his eyes, he looked more like the son of one of the local shopkeepers than the son of a rich count. She would take him no matter his station in life.

If he would have her.

Most days she imagined he would take her as his own, that he was just biding his time until Henrietta had married, thus clearing the way for his marriage to Katherine. But other days she felt certain that he was biding his time for a different reason.

The moon was dipping ever lower behind the tall skinny trees that lined the riverbank. They would have to go soon.

"Katherine?"

She started and blushed with embarrassment. Wrapped in hope-filled and tormented meanderings, she hadn't noticed him throw his last stone and join her on the driftwood. His laugh at her surprise was warm and deep, without mocking or condescension. "What were your thoughts all tangled up in?" He was curious and close, so close. The enigmatic gaze drew her in deeply and she found that she had forgotten the question. He was so awfully close. The cool spring air felt shockingly brisk against the heat rising in her cheeks.

With great effort she shook her eyes free of his power, turning her head as though something down the river held some curiosity for her. "Are you not speaking to me then," he laughed again, rolling down his sleeves and straightening his shirt.

The unseen tree frogs had begun their evening melody. She listened as the chorus grew and swelled to a distracting cacophony.

"Katherine," he said and it was more of a question. Her breaths came quickly and would not be calmed, despite her silent, internal lectures. Why was he so close? It was really improper. A heavy wind suddenly kicked up around them, scattering leaves and sending ripples across the waters. Katherine clamped down on her hat, looking at him with an amused apology.

"It seems," he breathed with a bit of disappointment. "That a storm is blowing in." Far down the river she could see where the already darkened sky was nearly black with swollen rain clouds. They were rolling down the river at a good pace and would soon set upon she and Viktor with all their turbulent fury. "I should get you home." With this his disappointment was clear and Katherine turned to catch sight of it, as though she was in need of more evidence.

The wind whipped stray hairs across her face. She fought to push them from her eyes but it was a losing battle. Viktor laughed at her predicament, and guiding her by the arm, he led her into the relative protection of the trees. "I think," he tightened his own hat upon his head. "We had best plan for speed. Those clouds are coming in fast."

"I think you are right." With a final effort Katherine removed her own hat, placed it between her teeth, and used both hands to smooth her hair back before replacing the worthless accessory.

Another wisp of Chestnut fell across her eyes. Chuckling at her failed efforts, Viktor lifted a long, elegant finger and brushed the strand from her eyes.

They both stood frozen in motion as the wind whipped around them, the suddenness of their predicament surprising them with more force than the oncoming storms. His eyes would not move from her shocked gaze.

"Katherine." This time it was a whisper, low and tormented. His touch lingered against her skin, brushing softly against the cooled curve of her cheek. The electricity in the air seemed to gather around them. The strength of his desire to take her into his arms was palpable and the apparentness of it filled her with sudden fear and excitement.

And desire.

Her own body felt it was being pulled and pushed toward his.

And yet, he did not reach for her. His arms returned rigid to his sides. Then he was gone, gathering his steed and deftly jumping into the saddle. "You'll excuse the improprieties, but we must hurry." He extended the hand that had just caressed her so gently and wrought such unexpected passions in her. "I swear I will tell no one." With a quirk of a smile he beckoned her to join him.

Katherine gathered her skirts, noticing Viktor's averted eyes, and took his hand. With a strong tug he pulled her onto the steed. Thunder rumbled overhead. The leaves scurried and danced in anticipation. "Hold on to me tight," he spoke loudly over the growing winds.

Improper indeed!

Riding astride and bareback with her arms wound tightly around his strong torso!

At his prompting the steed took off through the trees, down the old, worn path. Katherine had never held a man like this. The scent of him thrilled her senses as it mingled with the smell of promised rains. He drove the horse at full speed through the open field, reminding her every so often to hold tight or she should fall. She needn't be reminded. She only wished the ride home was longer. Her body melded into his, melting into the strong sinews of his back, appreciating the hard feel of his abdomen beneath her arms. He felt so substantial beneath the frailty of her arms. For the first time in her young life, Katherine felt truly protected, feeling the urgency and strength rippling through Viktor's body. Despite the danger of being caught in the storm she wished they could ride on forever, clasped together, dashing through the world recklessly together.

The jostling lessened as the horse slowed. Hopes dashed, Katherine looked up from the hard pillow of his shoulder. They were already at the edge of the trees beside her home.

She did not automatically release him.

He did not ask her to.

For a moment, they watched the gathering clouds, black against a blackening sky. His fingers gently stroked her wrist.

She could feel the depth and pace of his breaths change beneath her.

And then suddenly he was on his feet, offering his hand to help her down. She swung her leg over and clasped his fingers. He caught her at the waist as she jumped, steadying her as she landed.

Before the moment could take them, Viktor stepped away and tipped his hat. "Hang your proprieties and run, Katherine."

It occurred to her that she just might be angry with him. Why wouldn't he hang his own sense of propriety and just hold her? Silly games. Just like Henrietta! Instead of letting her tongue get the better of her, Katherine turned abruptly and sprinted across the swaying field, holding her skirts and forgetting her hat.

Fifteen

"Just rolling in?"

Kevin has been drinking again. It's nearly noon. He's stationed in what is supposed to be a recliner but looks more like a rhinoceros that was hit by a bulldozer. That chair has got to go.

Not that it's any concern of mine. Not anymore.

"Kevin, I *did* come home last night. You and Ms. For This Moment were already passed out."

He rises from his chair, sloppy beer in his sloppy hand. "Don't you talk to me like that little missy."

Oh, I am definitely leaving.

The creepy thing is I can't tell if he's angry or jealous. Most likely both. And that's more than an adequate enough excuse for me to get packing.

Kevin stalks toward me, offering me a better view of his two-day stubble and a smell of his unbrushed breath. "Don't think you're too old for me to turn over my knee."

Say nothing.

Any response will provoke him.

Things must not have gone so well with Ms. Last Night. The glassed-over, frenzied look in his wounded eyes (not to mention the empty bottle in his hand) tell me it's time to keep quiet and time to get going. The problem is, Kevin is standing between my bedroom and I.

Suddenly the recliner looks less like a rhino and more like an offensive tackle. This is a small room with too much furniture. He is still walking, setting the bottle down on the spattered old end table as he comes closer. My eyes are burning with moisture. Is it fear? Or sheer rage? Most likely a mixture of both.

Though I am not well endowed, my heaving chest makes me feel overly vulnerable as though it is stuck out there and heaving just for his notice.

I am frozen.

Kevin has never looked at me this way and the sick, perverseness of it has captured me in its grasp. His breath rolls over me, smelling of cheap beer and rotted meat and other things too obscene to mention and I can't move. My feet won't move and my brain has stopped processing anything other than what my five senses can tell me.

"Matter of fact," he drawls and the smell of it makes me want to wretch. "I think you're just about the right size."

Instinct.

If there is a God, I will thank Him for instincts. Kevin, stumbling drunk and seething with his injured man-pride, grabs hold of my waist and starts to pull me close. Turns out there isn't always a need for rational, objective thought.

Turns out that guy that came to give us the self-defense spiel in tenth grade was right. In times of crisis our natural instincts will take over.

I will send that man a postcard whenever I get to where I am going and tell him how right he is. And thanks for the nose drive.

My hand shoots up, palm flat and smacks Kevin's flushed and sagging face square in the nose. Stunned, he releases me and reels back, profanities hurling from him with his blood and mucus. Not bothering to wipe the gore away, he spins on me, trying to catch me as I dart past the immobile rhino and head for my room.

66

My room with its flimsy door and busted window.

For a jacked up drunk man Kevin is fast, too fast. He's at my back grabbing my hair as I try to leap the last few feet into my room, slamming the door behind me. White lightening slices into my brain and a scream rips its way out of me as those wide-awake five senses tell me everything I already know. My hair is caught in the door. The other end is still in Kevin's all too strong carpenter's hands.

Strong, unforgiving hands.

He yanks and yanks again, expletives flying without pause for breath. With back pressed tightly to the door, out of necessity because he has me painfully pinned, I turn the lock, scanning my brain for a brilliant plan to get out of this mess. My tiny room is sparsely furnished. The twin bed will only fit against the wall with the busted window. And my desk, my beautiful, white knight desk, is here beside me, crammed into the small space between the bedroom door and the closet door. Two nights ago I had started working on that stupid project for history. A battle scene, complete with corn syrup blood and cardboard trees. And there beside the last fallen soldier, still waiting silently for his place on the battlefield, are my scissors. New and sharp.

I have been growing my hair put for the last two years and it's knock out, sexy model hair. I'm not the vain type, but I'm vain about my hair. And I will admit, that mixed in with the tears of terror and anger and adrenaline now are tears of vanity as I cut my beautiful chestnut curls and separate myself forever from the man who had kept his promise to my dead mother for seventeen years.

Kept it but blew it all to heck today.

The cheap, hollow wood begins to splinter beneath the onslaught of Kevin's fury. Not waiting for him to think about the window and the possibility of me dropping out of it, I grab my messenger bag and shove another pair of jeans and a few t-shirts and my favorite plaid, some underwear and a jacket. I pause, for just a moment, and in a gush of teenager shallowness, grab Mrs. Henderson's copy of *Evening Shade* .

Fortunately, I think as I shove the window up and slip into the perfection of a late spring day, *I am not the sentimental type.* There is nothing here I want to remember .

Two weeks passed and not once had she seen him. He had not sent letters or kind regards. There was simply nothing. For once, Katherine was grateful for Henrietta's self-centered foolishness. Everyday she plagued their father with questions Katherine's own heart was demanding answers to. Even Mrs. Demure seemed a little rattled by the young man's absence. "What have we done," she often wondered aloud, perfectly vexed by this abrupt change.

"Mr. Demure did you say something to frighten Mister von Strassenberg away?" Mrs. Demure gently asked.

Mr. Demure sat down to his lunch. "Nothing at all my dear." He pulled a napkin across his lap. "He is most likely fallen ill again."

"Oh but wouldn't the Count..."

"Stop using that ridiculous title Henrietta. It has no bearing here. And no, Klaus von Strassenberg is not the sort of man to send notes."

What sort of man is he, Katherine wondered at her soup. Viktor had avoided the topic of his father, even *though it seemed they were the only two people they belonged to in the whole world. A pang of sadness coursed through her.* I would belong to him, *her brain declared but her heart answered more loudly that she already did belong to him. It just was not official yet. Her thoughts were replaying that night, as they dashed through the meadows and forests, her body and heart clinging to him as he raced against the elements.*

"Katherine?"

"Hmmm?"

"Are you well child?" Mr. Demure had been speaking to her and she hadn't a clue as to what had been said. "You look flushed, child, are you well?" The color rose in more violent petals. Fanning her napkin out more than what was necessary, Katherine dabbed at her lips. "Yes Father," she said into the napkin, taking a deep breath, hoping that would cool some of the heat she felt emanating off her cheeks.

"Well, I'm glad for it. But perhaps you should take a rest after lunch? Hmm? Yes, I think so. Mrs. Demure see that she does."

"Yes dear."

Mrs. Demure was unruffled by the faint change in her daughter's color. They had been through so many bouts of illness together. Mr. Demure, however, never grew accustomed to the frailty of his youngest daughter. Katherine looked across at him, his well coiffed, gray-streaked hair, the wrinkles around his eyes and the one deep score between his eyebrows. A jokester and a thinker, her father.

Henrietta caught her contemplative eye.

And just as Katherine was surveying what the physical clues could tell her about her father, so Henrietta was surveying her. Too many times Henrietta had taken the scenic route home from school and returned flushed. She knew all about rose-flushed cheeks and averted glances.

"Perhaps," Mr. Demure began, but Henrietta was on a conquest. "Perhaps," she intervened. "We should ask little Katherine about the Count's son and why he fails to grace us with his presence now."

Mr. Demure, being a lawyer, was not easily shaken from his yarn of thought. "Calling him `the Count's son' will not make him any richer dear and, pray, what could your sister possibly tell us?" Katherine waited for all three pairs of eyes to shift to her but her Father was challenging Henrietta, his wanton daughter. Katherine struggled inside the laces of her gown, trying to keep her breaths slow and shallow. She was losing. Her heart was tripping furiously. All those nights, Henrietta must know of all those nights. She must have seen me or heard me slipping back into the house. *Henrietta's minx eyes shifted toward her sister. There was not enough anger there. She was not certain, but she suspected, and that could prove to be enough.*

"Nothing Father," she smiled her pretty little smile, the one that had gotten half the boys in town in over their heads. "It was just a thought."

Mr. Demure was not amused. He took up his fork again. "Eat your soup, Henrietta and keep your unfounded suppositions to yourself."

Henrietta daintily sipped her soup, her hard hazel eyes never leaving Katherine.

"You little tart!" A pillow came flying across the room as Katherine entered her bedroom nearly an hour

later. She had assumed Henrietta had flitted off in pursuit of one of her admirers. She had assumed wrong. It was an ambush.

"What have you done?"

Most people treated Katherine with care, afraid she might shatter into pieces. She had to appreciate Henrietta's lack of indulgence, however irritating it could be. Henrietta never treated her like a glass doll. Katherine threw the pillow back. "Be quiet. Josephine is coming to undress me."

"Oh that's right," Henrietta rounded on her. "Father insists his little princess take a little rest, to rest her little lying face!"

They were nose to nose, but Katherine was not afraid of Henrietta. She worried over her father's opinion of her and didn't want to disappoint her mother, but she was never concerned over Henrietta. She could manage Henrietta. There was a small journal tucked beneath a loose floorboard under Henrietta's bed that Henrietta assumed no one knew existed except for her. She was wrong. And Katherine would tear it page by page and deliver them to their father if Henrietta so much as threatened her. They weren't Catholic, but Father would most certainly ship Henrietta off to the nunnery once he read the pages.

"I said, hush, you imbecile, Josephine is coming. And there is nothing to discuss."

"It was you, wasn't it?"

Did she know? Had she seen? But how could she prove it? "You and your impertinent manners and your smart little mouth. What did you say to him?"

"You're being irrational, Henrietta."

Tears rose to the desperate hazel eyes.

"I have said nothing to him. When have I had the opportunity?"

"You told him things! You told him horrible things about me because you want him but can't have him, you sniveling little brat!"

Katherine was tired. She pressed her nose against Henrietta's. *"Henrietta, you twit, maybe he talked to Caleb McDonnelly and discovered the truth of your virtue."*

"Girls! Girls!" Josephine had entered unnoticed and tried to push them apart, tenderly, so as not to break Katherine. *"All this fuss. I will send George over to the von Strassenberg's to ask after the boy. See,"* she started undoing Katherine's laces. *"Easy as that. No need to come to blows. Miss Henrietta I'm sure he will come calling again. Your father is right, the young man most likely just took another turn."* She lifted the dress over Katherine's head and smiled gently.

Did Josephine know? Katherine was beginning to feel paranoid.

"Now lay down there, Miss Katherine and rest yourself, and it will be all better." Josephine did know. The servants always knew. *"And you Miss Henrietta, I believe your mother would like you to practice that new music what came by post yesterday."*

Katherine could feel Henrietta's dagger eyes boring into her back. *"Fine,"* she snarled and stomped out of the room. Josephine pulled the quilt over Katherine's shoulders. *"It will all work out Miss Katherine. He will see that it does."* Before Katherine could question her, Josephine had scuttled away and closed the door, leaving Katherine in the shaded room. She knew she would not sleep. Her mind was overwhelmed with

—
73

everything she did not know.

Seventeen

"I'm coming with you."

"No Charlene."

"Kevin's going to come here looking for you and you know I'm a terrible liar. He'll know you were here and then the cops will come looking for you. And they will definitely know I'm lying."

I shift in the hard chair. Sitting still has never been a talent of mine. "But I never told you where I'm going."

Snip, snip, snip.

"No. But you did tell me about those weird lawyer guys. What was that firm called, Drexel and Westhoeler....something?"

"You are a horrible friend Charlene."

"Shut up or I'll cut you bald."

The greatest difference between Charlene and I is our feminine know-how. Charlene has older sisters that loved playing makeover. One of them is even a certified cosmetologist now. She had used Charlene as her guinea pig and, fortunate-Ely, some of those skills rubbed off on Charlene.

Maybe haircutting skills are genetic, I muse.

I'm trying not cry. In the face of all that's happening it seems pretty stupid to be so upset about my hair.

But it's a lot of hair. No matter what threats she makes, I know Charlene is going to have to cut pretty close to the scalp anyway, to remedy the chunk I had to whack off to make my escape. *Oh well*, I tell myself, *it will be easier to take care of during our little adventure. My little adventure*, I correct myself. *And it will help me be a little more incognito.*

"You need to stay and finish the school year Charlene. It's only a few more weeks and then you can come find me. I'll send you word of where I am. But this first part, I have to do it alone." Charlene steps in front of me, lifting my chin and testing the evenness of my remaining hair.

She's ignoring me. "It actually looks pretty good. I like this better than the porn star hair."

"It wasn't porn star hair, it was *Victoria's Secret* model hair."

"The difference? Anyway, I like it. It's edgy. You want me to tip it?"

"No, you've had enough fun."

She ruffles and adjusts my non-existent locks. "All right, stand up and have a look-see." I try to gauge the damage by her expression but she seems to be honestly pleased with herself. I turn slowly to face the dresser mirror and peer into the small space not yet littered with photos and movie stubs and various other memorabilia.

Sweet shocker!

After writing thanks to the self-defense guru I will be sending flowers to Charlene's annoying, pushy sisters and thanking them for imparting their skills to Charlene. "You know, Char." I say, smoothing the hair away from my eyes. "You could make a racket doing this."

She smiles, "Doing what? Fixing runaways' hair after they hack it off trying to escape their evil step-dads?"

"Exactly." I would turn to hug her, but not just yet, I need another moment of vanity to survey the new me. My hair is smooth and neat with the slightest wave, like a wisp of mystery, and I look like some corporate exec powerhouse. In third hand clothes. But no matter, Charlene has made me look the role. And now it's time to say goodbye. She senses it as I hug her and the wetness from her eyes soaks into my shirt.

"I'm so scared for you."

"Don't be. And I *will* call you."

"What if it's too far and I can't make it? What if something happens before you can call me?" Charlene has always been more emotional, in the soft, girly way of being emotional, than I am. I hug her hard, hoping that I wouldn't be responsible for ruining the final weeks of her senior year. "What about graduation?"

"Nothing will happen. I'm not going anywhere scary and it's really not even far away. Just please, Charlene, please. Don't tell anyone about the lawyers. It's all supposed to be hush-hush. And there's no one to come to my graduation anyway. So just let me go and keep it quiet."

"But why?"

"I could tell you, but I'd have to kill you."

"Rocky!"

"I am so kidding, you twerp." She looks so small and scared, more like a little sister than my peer. In our friendship I have always been the protector. It just made sense. I tower over Charlene by nearly a foot. She's soft and curvy with an ample rear and I am somewhat butch and nearly flat all over. Not that I'm some kind of Brunhilda, but everyone always expected me to play basketball or rugby, but that would have cut into my reading time and besides, someone had to work and pay the bills. "You'll be okay, kid. We'll be okay. And," I sling the messenger bag over my shoulder. "I will mail *Evening Shade* to you as soon I finish it."

She steps back, little hands on wide hips. "Running away is one thing Raquel Evans. Taking the only free copy of *EveningShade* is another."

"Dobson's was all out. I stopped by and checked

—
76

after I went to the bank, I swear. They're all gone. I will mail it to you."

"You're a real wench Rocky."

"I love you too, Char, but I gotta get going." We hug again. She holds the curtains back for me, "I won't tell them about the *Matrix* twins. Or the haircut." I land neatly between Mrs. Thomas's irises and violas. "Sweep it up and toss it in the bin down the street."

"I know, Captain. Take care of you."

"And you do the same." I turn and hop the chain link fence and never look back.

Eighteen

Getting to where I am going is going to take up most of my grossly inadequate funds. After going to the library and calling the Matrix twins, who were not in fact the attorneys Drexler and Westhoeler but two of their minions, I went straight to the bank and drained my account. The attorneys were willing to pay my travel expenses, but I prefer to show up unannounced and in my own time. Maybe it's just going to be like some bad daytime talk show, "You Don't Know Me But I'm Your Rich Old Granny." But maybe it isn't. Whoever I'm dealing with apparently has the money and the people. I have neither. All I have is $650 in my pocket and the brains in my head. Whatever that counts for. And I am going to make sure it counts for a lot.

Hitchhiking is out of the question. As is regular hiking. I may have smashed Kevin's nose but I'm not stupid enough to think that I can pull it off again if caught alone on a dark highway. But taking any public transportation, especially with me being a minor, would only work against me in the end.

Should I take what's behind door Number One: the possibility of a torturous death and my body being dumped in some boggy field, or what's behind Door Number Two : the unlikely chance that some bus attendant will recognize me despite the new do and report me?

I'll take the prize behind door number two.

After all, Kevin's drunk and nursing a broken nose and battered ego. There won't be any "Have You Seen This Girl?" posters for a few days. He would tell them that I was last seen wearing a baggy gray shirt and blue jeans, that I'm six feet tall with long curly brown hair and a mole by my lip.

There was nothing to do to help the height, but Charlene had covered my mole with concealer and painted my face to look like some throwback Cindy Lauper groupie. I look like Halloween trapped in the sunshiney land of Oz.

I had bought my first set of mall clothes and nearly choked at the price. Apparently not even Sears sold shirts for a buck. Kevin would describe a girl that no longer exists. *My* hair is short and smooth and my face appears mole-free and chemically altered by Maybelline. I've chosen to dress ridiculous enough to match my new face.

Combat boots and fashionably ripped, tight jeans that reveal striped stockings beneath. I've thrown out the baggy gray shirt and bought a long, tight black shirt that keeps falling off my shoulders, which I suppose is the point, but I'm not one of those spaghetti strap girls and my modesty is having a hard time keeping up with the plan. For good measure I've also added one of those retro, button-up vests and a jumble of long, gaudy necklaces.

I look like part of the Goth crowd, or the '80's reunion crowd, maybe a bad accident that happened between them. What I don't look like is the purposely shapeless, baggy, undone thing I used to be.

Rocky Evans?

Why no.

I am Maria Josepha Raquel Demure von Strassenberg.

Whoever she is.

Nineteen

She paused in front of the formidable doors.

The journey had been longer than she had imagined. Many times, too many times, she had to sit and rest. It took more than an hour for her to reach the imposing house with its high stone walls and iron gate. Only men with secrets need fortresses, *she thought. Her hand shook violently inside its dainty little glove, but the resolve running through her was iron. She would not turn away. It had been nearly a month now and no direct word had come from the von Strassenbergs. She would demand to know. It was cruelty to her heart and she had the right to know why she must suffer this agony.*

Katherine rolled the lace veil away from her eyes and pounded her shaking fist against the solid mass of wood. It took ages, or perhaps just minutes, before the door drew back to reveal a shadow of a man. He was gray and bent and looked as substantial as muslin. But his eyes, she noticed, were sharp and there was no lack of inner warmth in his countenance.

"May I help you, Miss?"

"I," she swallowed hard. This really was improper.

And what if the servants talked? "I have come to inquire after the young master's health? Please sir?"

The old man stared at her without flinching, making his silent calculations. When he spoke his voice was gravel and thunderstorms. "The master is away on business and shall be every day." He began to swing the door shut.

Katherine boldly stepped forward, positioning herself within the entrance. "Yes but, I am inquiring after the young master, Master Viktor? Is he home?"

Calculations, she saw them flit across his eyes. "He is indeed, miss, but the young master is not well."

"May I see him please?"

"He is not well."

Katherine had reached a point of immobility. "Yes, but may I see him?" It was a certain stalemate. Neither of them would be moved. He was stubborn in his protection of the master's home and she was just as certain that she would infiltrate the home if necessary. Best to handle things in a civil manner first, she had decided.

"You may not."

Not to risk being mistaken for the gentlemanly sort of butler, the old man swung the door to, sending Katherine stumbling back. She made a little "hmph" which sounded shockingly like Henrietta. "We shall see about that, old man," she whispered, clutching her parasol and heading decidedly toward the iron gates.

She knew he would watch her go, but she would not be leaving.

Katherine was considering becoming a suffragette. She would wear split-skirts and burn her corset and get a job as a clark in a bank. She would smoke those little cigars and shove her pretty white gloves down the throat of whoever had come up with the blasted idea in the first place.

"A man, most likely," she snarled in cursing tones. The wood behind the mansion was thick with under-growth, most of which sported tangles of thorns. She imagined he also had a moat with hungry reptiles lurking in its depth. "And he feeds them," she huffed. "In a pool in his dungeon where he has locked Viktor away. Because he knows," a mosquito dived toward her face and she swatted at it. "Viktor wishes to marry me, so he locked him up and threatened to feed me to the beasts if he escaped."

Her ramblings continued as she fought the thorns and briers and blood-sucking parasites. Was there no end to this stone wall? Her strength, she knew, would soon give way.

And then she saw it.

A groundskeeper's path just up ahead. She battled through the last clawing, snatching arms of undergrowth and breathed a sigh of victory, looking back at all she had come through. The door was hidden beneath the overgrown ivy. Maybe Count von Strassenberg was thorough about his security, but his groundskeeper was not plagued by the same paranoia. It was unlocked. Blessed serendipity! Katherine mopped her brow with a now worthless handkerchief. She was soaked through with perspiration. What good would it be to fight her way to Viktor if she was such a mess? But she would press on because Viktor needed her and he would be missing her, longing for the soft touch of her. He wouldn't care about her matted, undone hair and tattered dress. Maybe it would even make her look more romantic. It was a display of her violent affections for him.

She peered through the gate and the deserted grounds. The carriage house blocked her view of the back of the miniature castle. With another cautious sweep of the lawn Katherine hurried to the rough wooden wall of the small structure that housed the von Strassenberg's coach and motor wagon. She ignored the curious urge to peek in and see the motor wagon, having never seen one up close before, and continued toward the front of the building. It seemed abandoned everywhere she went, which was at once both a relief and a trifle unsettling.

There would be no one to hear her call for help. "Stop it," she scolded herself. "There will be no need." The landscaping had been done in English garden style, complete with a box hedge maze. She would have to come back under better circumstances to view the gardens, which felt somehow out of place in the otherwise foreboding environment. "It's only foreboding because you are not supposed to be here." The servants' door stood open. It was a hot, humid day and the kitchen was most likely hotter still. Gathering her skirts, Katherine ran on tiptoes to the door and stood, quiet as the little mouse she felt like, and listened. Nothing. No clanking of pans or tinkling of dishes and silverware. No cursing cook or scullery maid. Of course, for all she knew, the von Strassenbergs had neither cook nor maid.

Katherine edged into the deserted room and wondered where to go from there.

twenty

The short city of St. Louis greeted me with a wave of pelting rain.

The Arch was tucked away in angry clouds, though the bases were still visible. I imagine they must be much bigger up close than what they had looked from across the river. Maybe tomorrow it will be nice and I can go have a look-see, buy a postcard to eventually send to Charlene. Whether or not I will be going up to the top is debatable. Small places suffocate me and high places scare me and I imagine the Arch is a little of both. Charlene would drag me up there if she were here. In many ways Charlene is the brave one and I am beginning to regret not letting her come.

My original intention had been to spend the day exploring the city. I had looked up a few things on the Internet before leaving the library, but my plans hadn't included rain. My fall back is the typical answer for any teenager.

I will go to the mall.

Despite the veil of rain, I already know there are some differences between St. Louis and Nashville.

Nashville has a decidedly more Southern flavor than St. Louis and more gaudy bling.

People go to Nashville in search of their dreams; dreams of being country western singers or Christian musicians. It's like Hollywood for hicks.

But I'm not sure why people go to St. Louis. Maybe

it's more like they just get stuck here.

But St. Louis is not completely unlike Nashville. They both have train stations converted into malls/tourist attractions and Union Station is my new destination. There's a white cab at the bus station waiting for the opportunity to make some cash. I gladly oblige the bored driver and ask him to take me the few short miles to the mall. I may be short on funds, but walking in the rain in a city I don't know is not my thing.

Through the unfocused images of a city caught in the rain, I see a city of restaurants and corporations and baseball. The cabbie skirts us around the new stadium. I think he does it on purpose. He speaks in that strange sports talk, telling me about the start of the new season and asks if I follow baseball.

No. I really don't.

He assures me if I stay in town long enough I will become a baseball fan. It's a requirement of living in St. Louis. Everyone is a Cardinal's fan.

"Loyal," he tells me. St. Louis is a loyal town.

I allow him to go on his spiel, not interrupting his passionate monologue, and wonder if he had come here chasing a dream of being a baseball player or maybe a sports announcer. It seems likely. I'm just glad I didn't get into the cab wearing a Cubs shirt. Might have gotten me killed.

The streets of St. Louis are crowded with early rush-hour traffic speeding through the ever-increasing downpour. Through the rain and fog a tall, Gothic shadow looms.

"What is *that*?"

It looks like I've slipped through a wormhole or that maybe this piece of Earth existed in its own time-space continuum. The cabbie shrugs and looks back at me, waiting for his green light. "That's Union Station."

"That thing is Union Station?"

"Yea, cool huh?" The car turns onto Market Street

and I am shortly deposited in front of the mini-castle, forking over more cash and cringing inwardly as I do so. I crash through the rain and into the glittering castle-mall. It is more elegant than any mall I have ever been in and I wonder if I can even afford to breathe the air in here.

This is where my Plan B ends. Find some public place to get out of the rain: accomplished.

Now what?

Twenty-One

Katherine had never been in such a grand house before and believed that she was most definitely lost. There were twists and turns and long, dark corridors she was certain were only designed to entrap certain curious, young ladies. Her weight seemed to be growing heavier upon her tired bones and she was weighing the possibility of lying down on one of the Persian rugs and resting.

"Ah, but if the Count finds me he will drag me off and bury my corpse in the depths of his dungeon."

Vivid imagination won out and instead Katherine pressed herself against the coolness of the stone wall. The sound of her blood rushing through her was louder than her own ragged breathing. Calm, she told herself, slow down. She drew in a breath and held it for a few counts before allowing it to slowly roll from her trembling lips. This exercise was repeated for nearly five minutes before her breathing, and the rush of her blood, slowed and quieted.

"Better." She squirmed inside the infernal corset and, taking a cautious glance for modesty's sake, fanned her skirts. Sweat was rolling beneath the layers of cotton that constricted her. "One day," Katherine vowed. "Women will not be so insensible." She turned to continue down her chosen path.

And then she heard it--a mournful song cried out by the strings of a violin. It was unlike any song she had ever heard and the sound of it nearly broke her heart. The strings wept chords of pure melancholy. Katherine ached to hold their master, the one who made them cry out, for she knew the pain must be his.

Down the dark corridor she followed the woeful melody until she found the place where the music seeped through the door so loudly her heart trembled from it.

Should she knock? Should she wait? What if it was not him? "Well who else would it be, stupid?" She raised her gloved hand and dropped it again, her spirit overwhelmed by the wretched passion of the music. The chords rose to a crescendo and fell to a whisper of private agony and she could not imagine intruding upon his sadness, except for her own selfish reasons. She had to go in and hold him and offer him what comfort she could if only to quiet the pain she felt for him.

Katherine raised her gloved hand again while the music continued in its doleful whisperings and let it fall. The strings fell silent and she waited to hear his voice. It came and it was severe. "I told you I will have none of it! Leave me!" Stunned, Katherine considered tiptoeing away. But he doesn't know it's you.

Katherine pondered what to do next. Calling out would risk one of the servants overhearing her. Knocking again would only result in that harsh voice ordering her away again. With a settling breath, she reached for the ornate handle and cautiously began to push the door inward. Viktor was taking big angry strides toward the door. She noted in bizarre clarity his tousled hair, bare feet and shirt buttoned halfway down. In those few seconds, as he registered her presence she saw that his face was unshaven and that there were great, dark circles beneath his widening, storm-blue eyes. An unbidden smile broke across her face, revealing clearly the relief and joy she felt at the sight of him. Overcome, Katherine rushed to his frozen form and clasped his free hand in hers.

The violin clattered to the floor.

Everything in her wanted to press herself into him, to feel the strength of him supporting her and giving her strength. But there was none to be had. There was only fear in the eyes she had waited so long to see. At the realization of it, Katherine released his hand and stepped back. Viktor continued looking at her with those wide, disbelieving eyes.

All she could think to say was, "I had to know you were well."

The astonishment evaporated from his countenance and, to Katherine's dismay and confusion, was replaced with a fierce look she had never known in that gentle, mocking face.

In two strides he reached the door and swung it shut, twisting the lock. He went next to the windows, looked out over the grounds, and drew the curtains tightly together. When he turned to her, there was no softness there, but a hardness that showed the truth of the man he was becoming.

"Did anyone see you come?"

"Of course not, whatever on earth is wrong?"

Viktor paced the room, rubbing at the stubble on his cheeks as he considered their predicament. "You should not have come Katherine." Katherine's heart caught in her throat, but she would not cry. With as much stubborn pride as ever, she squared her shoulders and tugged lightly at her gloves. "Well, I see that you are not dying."

She turned to go and found herself suddenly caught in his grasp. "Don't be a foolish girl Katherine. I need you and all your stubborn bravery." Those gentle fingers stroked her sweat-cooled cheeks. "But not your silliness, Katherine. Those days are gone."

He held her tightly by the arms but she would not let him know his fierce grip caused her pain. There was a fire in him that burned through his flesh into hers with waves of fear and determination and the passion in it over-shadowed any pain she felt.

"I will be with you Katherine and I will come for you, but not just yet." Still grasping her arms, he pulled her in close, their faces so close their breath met in a torrent of barely checked urgency. Urgency to be as one, to be close, to protect and be protected. "You must go now. They will come again soon for me."

So many questions. She opened her mouth to give voice to all her curiosities when something rattled down the hall. Viktor went still as death. "They have come early."

Never releasing her, he looked around the room. "Curse you, you foolish girl." He shook her once and hard. Before she could fire back he hissed at her, "Do not speak," and dragged her into a dark anteroom. "Stay here behind the trunks. They will keep me for several hours. Wait until all is silent and then hurry out the way you came in." He shoved her roughly behind a stack of trunks and without looking back left her in the darkness.

Twenty-two

As was to be expected, the mall lost its appeal rather quickly. Whenever I have somewhere that I'm waiting to be I get so impatient that it creates this annoying physical reaction, like I get jittery and start pacing.

I tried to watch the people at The Fudgery as a distraction but even their fudge-whipping skills couldn't divert my attention. There were paddleboats at the little lake but that seemed more of a romantic endeavor and I was missing a partner. In the end I tucked myself into a corner and read my stolen library book for a very long half-hour.

But now the words slip by and I'm not even sure what happened in the last five pages.

It is only 4:30 and if I hurry I can blow my whole plan and let attorneys Drexler and Westhoeler know their client has come home.

It's very tempting. I'm just not sure how smart it is.

Twenty-three

Terror chased Katherine through the fields and the dust of the streets. She reached the steps of the Demure home without a breath of strength left in her. Stumbling and crashing through the door, sweat rolling in fountains beneath her dress and underclothes, Katherine slammed the heavy wooden door against all her imagined pursuers. At the noise, Josephine and Mrs. Demure rushed into the foyer, faces wrought with fright. "Miss Katherine!" Josephine exclaimed in an unwomanly volume, rushing to her mistress's side and catching her as she lost her last remaining bit of strength. Mrs. Demure dropped to her knees beside her daughter. "What is wrong, Katherine?"

Katherine limply batted away the soothing hands that, in their number, seemed to assail her. "Please I just need rest," she managed through labored breaths. "I have walked too far today."

"Josephine, what is this?" Katherine heard her father demand as he strode into the foyer. Another set of footsteps followed him. Josephine had pulled a handkerchief from her apron and was mopping Katherine's forehead and neck. "Miss Katherine says she has walked too far today."

She heard her father make his usual hmph of disgruntlement. Someone who smelled of expensive cologne and peppermint was behind her. The smell of him *made her nerves clench reflexively.*

"Let me see her."

"No!" Katherine recoiled from the soft, warm hand that reached out to her. It paid no attention to her withdrawal, but snatched up her trembling hand. The Count looked down at her speculatively, moving his awful, pulpy hands down to take her pulse.

Her father loomed over her and she imagined they looked like some tragic Greek statue. Maybe something like the painting of the death of Socrates.

"Is she delirious," barked Mr. Demure who was known to cover his fear with his authority.

The doctor, she knew, was done counting the beat of her blood rushing through her artery, but he continued to hold her wrist. Fear snaked through Katherine. Could he tell, that there were lies and secrets swelling within her? Were there some biological indicators of dishonesty? Would her racing heart reveal her fears or would he just take it as overexertion?

Herr Doctor would not immediately answer but surveyed the sanity in Katherine's eyes. And she knew, what he found there was certainly not delusional. "I believe," he began slowly, never looking away from her. "Her journey has exhausted her. She should be taken to bed immediately."

She snatched her eyes away from his prying gaze. "No I would prefer to rest down here. Mother, if you would play for me? It would help calm me." She sought desperately for another lie. What a tangled web, *she thought. "Truthfully, when I began to tire I was frightened I wouldn't make it home." Lie again. "It was awfully frightening. Mother please."*

Her eyes flickered unintentionally toward the doctor,

seeing if he was believing her lies. She saw it there, the dawning of his understanding. His grip on her delicate wrist tightened. Viktor had held her roughly like this, but she had felt in his grasp his desperate need to shield her. In the grasp of Count von Strassenberg she felt what Viktor had sought to shield her from. "I insist," he was saying in the midst of her realizations. "That you receive proper rest. I will carry you to your room." Mr. and Mrs. Demure were fussing about the lack of necessity.

Josephine was leaving her to fetch some cool cloths and a drink of water. But Katherine remained locked in the intrusive gaze of the unyielding Count. "A young lady of your...fragility should not be so foolish," a cruel whisper of a smile tugged at the corner of his wide mouth. He continued as though it was the same line of thought, but she knew he had spoken his only true meaning. "In exerting herself to such a dangerous extent."

Mr. Demure barked with laughter, his thumbs stuck in the pockets of his vest. "As I have said, either her stubbornness or her curiosity will be the death of her." Mrs. Demure gasped and chided her husband for such insensitivity. The doctor simply nodded, "I believe you might be correct in your assumptions Herr Demure." Her father chortled even louder over the shared sentiments. Mrs. Demure patted her daughter's hand. Their callous remarks had made her contrary and solidified her resolve. "If you would kindly take her to the lounge in the parlor, Mr. Demure. I would like to play for her. I believe she could use some music to calm her nerves."

You have been saved this time, *the Count's eyes whispered to Katherine.*

Her father's arms scooped beneath her and gently lifted Katherine to his chest. "I did not mean to upset you, child." He lowered his tone, "Truly your recklessness does frighten me at times. You must take better care of yourself." Katherine patted his hand gently and smiled up at him as he settled her onto the chaise lounge. Mrs. Demure descended upon her immediately, tucking pillows behind her and propping her feet up. Katherine thanked her and added, "I am sorry Father, I just always feel so confined." And this time, with all the intent in the world, she lifted her eyes to the waiting gaze of the Count. "It just feels at times that like I am locked away from all the world."

Twenty-four

"Yes, hi, I was asked to call this number?"

My impatience has won out.

"And who was it that requested you call?"

The Matrix twins.

"I don't know their names. They just gave me this card."

She is a well-trained assistant. It is almost quitting time on a Monday and some punk kid is calling and doesn't even know who she's calling for. The assistant doesn't even sigh. "One moment, let me check," is all she says before she gets my name and turns me over to the elevator music. At least it's straight up classical music and not some bad morph of pop music into easy-listening elevator tunes. It takes her less than two minutes.

"Are you calling from Nashville, Miss von Strassenberg?"

Well don't that sound impressive? "No ma'am, I'm in St. Louis."

"One moment please."

She's covering the receiver now, not even bothering to turn me over to the soothing lull of Brahms or Debussy.

"We will send a car to pick you up. What is your location?"

It makes me feel like some covert operative. Problem with that, someone on the other side always turns out to be a rat. For now though, I will have to forget Hollywood and trust these people. "I'm at Union Station. I'll be at the Market Street Entrance."

"Someone will be there in ten minutes." There is a click and she is gone. "Well that was weird."

The rain has slackened off to an annoying drizzle. I stand under the awning, trying to stay out of the way of the few people who still really feel a need to enter the building. A black Jag pulls up to the curb and the window rolls down. Matrix twin number one. I stroll through the drizzling rain and open the door even as the window is sliding back up. The car smells of leather and expensive cologne and something pepperminty. My foot is barely in and the door secure when he pulls back into traffic.

"We meet again, Miss von Strassenberg."

There is a comical edge to his tone and I imagine he is perhaps being well compensated for his part in wrangling me into the grasp of attorneys Drexler and Westhoeler. I situate my bag between my feet and strap the seatbelt across my chest, trying to pretend that whatever he has to say to me is of little to no importance. "Indeed we do, Mr. Smith."

Confused, he turns to look at me through his dark glasses and I see that he is not nearly as old as I had at first suspected.

"My name is Drexler."

"Oh," I say, watching the foreign buildings slip behind me. "Is it daddy's law firm then?"

"It's a family business. Just like yours."

I snuggle into the smooth leather of the car. "I don't know what you're talking about."

"Neither do I. But, I imagine we'll both know soon enough."

"If it's not your case, why did they send you? Are you their gopher boy? I would think the son of the big boss would be too important to send out to gather up a teenager." I don't know why, but I suddenly have the urge to irritate this guy to the best of my ability. His flashy car and him throwing around daddy's name tell me to strike at his pride.

"It's a show of respect to an old client."

My gut clenches. Maybe this *is* going to turn into a sappy daytime talk show. Maybe there is an old estranged, ridiculously rich, old granny winding her way through the wet streets of St. Louis.

One could only hope.

"So who is this old client?"

Mr. Smith clears his throat and focuses really hard on the changing yellow light. "I don't know how much I'm supposed to tell you." The light was still red. I put my hand on the lever to open the door. "Then maybe should I get to steppin'. If this is some hush-hush operation, I don't trust it." The light turns green and I can tell he's just holding back from plowing over the Audi in front of us. "There is nothing for you to be afraid of. There is something we need to present to you. It was put in our charge....many years ago."

"Is that why it's a family business? What are you guys? Like the Knights Templar or whatever?" Mr. Smith doesn't respond. He pulls into a parking garage and follows the path around and around until we are on the top level. "Do we go by helicopter next?"

"You don't need to be nervous."

"I'm not nervous."

"I think you are, and I think that's why you run your mouth like that."

The Jag stops in front of a sign declaring that this spot belongs to Mr. Drexler III. He steps out of the car and slams the door a little harder than intended. I scoop up the handles of my messenger bag and check to make sure nothing spilled out on the floor. When I sit back up to grasp the handle I find my door already opening.

I suppose there is a first for everything.

The sun is starting to creep out from behind the clouds. As a kid these moments would always pull me outside in search of the fairytale rainbow. There was something about their surreal beauty that drew me to them. But I've given up searching for fairytales. Mr. Drexler steps aside, umbrella in hand, opening the door wider. No one has ever opened a door for me before. The simple gesture has knocked all of the snark out of me. I mumble my thanks and step out of his way. He walks beside me, being careful to keep the umbrella over my head, and leads me to double doors where he places his thumb on a scanner.

"Wow," I say with noticeably more humility than before. "That's pretty high-speed."

"Indeed."

The doors swing open and we step inside, hearing the doors audibly lock behind us. The place smells clean, but not in a sterile hospital kind of way, more of a Pledge or Mr. Clean kind of way, like they have the carpets cleaned every week. The plush rug feels luxurious beneath my boots and I wonder what kind of family I must come from if they can afford lawyers like this. Mr. Drexler III leads me down a short corridor that turns and opens up to a lavish waiting area where, I assume, no one is ever kept waiting long. A well-dressed assistant hops up to take Mr. Drexler's coat and dripping umbrella.

"Any calls, Abbie?"

"No sir," the young woman replies, already moving toward a coatroom. "I set out refreshments in conference room three. Your father..." she stops herself, they've obviously had this conversation before. "The other attorneys are there already." For the first time she pauses to look at me. Her expression tells me that this is not how she had imagined the infamous Miss von Strassenberg.

Mr. Drexler motions to me and nods to his assistant, "Thank you Abbie."

"Yes sir."

Historic photographs line the walls but he moves me too quickly for contemplation.

Kevin's rented house could fit in conference room three and if we had owned a car it would fit nicely on the

—

99

highly polished table that is centered in the room. "Don't be afraid," the third whispers to me. Two other men are moving through the dimly lit room toward me, one is old and the other is ancient. Both men are tall and pale with silver hair, although the younger one has more to boast of than his father.

I can play this part, I tell myself.

"Mr. Drexler, first and second?" I smile, extending my hand for whoever reaches me first. Surprisingly it's the ancient one. His movements are nearly electric with excitement. He takes my hand; his feels wrinkly and papery, accentuating the wet clamminess of my own. He looks at me as though I am the *Venus de Milo*. "Miss Maria Josepha Raquel Demure von Strassenberg."

"So I've been told."

He pats my hand in a grandfatherly sort of way and moves so that his son can have the honor of shaking my hand. The Second is more composed than his father but I can tell he is less ecstatic to see me. "Please have a seat," he pulls a leather chair out for me. "I trust William was polite?" I take the offered seat, assuming that William is the Third and then realize that they all must be William. It's enough to make a girl laugh out loud, but the Third is right. I am a little nervous and I clamp down tight on the bubbles of laughter before they can turn into a regular giggle fit. The Second walks around the table to sit across from me. The First takes the chair beside me, admiring me openly as though I am some exquisite, rare find. Feeling a little more than slightly uncomfortable I turn to look for the Third. He is at the bar, opening a bottle of water, his back to us.

"He was very nice, yes, thank you."

"William get Miss von Strassenberg some..." He lets the sentence hang for my benefit.

"Water's fine. I can get it." I start to push away from the table but the Third is already walking toward me, he sets the bottle down in front of me. "Thank you," I whisper, feeling like a jerk for the attitude I gave him in the car. Maybe it wasn't so easy working for daddy. William walks away, most likely to get himself another water or just get away from his father.

"Miss von Strassenberg," the First begins.

"Please sir, I'm used to being called Rocky. Or, Raquel would be fine."

He laughs kindly and pats my hand again. "All right, *Raquel*, I'm sure you have a lot of questions for us, but unfortunately..."

"We don't have a lot of answers," the Second finished for his father. William comes back to the table, a wooden box in his hands. He hands the box to me and our fingers inadvertently brush. My nerves jump, startled at his touch, and I look up to find that he has removed his dark glasses. I have never been to the ocean but I have seen pictures. His eyes remind me of the seas of green and brown seaweed swaying in the gentle waves. I've never seen such green eyes. "What we have," the Second continues, completely unaware of the electricity passing between his son's fingers and my own. "Is what's in this box. William, the key."

The green-eyed young man, whom I will never again think of as the Matrix twin, seems a little disconcerted as he withdraws his hands from the box and my touch. He stiffly crosses the room again and stops in front of an oil painting, which he removes. A safe, with a flashing red light is nestled into the wall. William steps up and places his eye in front of the light.

The Second looks at me and smiles proudly, if not smugly. "Biometrics. We're the only three that can get into that safe."

"Nice," I say with what I hope is the acceptable amount of admiration.

There is a click and William pulls the safe open. When he turns back around there is a small, antique key between his long, elegant fingers. Back when I thought he was stalking me in Nashville I hadn't stopped to notice it, but William is not at all bad looking, especially with those ridiculous glasses taken off. He looks at me, weighing something in his thoughts, and hands the key to his father. Best not to get a teenager's heart all a-twitter, I guess.

"This," the Second says with a bit of dramatic flair. "Is the key to knowing who you are, if you'll pardon the pun."

I won't, especially since he planned it. Corndog.

The key he holds looks like something from a movie with trolls and shrinking and growing little blonde girls. I look at the box for the first time. It looks impenetrable. A golden plate is on the front. In elegant script are the entwined initials *KRD* and the year 1875.

I'm not so certain about the *K*, but I have a pretty good idea about the *R* and the *D*.

Raquel Demure.

Twenty-five

"Katherine Raquel Demure," Mrs. Demure patted a cool, wet cloth against her daughter's forehead. She had gone wrong with this one somehow. Henrietta may be a forward, overly vivacious girl, but she was still womanly. Katherine, on the other hand, was too adventurous and inquisitive for a girl. No respectable young man would think of her escapades, let alone her illnesses, as evidence for a good wife. "One day, I'm afraid your father is right, your curiosity will get the better of you."

"Better to die curious, " Katherine whispered. The fatigue had begun to overwhelm her. "Than to die an insufferable old bore."

"And what of dying a penniless old bore?"

"I will become a great novelist and write of my adventures."

Her mother sighed heavily, leaving Katherine's side. "Such dreams are nonsense and best left to old age, after you have secured a house and husband for yourself." Katherine did not respond. Her mother had come of age in a time when women had no other choice but to marry and marry well, when marriage was an exchange of money and property and not love. But things were changing and Katherine knew she would only marry for the fiercest love.

But would Viktor have her?

She was beginning to wonder if this pain she felt, this

pain that cut through every ounce of her reason and sensibility, was the reason people had degraded marriage down to nothing more than money. Maybe love, unfathomable love, was too much for people, so they had traded it for something easier. "But I will not give up on him."

"What was that dear?"

Katherine looked up to her mother. "Nothing mother." Mrs. Demure smile tenderly. What a thing to risk, *Katherine thought,* to ask a man to love you. My own mother loves me, despite my flaws and failings, but could a man who had had no part in bringing me into this world, a man who does not share my flesh and blood? Could a man truly love a woman like that? Maybe what Henrietta seeks from men is so much safer than what I ask.

Katherine returned her mother's smile and, certain her daughter was comforted enough for the moment, Mrs. Demure retreated, leaving Katherine to listen to the whispers and quiet chortles of the men in the foyer.

"Love is a dangerous thing." Katherine stretched and her eyes fell on him. The Count watched her intently from the light of the foyer. You have become my enemy, *she thought, locked upon those cold eyes. "I must return home," he was saying to her father, "My son is not well," but his eyes never strayed from Katherine's. "I have been gone from him too long."*

"Of course, of course," Mr. Demure was saying, he did not realize that this truly was not his conversation. "You know I understand all too well," this he added with a gesture to his feeble little daughter.

The Count placed his hat upon his head in a grand, sweeping gesture toward Katherine, "I will return to see that you recover well, my dear." He smiled his reptilian smile and Katherine, unaware of its origins, found herself smiling in return. "I look forward to it, Doctor."

Before she shifted to turn her back to him, Katherine noticed Herr Doctor's eye twitch ever so slightly, "As do I."

twenty-six

The Second continues to hold the fairytale key up for my viewing. "There is one thing we must ask of you." Ah, so this wasn't going to be so easy. Without meaning to, I look to William for encouragement. He's looking at his father, apparently as befuddled as I am. "Father you said all we needed to do was find her and give her the box and the key."

The Second smiles at me and suddenly I find him to be a very schmarmy sort of lawyer. "It's a simple thing. A DNA test. We just need a little blood sample. If you can wait a week for the result, I think you'll find your patience will be rewarded in dividends."

I look from First to Second to Third.

The ancient one still looks like the doting grandfather, as though all is right in the world. The old one looks suspicious of me and somewhat disappointed. And the young one, the one with the startled green eyes looks uncertain for the first time since we met. I look to him for the answer I should give.

He goes to bat for me. "Father, who else would have that name?"

The Second waves off his son's deductive reasoning. "We need to be absolutely certain son, and DNA is the most certain way I know of."

"But where will we even get a sample to compare hers against?"

The million-dollar question.

"We have one."

I wonder who should feel more betrayed at this point. I'm starting to feel a little duped and on edge about the whole thing. Bringing needles into a situation can never turn out to be a good thing. But William has invested a lot of time and effort into finding me and bringing me in and he seems to just be discovering that there are answers the Second and First have that he does not.

The wooden box is cool and hard beneath my trembling fingers. So many secrets and answers inside such a small box. What's a little blood? And I know the Second is right. Despite how unlikely it is that anyone else on the planet is cursed with the same awful name, the most responsible course of action would be matching DNA. And the man's security system says he definitely favors biological evidence as proof of identity.

"Miss von Strassenberg?"

I look to William for an answer but he is staring hard out the tinted windows. Well, it's all me then. "All right then," I hear myself saying. "Let's do this thing."

The First claps once, loudly and I almost expect a, "Yeehaw!" to follow it. Maybe a, "Shazaam!" Instead all I get is the Second speaking into some spaceship-looking intercom. "Abigail, please let Dr. Harrison know we're ready for the sample."

The disembodied voice of the young receptionist chimes back, "Yes sir." I sit back, waiting for Dr. Harrison and his needle.

Twenty-seven

She had awakened feeling every muscle in her frail body. The drapes had been pulled tightly together but edges of sunlight had shone through. By the brilliance of the sneaking light she had known she had slept the morning away. Katherine had tried to sit up but the fatigue and pain in her body had overwhelmed her. It had seemed like hours before Josephine had come to check on her.

"What time is it?" she had asked.

Josephine had wiped at her forehead, for this surely cured all ills. "Oh Miss Katherine, you slept all through the day and today is Wednesday."

Katherine had been stunned and her first thought had been of the count/doctor. Had he given her something to induce sleep? But no, he had not had the opportunity. Josephine had plumped the pillows around Katherine's head, "You slept something frightful, tossing and sometimes screaming."

Katherine's blood had paused in its course through her body. "What did I say? When I was screaming?"

"Nothing miss, you just screamed. The Count, I mean, Dr. von Strassenberg came to look in on you."

So he had been given the opportunity. "Why didn't mother and father tell the good doctor I already have a perfectly capable physician?"

Josephine had continued to fuss and fret, straightening and tucking in blankets, smoothing Katherine's tangled hair. "I imagine because they do not wish to insult the good doctor. He is becoming quite the item of talk in town, you know? He has been given a position at the University."

"That is all well and good Josephine, but being a professor does not make him my physician and Dr. Craig is more aware of my condition and its intricacies. Besides, the professor/count/doctor may take it upon himself to turn me into one of his experiments." Josephine had gasped at her mistress's impertinence.

"Now miss, that man has been nothing but good to you. You should not speak of him so harshly."

There was little point in continuing. Katherine had sighed, "May I have some broth, Josephine? I am frightfully hungry." Josephine had smiled, glad to be done with uncomfortable conversation, and hurried off to fetch the broth.

Five days had passed since that early afternoon. Any time Katherine had attempted to stand waves of gray and nausea swept over her. She had caught herself wondering more than once as to what the good doctor had done to her during his visit. He had not come again during her recovery. "He is most likely satisfied that he did sufficient damage to render me useless these many days," Katherine muttered to the empty room. Henrietta was rarely in her company, not that she missed the rants and ravings of her older sister who was certain she would die an old, blue-stockinged spinster if she did not marry soon.

Katherine sat up and waited for the torrents of unconsciousness that would assail her, but none came. "Perhaps the drug has worn off," she whispered.

The door flew open and Katherine instinctively yanked the sheets off the bed to cover herself. Henrietta whirled into the room, screeching in near-hysteria. "Mother where has my petticoat gone? And my silk hat?" She noted Katherine standing there, frozen with the sheet spread across herself. "Don't just stand there, do you know where they've gone?"

"I have been in bed for five days Henrietta."

Henrietta huffed, "Well congratulations, Katherine. Now help me find my things."

"What on earth for?"

Henrietta whirled on her, those hazel eyes crazed with excitement and possibilities. "The Lemps are having a ball this very night!" That was nothing so unusual. The wealthy owner of the brewery and his wife often had balls and teas that were reserved for only the height of St. Louis society. "It seems they have a ball nearly every month Henrietta."

Skirts and petticoats were flying from the armoire. "Oh posh! Katherine you are such a simpleton." With unbridle energy Henrietta continued her violent rummaging. "He will be there you dolt."

Katherine's heart clutched and she was certain the waves would begin. "He?"

Henrietta turned, her precious new petticoat in hand, triumph in her eyes. "Viktor. He will be attending the ball and all the town is talking about it." With a lunatic frenzy in her eyes, Henrietta approached her trembling sister. "Tonight, dear little frail Katherine, Viktor von Strassenberg shall be mine."

twenty-eight

They are sticking me in a hotel for the next week. No one even bothered to ask where my adult supervision was. Since they know everything else about me I figure they probably know my birthday is in two weeks anyway. I will be eighteen and no adult supervision will be necessary. Not that I really had any supervision anyway. I don't think Kevin really counted. Being passed out drunk doesn't exactly make one the ideal caregiver.

The attorneys Drexler are holing me up in the Marriott. What better place to dump a teenager than in a hotel attached to a mall? I'm not going to complain. It's better than the seedy places I had imagined would be necessary on my tight budget.

William sits in the car beside me, waiting for the light to change. I'm not sure what to say to him anymore. He's not the comical figure he once seemed to be. He may be working at daddy's law firm but he certainly isn't high on their totem pole.

"How old are you William?"

He doesn't turn to me, but keeps his eyes on the now slowly rolling traffic. "Twenty-two."

What?

"And you're an attorney? Are you some child genius or some crap?"

He laughs bitterly. "No, I'm just interning at the firm. I just finished my first year of law. I took the fast track through undergrad and went straight to law school."

Impressive. "So do you go to school around here?" Another red light. I can almost hear him cursing in his head, but instead of voicing his expletives he smirks, "No, not around here."

I turn to watch out my window as groups of business professionals and romantic couples stream into the restaurants lining the street. I envy them their normal lives. "Where then?"

He waits to answer. "Where do you think?"

Where would rich daddy send his gopher son? "Harvard?"

"Close, but no. Yale."

I choke on the breath I had been inhaling. Harvard had been a joke. I have never known anyone intelligent enough or money enough to even think about going to Harvard and here I sit in a dark car with a handsome guy who is only four years older than me and he goes to Yale Law School? Fate is laughing at me, toying with me while my blood is shipped off to some lab to decide my path. Would the answer from the test put me in the running for someone like William?

Stop it! I shout silently at my thoughts. *Don't be a stupid girl. Focus.*

I'm trying so hard to not look at him, to not stare at that perfectly sculpted silhouette but the events of the day have made it nearly impossible not to admire him. The sight of Union Station at night, however, succeeds in pulling my thoughts away from the intriguing Mr. Drexler III.

"Oh my gosh, it's beautiful."

It does look like a castle complete with fountains and statues. It is the most romantic place I have seen in my life. The idea of it puts me on edge a little, but not in a scared way. There is an excitement crackling through me and I can feel my stupid hands beginning to shake with some unknown anticipation.

"We thought you would be comfortable here. There's a lot to see and do and all in walking distance. Unless of course," he adds quickly. "You want to go somewhere else, we could send a car."

Ah, but will you be driving it? Arg! Stop it! "Oh, thanks."

William parks the Jag and this time I know to wait while he walks around and opens the door for me. Suddenly, ridiculously shy, I smile and focus too intently on the architecture of the entrance. It's too grand for me. I'm now very aware of my Cindy Lauper/goth look and how it doesn't fit in with the rest of the clientele or the décor. As William escorts me into the staggeringly elegant lobby I pull my messenger bag across me in a feeble attempt to hide myself. He notices I'm lagging behind, my embarrassment slowing my steps, and waits for me to catch up. Placing a hand on the small of my back, he leads me to the receptionist's desk. I feel the pressure of his long fingers against my back and can't even yell at myself to stop being a moron. I'm too busy wondering if he can feel me trembling at his unexpected touch.

Stupid girl, stupid girl, is all my brain can eek out. But I can't help it. There's just something about him, something so unlike any boy I have ever met. Nashville was filled with hot young wannabes and university students. Charlene would drag me downtown so we could watch the hotties go by. I had never seen the point in it and usually wound up sitting against a tree with a good book while she daydreamed about the future country singer that would one day whisk her away. But William, I was finding, is more than all those boys. There is something tormented in his sparse laughter and I just want to crawl inside his brain and find the cause of it.

"Ready?" He's talking to me and I have no idea of what he's saying.

"I'm sorry?" I notice for the first time that he has slipped his dark glasses back on. Odd that. Maybe he has to wear them so as not to blind the ladies with the brilliance that is him. *It's probably some medical condition you idiot.* "Whatever."

Oops, that was audible.

"Sorry," he asks, and I can see he's trying not to smile. I'm confused because sometimes he just really irritates me and other times I just want to fall at his feet and beg him to runaway with me. Right now, I'm caught somewhere in the middle of the two.

"Nothing. Yea, I'm ready."

He smiles at the distraction in my words and I think of how good it would feel to just slap him really hard across his smug face.

Twenty-nine

"Katherine I really do not believe this is a wise decision." The carriage pulls to a stop in the crowded street. Katherine tugs at the frilled neckline of her gown, wishing the fashions of the day were not quite so plunging. Henrietta twitched impatiently beside her. "Mother I will be fine. I am quite well." And I would not miss this but for the death of me, she told herself fiercely. Henrietta checked her reflection in her small looking glass. "Oh no, let her come mother, I want her to be there to see how Viktor prefers me over all the others." Katherine restrained herself, whether it was laughter or a sudden urge to yank her sister's curls, she held it in.

The summer dance at the Lemp Mansion was beginning to look like the event of the season. The streets were jammed and the house looked like it was stuffed to overflowing. Katherine waited impatiently while Mr. Demure and the driver descended and carefully helped the women and their skirts and bustles from the carriage and into the streets. The evening was warm but Katherine pulled her shawl over the nakedness of her pushed-up cleavage.

Lively music poured through the opened windows. Mr. Demure took his wife's arm and led her into the frivolity. Henrietta, forgetting the dictates of feminine behavior, *gathered her skirts and fled up the steps before her parents and disappeared into the throng of the St. Louis elite.*

Mr. and Mrs. Demure had forgotten their daughter's frailty in their excitement. Katherine slowly managed the steps, gripping the rail and praying her limbs did not begin to give way. Another step and another and then suddenly an arm wrapped around her waist, holding her up as she attempted another step. Tears of relief nearly sprang into her eyes as she turned to thank him. The old man smiled back at her. "I do apologize," he whispered cordially. "You were expecting someone else perhaps?" Count von Strassenberg cackled at the shock so clear upon her face. "A younger gentleman perhaps?" His free hand gripped hers, rubbing across her knuckles. Katherine wanted to pull away but he was too strong for her. "Ah," he smiled. "I thought so." He rolled his fingers over the ring hidden beneath her glove. "I will be needing that back, my dear."

She found she could only whisper at him despite the volume of the music and the laughter that filtered from the house into the streets. "Viktor said you wished for me to have it."

They were almost at the top. Others were streaming around them. She cursed her weakness. She could be safely inside by now. "Why would I want a foolish, frail girl to have this ring? Viktor lied. He stole it from me."

They reached the top. Katherine straightened herself despite the fatigue that was creeping in. "Then you will have to steal it back. Viktor gave it to me and I will keep it until he tells me otherwise." The Count stepped closer to her. She smelled his cologne and his peppermints. "I am not afraid of you doctor."

116

He merely released her and tipped his hat, "As I said, you are a foolish girl." And then he left her.

"This is your room." William slips the card in and unlocks the door for me. *Room?* It's more like an apartment, minus the kitchen. But who needs a kitchen when there's one fully staffed downstairs?

"Great Caesar's ghost!"

William walks in before me and I can't believe he doesn't feel as nervous as I do. Probably because he isn't crushing on a twit teenager. "Well, father said to make sure you were comfortable. I had Abbie call and reserve the best room they had available."

Abbie...I wonder if they are secretly an item?

"Thank you, but this really isn't necessary." I close the door behind me and follow him farther into the room. "Well," he shrugs. "I know you weren't planning to hang around doing nothing for a week, so I hoped this would make up for that and," he pauses and now he seems uncomfortable. Leaning back against a square column, he loosens his tie. I place my bag down on the shiny little coffee table. "I really am sorry. I didn't know they were going to ask you for..."

"My blood," I smile, lifting the tangle of necklaces off. I hadn't realized how much they weighed.

He smiles that sweet, smug, smirk of his. "I didn't tell you before but I kind of like this new eighties meets nineties pop star look of yours. It's an improvement."
I don't look up from the buttons of the retro vest as I struggle to undo them. "You're a jerk."

"I take it your step-dad didn't approve of you leaving?"

I shrug out of the vest. " I didn't exactly ask." He's still smiling at me in that infuriating way of his and I'm not quite sure where to go with this. "I need to, um, powder my nose. Do you have a map for this place?" He laughs, a real laugh this time, and points me in the direction of the bathroom. "Great Caesar's ghost!" I exclaim again and hear him laughing as I close the door.

The bathroom is bigger than my old bedroom, complete with whirlpool tub and separate shower and mirrors and closets. Maybe the DNA test will take longer than they expect? I hope.

My reflection startles me. It has been hours since I have looked at the short-haired girl with the piles of make-up. "In a minute," I say to the strange girl's reflection and head for the toilet, which has a room of its own. It is good to be rich, if only for a week. As I head to the sinks I thank my eccentric ancestors for their persistence in finding their heir.

It takes five good washes before every last trace is gone. It never occurred to me or Charlene to pack make-up remover in my bag. Now with it all scrubbed off, I look suddenly younger and curse myself. Smoothing back the wet edges of my short hair I head back to the column where I left him. He's not there. He's sitting on the yellow leather couch, feet resting beside my bag. Startled, he snaps off the television and hops to his feet.

This is awkward.

"There you are." And I know he's not just talking about my reemergence from the bathroom.

"Yea, I could've been done sooner but they didn't have a power washer."

"And I thought they had everything in this place." His hands are shoved in his pockets and I wonder if that's to keep him from fidgeting in the awkwardness of the moment. "Well, it's good to see you back." He clears his throat and with nothing else to offer I throw out,

"Why do you where those glasses all the time?" I wait for him to be offended but he just stands there, smiling and watching me.

"I have a sensitivity to light."

I flop down on the couch and look up at him. It feels good to sit. "Are you a vampire? You're almost pale enough."

He laughs again, "No, just bad genetics."

I flip the television back on and quickly change my mind. With a sudden realization, I blurt, "I'm hungry."
He gestures toward the phone. "You can order anything you want from room service, we'll cover it."

"Okay," and I know my weak smile of gratitude lets on too much. That wasn't exactly the answer I had been hoping for.

"You're probably worn out. Running away. Strange meetings with old men. Giving blood. I should get going."
I hop up, not wanting him to leave, and follow him to the door. He turns on his heel and we crash lightly into each other. Laughing nervously he pulls out his wallet. "Sorry, I just remembered, the First and Second, as you call them, said I should give you this. If you have any trouble have them call the office." He places a platinum credit card in my hand. "They thought you might need to do some clothes shopping. And," he smiles that enraging smile "For once, I think I agree with them."

"Shut up, Mr. Smith." He ignores me, reaching into his pocket. "The old man gave me this to give to
you." Producing a cell phone from his pocket he places it in my hand. "Our numbers are already programmed in, call us whenever you need to." Motioning behind him he adds, "There's a DVD player, maybe you could get some movies at the mall or something."

"Yea," I say, opening the door. "I was thinking about getting *The Matrix*."

He tips down his glasses, those green pools shining at me over the dark rims, "Goodnight Miss von Strassenberg."

I smile, a little too coyly I think, and close the door.

Thirty-one

It was not his desire to attend a soiree. He had not recovered quite yet and still tired too easily. It was only his father's insistence that brought him to the Lemp's home this evening. If he had believed she would be here, there would have been no debate. As it was, his father had assured him that she would still be too weak. This was mentioned days ago, when the count was certain his son was safely secured and could not be a threat to him. His father knew there was an uncommon strength that coursed through his son and he was careful not to provoke Viktor because of it.

He had already been invited to join the others at cards, but he had no heart for it. This appearance was only for his father's profit. The coffers, he knew, were low. It was the only reason his father had accepted the position at Washington University. Or perhaps, he thought, it was also for the chance to increase his status with the upper echelons of St. Louis society. There were whispers of moving the nation's capital to the gateway city and the old man craved power as much as he craved wealth.

Although, *Viktor mused bitterly*, popularity does not concern him.

Tucked into the shadows, Viktor watched the swirling skirts and the bright smiling faces and wondered what it would be like to be so free of concern. He thought of the splendor of the courts in Vienna and how the young ladies had winked and carried on at the sight of him. His father had chosen his bride long ago, the daughter of a wealthy baron. She was an uncommonly tall and solidly built girl who excelled in music and showed an interest in science. Klaus von Strassenberg had maneuvered and plotted until the girl, who had no shortage of suitors, was guaranteed to be his future daughter-in-law.

But that had all changed and they had fled Austria and then France and then Spain and then finally given up all hopes of a life in Europe. They had set sail for America when he was fifteen. He wasn't certain of all that had transpired. Klaus had never bothered to tell him. It was none of his concern, he would go where he was told. He only knew that something had gone wrong at the University in Vienna and that his father had made powerful enemies. They had fallen from grace in the eyes of the royal establishment, though once their family had been under the Empress Dowager's own employ.

They had fallen and fled to the promising city of St. Louis, sending money ahead of them to build their new empire. St. Louis, the Count had heard, was a place of science and society with a bit of the West still left in its blood. Viktor had followed with the hope of attending the University and becoming a physician himself. He was determined to find an answer to his illness.

The answer had finally come but not from the halls of academia.

Viktor was caught up in his musings until the sight of chestnut curls and skin so pale it seemed translucent caught his eye. The laughter and tinkling and music died around him. She was here. He was at once elated and *terrified. Had the old man seen her? What would he do if he had? Viktor pushed himself off the wall and waded through the sea of bustles and skirts and admiring gentleman.*

Thirty-three

I woke up to some travel show, some guy climbing mountains and buying goat cheese or something.

It was still dark outside and the TV seemed shockingly loud and obnoxious. I flicked it off and listened to the quiet around me and turned the noise back on. Remnants of my dinner and dessert sat on the coffee table in front of me. I hadn't even made it to the big four-poster bed. Fortunately the couch was comfortable and my neck wasn't screaming in pain. Drexler the Third had apparently been right. Running away and giving blood could make a girl tired. The sleep had been good and very much needed.

I stand and look around the expansive room and feel the dirt of the previous day hanging on me. The ridiculous bathroom is there just waiting for me. I stand on the tiles, contemplating climbing into the big tub, just for kicks and giggles. But I am not a soaking in the bath kind of girl and opt for a shower instead.

The water comes out hot and hard and my knees nearly buckle from the relaxing wave that sweeps over me. I could live like this the rest of my life and be quite content. The little bottles of shampoo and conditioner fill the shower with an intoxicatingly fruity smell as I wash the new do, noting all the while that short hair is infinitely more efficient. But I don't care about efficiency today. I'm gonna see how long it takes to run these people out of hot water, if it's even possible. The hotel even provided a little poof ball. I use it to scrub off the dirt from running in the streets of Nashville and the stank of the six hour bus ride. I shave and rinse and wonder what to do next, reveling in the fact that Kevin was not outside the door, banging his fists and reminding me of the water bill. And the electric bill, because he was pretty certain I wasn't takin' no cold shower for no fifteen minutes.

It is good to be here. I sink to the shower floor and let the water roll over me and the steam make a blanket around me.

The hot water outlasts my attention span. I shut it off and wrap myself in a towel that is not thread bare or faded beyond recognition. Everything here is soft and perfect.

And quiet.

I pad out to the living area. The sun is rising and I don't know if it's ever looked more stunning. Out the window I see the city of St. Louis, bright and fresh after the rains. Today I will go exploring. This thought reminds me of my wardrobe. The jeans and shirts in my bag seem grossly improper. I know I will have to wear them one last time, just long enough to go on a shopping spree. The thought makes me laugh. The sales girls will most definitely be calling the credit card company to make sure the scraggly thing in poor-girl clothes didn't steal the company credit card of Drexler and Westhoeler.

Thirty-three

As ever, Henrietta found him first. It was her unnecessarily loud exclamation that drew Katherine's attention to him. "Viktor! Darling! There you are!" Katherine stopped and spun in the direction of her sister's obnoxious trilling. Dancers spun gaily around her, disregarding her desperation to see him. With the last turn of a well-dressed man, she saw him. And Henrietta's stupid little head was in front of him. But he was paying her no attention. His eyes were scanning the crowd.

I'm here, she thought desperately, fighting her way through the couples.

Breaking through the twirling crowd she nearly fell at his feet. Henrietta glanced down at her and made a disgusted little sound. "I told mother she shouldn't come, you know. She is still too weak...." Her snide comments trailed off as Viktor turned from her and grasped Katherine's arm, holding her steady. But Henrietta would not be dissuaded, not even at the sight of Viktor locked in Katherine's gaze. "She should really sit, you know? She has been ill all this week."

With his support, Katherine straightened, her shawl falling from her shoulders. With her free hand she slipped the shawl off and held it out to her gaping sister, never taking her eyes from his, "Hold this Henrietta dear."

Henrietta stammered and yanked the shawl from her sister's hand.

Viktor stood very close to Katherine. Henrietta watched as he leaned forward and whispered in her little sister's ear, "You are beautiful Katherine Demure," and pulled back to smile gently down at her. "Dance with me Katherine." It was not a question but a plea, which Henrietta knew from the look on her sister's face, need not even be voiced. Katherine only smiled in answer and placed her tiny little hand in Viktor's strong grasp. They stepped away into the dancing, heedless of the music the others were moving to. They danced to their own melody, without speaking and without noticing the envious eyes that followed them across the dance floor.

When the music ended, it was too soon. Viktor held her, not caring if he did not have the music as an excuse. "He told me you would not be here."

Did he know then?

She weighed the tragic look in those stormy eyes and knew that he did. "What has he done to you Viktor?" Gossiping eyes continued watching them and whispers passed through the crowd like a hot breeze on a summer day. He shook his head, wanting to tell her but unable to give words to the horrors he had discovered over the last month. "I cannot say Katherine. Only," he saw the unabashed stares then and the gossiping lips moving passionately throughout the crowd. Viktor dropped his hand from her tiny waist and stepped back. She saw them then too and decided there was nothing less important in the world.

"Ignore them Viktor and tell me what he has done to you. You are not well, anyone can see that." Despite his dapper attire and his squared shoulders, he did look ill.

The dark circles, while less obvious, still hung beneath his eyes and he was thinner than before. His skin was sickly pale and looked devastatingly weary.

"It is not them, Katherine. I simply cannot. But," he whispered, mindful of the dancing couples who were purposefully directing their paths near them. "I do need to speak with you Katherine. Privately. I need to ask something of you. Something very... important and it is no small thing to ask."

Katherine had forgotten to breath. Could he possibly mean? But he had to know her father would never allow it. Viktor had not even begun at the University yet. And Mr. Demure did not believe in a man who lived off his father's wealth. He considered such nonsense a bit feminine. It was for a woman to live off the wealth of a man. Any good man earned his living. Katherine smiled in the midst of her thoughts. Her father was a bit of a progressive man.

"Katherine?"

She looked back up to him. He sighed in frustration and took her by the elbow, leading her to the less crowded patio.

Thirty-Four

"Hey there, I thought I might find you here."

"Yea, wasn't it just like sixty-five degrees yesterday?"

"Welcome to Missouri."

I am not usually a poolside girl but after the dreariness of yesterday it seemed only natural to seek out the hotel pool. "Is the weather always this manic?"

"Always."

He smiles down at me through his dark glasses. Here by the pool, in his tailored suite and shiny black shoes, he looks more out of place than I feel. An awkward silence grips us. Hot little things in itty-bitty bikinis stroll across the patio in the hopes of procuring an early tan. He never shifts in their direction and I find a new respect for young William. "Not getting in," he asks, teasing because he knows the answer.

"Absolutely not. I forgot my swimsuit." I begin to struggle out of the lounge chair and he extends a hand to me.

"I see you did go shopping."

His long fingers wrap around mine and he easily hoists me up.

"Yes, it was nearly torture but I managed to survive."

"I'm glad of it."

I can't look at him when he talks like that. Reminding myself that William is just a very chivalrous kind of guy, I shake off the struggling desire to fantasize

---

about the possibilities.

He's just smiling at me and I want to slap him. I've never known any person, any decent person, that I have wanted to hit so much.

The awkwardness begins to settle again. I blurt, "So what're you doing here?"

"The other attorneys suggested I check in on you."

"You mean they wanted to make sure I hadn't bolted?"

"Most likely."

"You could have just called." Ug. Why did I say that? I'm caught in this ludicrous, internal battle, hurt or flirt. He needs to stop smiling and being so dang nice. I would rather he just mock me and keep me in hurt mode. "So you decided to forego the Goth-wannabe look?"

"Yes. I figure this extreme or that is a far enough stretch from where I was. I'm still incognito."

He laughs. "And you're still shorter than me. How tall are those heels?" Looking all the way down to my clodhopper feet, I swivel my legs to admire my first set of heels. "Shut up. The sales girl helped me and she said if I was going to buy this dress then I just had to get these shoes to go with it."

"I'm sure she did. So is this the going-safari-in-heels look?" He finds himself amusing but my solid confidence created by the attentive gushing of the salesgirl is starting to crumble. "I thought it was more of an ultra-casual trench coat, business kind of look." William laughs again and I poke him hard in the chest, which only makes him laugh harder. Forget slapping him, I crave hauling off and decking him. I had taken a risk, dressing all rich-girly and he was mocking me. Instead of bruising his stupid, beautiful face I settle for shoving his shoulder. With amazingly fast reflexes for a twit pencil-pushing lawyer, he snatches my hand and steps closer. I try to yank away but his grip is too strong and I'm beginning to realize that my balance in these shoes isn't the greatest. Stupid salesgirl. She preyed on my ignorance.

"Miss von Strassenberg," he whispers, still holding my hand. "You are stunning. It's only," he releases my hand and looks away and I think that maybe he is having the same epic internal battles that I am. "I did some digging last night and thought I might take you on a little field trip."

My inclinations toward him shift as violently as the St. Louis heat. "Where are we going?"

"It's not far from here and I think you will enjoy it a lot more than the mall."

"Well, that isn't saying much."

He extends an arm and, unfortunately, I think it's only because he's afraid I will topple over. "But I think, despite how flattering those shoes may be, you'll want to change into something a little more comfortable."

I hate him.

William Drexler III parks his Jag in front of a building that is an oddly cohesive mélange of glass, steel, and stone. "What is this," I ask. "Some kind of lock-up?"

"Not at all," he points to a sign I had missed during my musings. "You're quite paranoid."

"I get that a lot."

Missouri Botanical Gardens. I don't know what he's plotting but I'm willing to follow. The Third helps me from the car. "Why here?"

"I'll get to that." He smiles that mysterious smile again. He loves making me wait for things. Maybe it's an attorney skill. Whatever it is, it annoys the crap out of me. I try to untangle the mass of confused emotions while he walks me inside and pays for our tickets. There's a glittering gift shop but so far everything else looks gray and I'm glad for the lack of romance in the place. It would help keep my ridiculous teenage thoughts in check. Maybe.

"All right," he says, resting his dang hand on the small of my back again. "Let's go see the gardens." I can't respond, witty or otherwise, knowing my tongue will trip all over itself. His long fingers burn an impression into my skin that lasts even after he steps aside to hold the door open for me.

It's a beautiful place. A mixture of statues and trees and flowers, but I am not easily distracted, at least not usually. "So you said you did some digging last night?"

He smiles at my singular mind. "You don't want to just enjoy your surroundings?"

"No, I want to know what they have to do with me. Or am I allowed to know that?" I think he senses the edge in my voice. While I appreciate what I think is their attempt to help me I'm also a little tired of the run around. If there is no living survivor of the original will or whatever it is, is their uber-discretion really so necessary? The Third may be gorgeous and make my mind bend in ways it never has, but I need answers if we're ever going to progress. And, beyond all that, the sun is getting higher and hotter and my dress is starting to feel very heavy.

We stop beside a long, rectangular pool. He seems to be admiring the statuary. I think he's really just trying my patience. Attorneys and their Jedi mind tricks. I clear my throat and he sighs.

"Have you ever been to a tropical rainforest?"

"Don't try, attorney Drexler the Third. I'm onto you." It's good I can't see those infernal green eyes. I know they're toying with me.

"Have you ever been to a tropical rainforest?"

"Why no," and I know my snide tone informs him that I am not really interested in his rainforest.

"Then let's go, shall we?"

"We shall."

He leaves me to stroll behind him as we approach a big dome of glass and steel.

"What is this? Like Future World, or whatever it's called?" He doesn't answer. Fine. He opens the door for me and we step into the wet warmth of the rainforest. Little birds skitter away into the dense foliage as the sound of rushing water reaches my ears. Okay. So it's impressive, but it doesn't answer my questions. "So do my people come from some South American rainforest? Is that your point?"

He leads me down a narrow, winding trail. "What makes you so certain, Miss von Strassenberg, that you want to know where you come from? Maybe some things are best left unspoken?"

"Then why did you bring me here, attorney? Just for my good company?"

Looking back over his shoulder he smiles enigmatically and I hate him for it, "Maybe."

I have no patience for games. "You know what, knock off the banter and just tell me." We round the corner and suddenly there is a loudly rushing waterfall. He stops abruptly and turns to face me, just staring. Little kids play in the fountain's pool but we ignore them. Their mother, wise woman that she must be, notices we're staring a little too long. Most likely mistaking this for some kind of romantic moment, maybe she thinks he's about to pop the question, she pulls her unwilling children away.

He's just staring at me and I wish he would stop it. "There was a man, in the late 1800's who worked closely with Henry Shaw for a period of time." He feeds me a little bit and walks away, ignoring the tank of brightly colored poison dart frogs and entering the dome's educational center. As I fall into step beside him, he continues. "That man was actually a professor at Washington University. A member of the College of Surgeons and Physicians."

He leads me through a double set of doors into a tropical mezzanine. "And who was this mysterious man?" We wind down a staircase, following a trickling stream.

"His name was Klaus von Strassenberg. A well-known Austrian physician."

"Okay, so what's a physician doing in a garden?"

The Third stops to watch the stream trickling down its path. "Klaus von Strassenberg was an early geneticist. The late 1800's was a time of explosive research into the field. Maybe you've heard of Gregor Mendel?"

"The monk with the pea plants? Yea."

The Third nods and moves toward the exit. I tag along, always feeling a step behind him physically and intellectually. I'm beginning to think that's how he likes it. That or he's telling me things the First and Second wouldn't approve of. But I could have Googled all of this. As a matter of fact, I had. At the Third's insistence, even.

"Mendel and von Strassenberg were actually at the same University in Austria for a period. Mendel left the University."

"Ok, ok," I huff impatiently as we break out into the sunshine of the early afternoon. "So what? This von Strassenberg was your client?"

He continues to walk, escorting me away from the concrete and into the lush greenery of the Garden. "No. Our client was a Mr. Demure."

"And he was?"

He takes a breath and I know this is going beyond what he has been instructed to tell me. I wonder if they know that he knows so much. "The father of Katherine Raquel Demure."

KRD. It was her box.

Seemed simple enough. "And she married this geneticist Klaus?"

He stops. The waters of a lake shimmer in the distance. A picnic basket would have been nice. William pulls me into the shade of a tree and lifts his glasses off so that I can see that the seriousness is back in his green eyes.

"I don't know that I'm supposed to tell you this, but there's something...off about all of this. I don't think I'm even supposed to know it and there are still parts I don't understand."

"Then tell me and maybe we can figure it out together."

Together.

"You have to promise you won't let them know I've been..."

"Shut up Mr. Smith and tell me." Unable to resist my sparkling wit, he grins and this time I can see it reach his eyes. Be still my stupid heart. "The strange thing is, there is no record of Katherine Raquel Demure ever marrying or having a child. She disappeared in 1877."

Thirty-five

"Katherine," he whispered fervently. "It cannot be now, perhaps not even soon, but when we are both well, when we are both strong, come away with me." The other couples on the patio watched them without bothering to be discreet. Katherine caught their eyes in a panic, wondering if they had overhead Viktor's urgent whispers. "I have a plan Katherine but I will not go without you."

She leaned back against the coolness of the wall. "Viktor, what are you asking?"

He stepped closer, his clothes nearly brushing against hers. He was so close. Well aware of the prying eyes of St. Louis's elite, she turned her head away from him.

"I am asking you to leave everything and runaway with me."

"But why Viktor?" she asked the darkness beside her. "Why is it necessary to go to such extremes?" She dared a sideways glance, seeing both his frustration and the curiosity of strangers.

"I cannot say."

"You cannot say," she hissed, "But you will ask me to leave everything and runaway with you? Can you not appreciate the scandal it would cause for my mother and father? They would be humiliated. What you ask, you ask not only of me, but also of my family." She could feel him wanting to grab her and shake her. His fingers balled into fists against the urge. "Katherine, I would not ask if there were any other way."

"What is he doing to you Viktor?" She turned to him, disregarding the ever-growing crowd of spectators.

"It is not proper," he whispered.

She retorted a little too loudly, "What you are asking is not proper!" The ladies closest to them gasped in shock. Suddenly aware of them, Viktor straightened and took a step away from Katherine. Another figure approached from the open doors. He stepped in front of the others, a false smile on his deceitful face. "Ah, Viktor there you are," he said loudly for all to hear. He sounded warm and concerned but Katherine could see the rage and malice in his eyes. "We should be getting you home dear boy. We wouldn't want you to overtire yourself and have you fall ill again. The young ladies would never forgive me."

Giggles and little gasps of pretended shock. Katherine hated them all. Did they not see that he belonged to her and only her? Klaus reached a strong arm up and clasped his son's shoulder. "Bid the young ladies goodnight, we must get you home."

Viktor poured all his pleading out to her, staring hard until she disappeared from his sight. Katherine was left standing in the midst of the gossiping and giggling.

thirty-six

I wander away from him, retreating to the shade of a gazebo by the lake. "I'm just a little confused." William follows me into the coolness and smiles bitterly at me. "I wish I could explain things more thoroughly but, apparently, it's above my pay grade." He sits beside me on the bench. "Somehow the two families merged, or at least, that's how it seems due to..."

"My awful name."

He laughs before he can politely stop himself, "Your awful name." Ducks and geese glide effortlessly across the glistening lake. Families and couples stroll along the manicured paths, stopping here and there to smell a flower or observe a statue. For me, it seems life was easier in the rundown rental in Nashville. Having a family, even the notion of one, is turning into a lot of work and even more unanswered questions. "All right," I say, turning to face him. "We have some Austrian guy, genetics guru, comes to work here." I gesture across the garden.

William holds up a long, elegant finger in correction. "Through the University."

"Through the University. His last name is my last name. The lawyer who hired you also had one of my names. His daughter, who went missing in 1877 before getting married or having children also had one, or actually two, of my names. Her name is on the box in the safe."

"Which only leaves..."

"The first part of my name unexplained."

"I did some Googling."

"Did you?"

"I did. I would have printed the papers off, but it seemed like too much of a risk." William looks at me through the blackness of his expensive shades. "Maria Josepha was the ill-fated daughter of Francis I, the Holy Roman Emperor, and Maria Theresa, the Holy Roman Empress and Queen of Hungary and Bohemia. She was born in 1751 and died at the age of 16."

"From what?"

"Small pox."

"She actually died on the day she was supposed to leave to marry the King of Naples."

"Whoa, tragic. But I still don't see what it has to do with me."

"Neither do I. I tried tracing von Strassenberg's name in Austria but didn't find anything that seemed relevant. And, frankly, I got tired and gave up." I wish he would look away from me but he doesn't. I don't know if he's searching me to see if I've told him everything I know or what he's doing.

Whatever it is, it's a look I'm not use to getting. I turn away, pretending to find the local wildlife a lot more interesting than I actually do.

"Whatever it is, we'll figure it out. Maybe the old men are just waiting for the DNA results before telling you everything."

I can feel his gaze fall away from me and follow mine to the skimming and diving geese. "Maybe," I whisper, unconvinced. Something about the whole thing doesn't sit well with me and I'm beginning to wonder if my genetic make up is trying to tell me something. I had watched this stupid show one time at Char's house about memories being stored in our DNA and that's why some people have past-life experiences, déjà vu and all that. It had seemed like idiocy at the time but I'm beginning to wonder. Either it's my DNA or my savvy street smarts, whichever it is, I don't like where this whole thing is going. In my musings about memory-encoded DNA I miss whatever William says.

"What?"

"I said, what would you like to do next?"

"What is there?"

He shrugs, a bit too nonchalantly. "Lunch."

"I could do lunch."

"Good, there's a place I think you'll like."

"McDonald's?" His laugh actually sounds as though he pities me and my culinary inexperience.

"No, not quite."

We begin down a path that winds its way through groves of trees and past statues of happy little girls, statues I obviously hadn't modeled for, and head for the front of the park. "*I like* McDonald's. Wendy's?"

He sighs dramatically. "No, we are going to expand your culinary horizons."

"Well, you can try."

"Don't you trust me?"

Do I? He seems to be giving me information he pilfered from the family vault and he Googled information on my case because he's trying to help me figure out what his father and grandfather won't tell either one of us and he's sharing it with me even though he doesn't know if *he* can trust *me*. And we were alone in a hotel room together and he didn't even try for a hug. Of course, that could just be because he's older and hotter and has better prospects than an almost-eighteen year-old charity case.

He laughs suddenly, breaking my rambling chain of thought. "You've had to think way too hard about your answer to that. I guess I will need to work harder to prove myself."

What does that mean?

"Well," I say, trying my hardest not to smile. "We'll see how this lunch idea of yours goes."

Thirty-seven

She had fainted dead away.

Two days had passed since the ball at the Lemp's home and there had been no word from Viktor. She had gone down to the breakfast room that morning, determined to believe that Viktor was recovering and plotting their course for a new life of adventure, free from maniacal fathers and annoying sisters. Yet there was inside her some great shadow of dread, whispering to her that Viktor would never recover before they had a chance to escape. It hissed at her, insisting that Viktor had only spoken out of desperation and that he would never dare leave the wealth of his father's estate. What could possibly be so horrid as to drive him from such wealth? Such was the state of her thoughts, journeying from tremendous heights and depths with such great speed,
she could not discern whether she was famished or ill from the violent torrents of emotions. When she had sat at the table that was laden with cold meats and bacon and toast and jams and jellies, the pirouetting of her stomach informed her that she would not be eating. At least, she would not be eating anything more than plain toast, and that would only be for the sake of appearances.

"Good morning my dear," Mr. Demure had beamed at her, folding his morning paper and laying it on the

table beside him.

"Do not listen to our father, Katherine," Henrietta snapped, her words catching on a sob at the end. "For there is nothing good about this morning."

Mrs. Demure had tsked at her eldest daughter's overwrought emotions. "It is, indeed, somewhat disappointing, Henrietta dear, but we were never led to believe..."

Henrietta had pounded the table then with such violence that Mr. Demure's fork hopped from his hand and onto the floor. "Now that will be enough, Henrietta!" Mr. Demure, who had trained himself to never shout unless it would be helpful during a trial, had bellowed. The force of her father's voice, however, was not enough to calm Henrietta.

"But he did, father, he did! I know he preferred me! And he must still!" Henrietta had leapt to her slippered feet, face enflamed. Mrs. Demure, more practiced at handling such romantic tantrums from Henrietta, had remained unruffled. "It is a disappointment, to be sure, but your father is right, Henrietta, neither gentlemen ever...."

"Ask her!' Henrietta had thrown a violent gesture toward Katherine. "She has seen the way he preferred me, the way he played with my emotions. It was most improper!" Like the spoiled girl she was, Henrietta had pounded her foot on the floor. Mr. and Mrs. Demure had looked to Katherine for confirmation of her sister's accusations.

Katherine had placed her plain piece of toast back upon her empty plate. "I am sorry, I do not know what any of you are speaking of." Mr. Demure had turned his attention to Katherine but Henrietta rounded on her, face

143

red with rage, eyes overflowing with torment.

Mr. Demure had cleared his throat, seeming to calculate whether or not he would have two hysterical daughters on his hands and, if so, if he should just leave the matter and retreat to his study before inciting further emotional tirades. Deciding his youngest, most sensible daughter could be trusted, Mr. Demure had begun to explain. "At the dance the other night Doctor von Strassenberg asked if I would prepare various legal documents for the upcoming nuptials of his son."

"His son!" Henrietta had shrilled.

Katherine had not realized she had risen to stand beside her seething sister. "His son," she had whispered, unsure of what it all meant. Nuptials to her? Nuptials to another? Is that why he had been locked away? Was that why he was so desperate to escape with her?

Mr. Demure, having assumed Katherine was sensible enough not to be affected, had stabbed another bite of ham and spoken around it. "It seems we were all making incorrect assumptions, The young man has apparently been betrothed since his youth to some girl from the Austrian court."

Katherine had gripped the edge of the table.

"Some Austrian tart," Henrietta had spat.

Mrs. Demure had gasped.

"Austria?" Katherine had whispered.

"Yes, of course, Austria," Mr. Demure had begun to retrieve his paper. "Austria," she had whispered again, her voice breaking with the sharp realization.

Katherine awakened upon the chaise lounge, her mother's face floating above her, the sound of her father bellowing about senseless girls filling her ears. He was

144

worried, she knew, he was always too worried about her. Mrs. Demure wiped a cool cloth across Katherine's forehead.

"Mother," she wept, unable to contain her tremulous words.

"Yes dear?"

"I shall die an old spinster."

There was a look of confusion across the elegantly aged features. Mrs. Demure was just past forty and, Katherine thought, she seemed to become more elegant and beautiful with each passing year. Katherine was certain she herself would never look so lovely at that age, she would crack and wrinkle and go all gray from loneliness and heartache.

Mrs. Demure, though, was not simply beautiful, she was wise and realized then what she had been missing all these months.

Henrietta was carrying on about her own death and spinsterhood, disregarding their father's demands to quit this insensible nonsense. Mrs. Demure ignored them both. "Sweet Katherine," she began.

"No mother, do not bother yourself. You cannot comprehend, you do not know."

Mrs. Demure smoothed her daughter's curls away from her face. "I may have been blind to it before Katherine, but I see it now. All those nights he came to call upon you and last night his only concern was to seek you out. Oh, daughter, he treated you poorly. He must have known of his betrothal. Oh Katherine," she planted a light kiss on the wet cheek. "I see it all now."

"He does not want her mother, whoever she may be. He cannot."

Pulling her in close, Mrs. Demure tried vainly to

comfort the small, shuddering form of her daughter. "Most likely, dear, you are right, but if it is his father's desire, he cannot turn his back on it. No sensible man would shun so great a fortune, not for any amount of love."

Acknowledging his common sense would not prevail, Mr. Demure left the room, causing Henrietta to carry her tantrum to her mother. With an unfeeling glance at her weeping sister, she demanded, "Whatever is she crying about? I am the one who has been wronged!"

Without a glance at her insensitive daughter, Mrs. Demure said quite coolly, "Oh shut up Henrietta."

thirty-eight

William dropped me off at the hotel almost entirely without incident. It was kind of disappointing. We went to this swanky bistro, with checkered tablecloths and French-window-style front and everything, run by one of the city's top chefs. William raved about the guy the whole time we sat there on the patio, waiting for our food. Everything's local as can be and in season and other such things I had never given thought to when eating at the burger joint back home. After twenty minutes a waitress brought out what looked more like art than food. He watched me pick at the various elements, waiting to see my reaction when I finally manned up and took a bite.

I chewed slowly, playing my best poker face. It was a stupid, childish game but it was the only game I had. Being four years younger and still a teenager is seriously beginning to cramp my style. So I had chewed and pondered and made him wait, which he did, and quite patiently. Upon swallowing I continued to stare at traffic and the pedestrians strolling down the street in search of their own lunches. He was getting impatient and put his fork down so that he could rest his chin on his fist.

I hadn't had any siblings to annoy growing up so I had borrowed Char's. For her sisters it was more like dealing with a younger set of twins than just the one obnoxious baby sister. As a rule, there was only one phone in the house, and only Char's dad had a cell. Breanna, the oldest, was seventeen when we were seven, and she had a boyfriend. He was an aspiring musician, not a hard find in Nashville. He would call and croon to her over the phone while she pretended to be paying attention to him. She had tried listening to his cheese-sauced lyrics but Char and I would find a spot just out of reach of the phone chord, (Mr. Weathersby is a frugal man, and that phone, old as it may be, still works) and just stare at Breanna while she tried to talk to her boyfriend. It drove her insane, to the point that she would put the phone down while he was singing and chase us out of the house, sometimes locking us out. Having a multitude of sisters, Char and I were able to continue our practice on the others when Breanna practically ran from the house to her own apartment on her eighteenth birthday. It was two months shy of her graduation, but Mr. Weathersby was a practical man. One less mouth to feed. One less shower per day. And so on.

So William stared, waiting, underestimating my resolve. And he broke first. "Should I demand a refund?" I sighed and looked sideways at him, "No. It'll do."
He laughed and took up his fork. "It'll do?"

Taking another bite, this time obviously savoring it, I finished with, "I thought fru-fru food would taste rancid, but it's actually...I don't know...complex?"

"Fru-fru?"

"Yes, fru-fru."

We went on like that through all lunch and a small dessert. It was a long, lingering meal and I was seriously beginning to wonder if he *had* been sent to keep an eye on me, to keep me alive and keep my nearby. Otherwise, he must have more important things to do than entertain a teenage runaway.

He walked me around the city, taking me for a stroll down to the Arch. "Do you want to go to the top?"

Small spaces. Heights.

I really wasn't tempted. But then I rethought things.

Small spaces. With William.

Being scared. With William.

Certainly it was the old, "Let's go see a scary movie so I can press myself against you while I pretend to be terrified," routine, but it seemed like a good tactic. Girly as it was. Having never really been interested in a boy before I was beginning to understand why girls do the silly things they do.

So up we went in a tiny little elevator with four other people. And we were close. When the others were shuffling in around us William had maneuvered me to stand in front of him, his breath, spicy with cinnamon gum, rolled in waves of heat onto my neck. It sent chills down to my toes and I thought my knees had melted for a moment. Fortunately the little girl in front of us didn't really like small spaces either. In the moment when I thought my knees would give way from his unintended seduction, the little pig-tailed thing jerked away from her mother's grasp in a sudden tantrum and fell against me. It was just like Dominos. She fell against me and I fell against William.

He has surprisingly quick reflexes.

Before my weak-kneed, stumbling form could fall all the way back, his arm had encircled me, pulling me close as little Hillary (her mother was chastising her rather loudly by then) crashed at our feet. The mother apologized repeatedly, scolding Hillary five times over just for good measure. William assured her that it was all fine and not a problem.

His words were floating around me. The only thing I was sharply aware of was a strong arm locked around my waist and a rather firmer upper torso than I had expected pressed against my back.

"Are you all right," he whispered, his lips brushing the tips of my spiky hair. Granted, I knew he was only being discreet so as to save poor Hillary from being reamed again, but my knees didn't know the difference. They betrayed me, buckling under his hot breath on my ear and the deep whisper that tickled my senses. My fingers unconsciously gripped his arm, making matters worse, because, Heaven help me, he really must have a gym membership. There is nothing soft or doughy or paper-pushy about him.

Every ounce of sensibility in me was under assault. Whatever nonsense it was, I couldn't get it under control. Poor, sweet William must have thought I was having a panic attack or an inner ear problem or something rational like that.

If there is a physical moment of realization of falling in love I imagined it must feel like that. In his ignorance and innocence he coaxed me around, turning me to face him. Fearing for my health, he removed his shades and looked me hard in the eyes. "Raquel, are you all right?"

I had never really taken up the habit of swearing but with those blasted green eyes searching mine for signs of ill health I wanted to start screaming profanities at him. My idiocy was surely his fault. He was older, wiser to the ways of the world. He had to know what a man like him was capable of doing to a silly teenage girl like me.

Instead, I merely nodded and choked out, "I'm not so good with heights."

He laughed softly, squeezing my arms reassuringly with those dang strong hands. "You can't even see out."

"I know," I looked away from the flecks of gold dancing in the pools of green. "But I *know* how high up we are. And I'm not a fan."

"Then why did you agree to come up?"

Because I wanted exactly what is happening to happen? Hello? My plan had worked perfectly, even if it had gotten away from me a bit. The movie theater plot was safer, I realized. At least I would have been seated. There was a lot to being a girl that I had yet to learn.
"I didn't want to seem like a coward."

The elevator came to a stop, my fingers clutched at his shirt as the confounded contraption settled. "Just breathe," he whispered, but I could hear the suppressed laughter in the gentleness of his words. I dropped my head down to try and get an even breath and hoping to hide whatever blush might be rising to my face. The door slid open and Hillary all but bolted for the exit, glad to be rid of her close confines. As she ran she bumped us again, causing me to fall against him, my cheek neatly smacking his shoulder. "I'm so sorry!" Hillary's mother offered as she raced after her mischievous spawn. I tried to smile encouragingly at her but she was gone before I could swing my head around. A light, cool touch brushed against my burning cheek and my own trembling fingers flew up to investigate, brushing against his as they fell to grip my elbow.

"I don't think it will bruise. Let's get you out of here."

I allowed him to escort me out, feeling more like a psych patient being ushered by her nurse than anything else. Could I be more ridiculous? William led me to the windows, staying strategically close, just in case.

The view from the top was beautiful and revealing (one hotel boasted a rooftop pool) but also dizzying. William pointed out his building and various other points he felt would be interesting, but I really just wanted to get back down to solid ground.

Sensing my discomfort he took me back down in an elevator without Hillary.

And so now I sit, all alone in a hotel room that I swear is bigger than my last home, replaying all the day's events. He had driven me back to the hotel after the Arch incident, feeling that a nap would help calm me down. Really the only thing that would calm me down would be getting away from him and whatever strange voodoo powers he holds over me.

I'm a stupid girl.

But when he had gotten into the hotel elevator with me I was dying for him to invite himself in to maybe watch a movie or just sit there so I could stare at him.

Instead, he had walked me right to my door and smiled. "I hope you feel better. We'll stick to ground level next time," he said and smiled. I laughed and agreed and then he turned and was gone.

"But he said, next time," I whisper to the empty room. "Next time."

Thirty-nine

Mr. Demure owned a Smith & Wesson .45 revolver. Being a sensible man he was not given to violence but understood and accepted that the civility of the East had not thoroughly penetrated the wilds of the West. And he had seen enough during the War to know that even civilized men had barbarians lurking within. He kept his weapon meticulously clean and fired it regularly to keep it in good order, but most days it remained locked in his desk drawer. The key was tucked safely into the pocket of his vest. He had never shown the revolver to his daughters, believing it would only frighten them, but they knew what the locked drawer contained.

Katherine stared intently at the cold, hard steel. She knew it would be loaded. And that, if need be, there was extra ammunition in the back of the drawer.

She would not be one of those girls; the ones who sit idly and wait for the answers to come to them.

Though it took a day of sobbing and carrying on, Katherine was well enough recovered. She would go to the von Strassenberg's and free Viktor from whatever torture was being inflicted upon him. And they would run, just as he had said. There was no time to be wasted. Rumor was spreading rapidly through the city.

Her tiny fingers, no bigger than a young child's,

closed around the smooth metal, testing the weight of it. She had not the slightest inkling of how to use the thing but imagined Viktor would. Men always knew of such things, no matter how refined they might be.

"Miss Katherine!"

Startled by Josephine's shout, Katherine slammed the drawer shut and turned the key, tucking it into the ample bosom created by her corset.

"Miss Katherine!"

As the door began to swing open Katherine jumped from the chair and turned, fixing her eyes on the rows of books behind the desk. "Ah, there you are, child. Goodness me, your mother has been asking for you. She's bought you some new things and wants to see how they look on you." Josephine motioned for her to hurry along. Katherine obliged her, nearly bumping into the portly maid as she passed through the doorway. "Well don't be all that eager, Miss, they aren't Paris fashions, you know?"

Katherine paused on the steps. "I do apologize Josephine."

"It's all right child." Gripping the banister, Josephine tugged herself up the steps behind Katherine. "Oh and your father, he says he's missing a small key, been lookin' for it all morning. Have you seen it?"

Katherine continued on her course as though this had nothing whatsoever to do with her. "No. What does it belong to?"

Behind her, Josephine has huffing with exertion. "Who could say? That man has so many keys."

"Indeed he does, Josephine."

Beyond being caught up in a flurry of fashions, Katherine's plans fell victim to her father's insistent demands that somebody find the key to his desk. Quietly, she slipped away and planted the key beneath the bed of Mr. and Mrs. Demure. She sneaked away, knowing another means of defense must be sought. Mr. Demure would not allow the key to disappear twice in a day's time.

The study, most fortuitously, held other available options for defending one's self. There was a silver dagger her father had worn during the War. He would most likely miss it, but only after she had made her escape. Perhaps he would find comfort in knowing that his daughter was sensible enough to take along some form of protection.

Katherine waited through dinner and a tedious dessert. Henrietta had fallen mercifully quiet ever since their father's news of Viktor's impending nuptials. She barely spoke except to complain that she would most likely have to marry Caleb, though she did not prefer him quiet as well as she did Viktor.

"It is good to see you have your appetite back, my dear," Mr. Demure smiled at Katherine across the table. "Must keep up your strength."

Katherine only smiled and nodded, knowing he was certainly correct. She would need all her strength tonight for she was leaving on a long journey.

forty

It's six-thirty in the evening and I am so bored out of my mind that going to the mall is starting to look favorable.

Until now I had never realized how work and time at Char's had filled up my life. Without work or my best friend or a good book, I don't really know what to do. In the few hours since William left I have replayed the elevator scene numerous times, knowing it can come to no good. Recalling the feel of him against me and the heat rolling from him to me only makes me want him more. If I'm going to clamp down on this nonsense the daydreaming will have to stop.

I will need a good book, some angsty teenage romance for a little bit of vicarious living. Despite the sales girl's warnings about my outfit and the proper shoes, I slip on some flip-flops and grab my room key and Attorney Drexler's credit card. It's his fault I'm holed up in this big empty suite, he can pay for my entertainment.

Reaching for the door handle a sudden, barking rap sends me jumping back. "Who the crap?!"

"Miss von Strassenberg?"

A quick peek reveals a fish-bubble view of the owner of the flashy credit card. I throw back the latch and unbolt the door, opening it just enough for us to chat. Without thinking about it, I instinctively leave my foot pressed firmly against the interior side of the door. Paranoia dies hard.

"Mr. Drexler, hi."

"I came to make sure everything is suitable, that you are comfortable?" It seems he would like to personally check and make sure everything is suitable and comfortable. But I ain't budging. The old man and I are not going to be alone in a hotel room. His hot, young abominably well-mannered son and I, yea, sure. But him? Absolutely not. "Everything is great. I was just actually going down to the mall." I edge out of the room, tucking both cards into a front pocket. I pull the door closed and step into the middle of the corridor, away from Mr. Drexler the Second.

"Have you eaten dinner yet?"

My stomach slams into my toes and in the ensuing lack of blood flow to the brain, I am unable to generate even a shoddy excuse. All my reflexes can manage is a weak twitch of a smile.

"Neither have I," he says, coming alongside me, placing his old, wrinkly hand on the small of my back. The tremors his touch sends crawling up my spine are quite different from the ones sparked by his son. Where was his son? Why wasn't he here?

I am led into an elevator against my better judgment. *Creepy old man, creepy old man*, is all my brain can think to say to me. He pushes the button and smiles at me with his too white teeth and his perfectly coiffed, overdone do. "I must say, Miss von Strassenberg, you clean up nice, as they say." He smiles again.

Ach. Somebody make it stop.

"As who says?"

He shrugs, amused that I am such a simpleton. "People." Whatever my face does, it's something like a smile, a very pained, slightly disgusted smile. He's a lawyer, I consider, he has to pick up on all these weird facial ticks.

The door glides open and I step out in one grateful lunge. "How about some steak? Or are you a vegetarian?" He thinks he's charming. He isn't. Maybe his money is,

157

but him personally, he just gets sleazier and sleazier with each precisely spoken word he speaks.

"I'm not a vegetarian."

"Good, neither am I."

"But I'm really not that hungry. William took me to lunch earlier and.."

He wants to seem unruffled but his gait stutters and he cuts me off too quickly. "Did he?" Apparently lunch wasn't Daddy's idea. "I hope he isn't harassing you? William can be overzealous."

"No, not at all."

The Second leads me into an expensive looking steakhouse. The head of house seems to know we're coming. The Second doesn't even need to announce himself. They know him here and he has a private table for two waiting.

"He wanted to make sure I hadn't skipped town, I think."

"Was that necessary?" He helps me with my chair, which makes my skin crawl, and takes his place across from me.

"We'll see how bored I get."

He joins me in a little chuckle, but the rat in his eyes tells me he doesn't believe anything I've said.

"Perhaps if we feed you well enough, you'll stay. Hmm?" From his limited vantage point he rakes me over with those cold, gray eyes. Turning to the *maitre de* he simply states, "The usual for both the young lady and I."

Cocky son of a gun.

He resumes his appraisal of my physical form. "A few more pounds here and there would suit you nicely." Trying not to squirm under the cover of the tablecloth I blurt, "Does William get his green eyes from his mother?" The Second is thrown off from whatever path he wanted his conversation to follow.

"No."

His beady little eyes gleam malevolently, watching me now, testing me. "My grandfather."

"Oh. I've just never seen such green eyes. Would that be your mother's father or your father's father?" Rambling, utter nonsense, but I can't stop myself.

Nonsense that it may be to me, the whole air around the Second has shifted from purely creepy to something much more malignant. "It's just, your father's eyes, I think they're hazel...and I just..."

"And your blue eyes," he leans across his bread plate, investigating my irises. "Are those from your mother?"

"I couldn't tell you. She died in childbirth. But you know that all ready. There weren't any pictures of her. I guess maybe that's why the whole family thing, genetics," *don't say genetics,* "Interests me." I look down at my little plate and snatch a roll from the breadbasket. "I don't know who I look like or even who my father was...or is, I guess he could still be out there somewhere."

He stares at me and I hope desperately that the pity story worked. "Would you like us to find him for you?"
I concentrate on my butter. "Find who?"

"Your father?"

"I could never afford you," I laugh.

"Don't be so sure." His eyes flick away from his bread and butter and bore purposefully into mine.

"Even if I could, there's absolutely nothing to go on."

"We found you."

"Yeah, but I had a name. An uncommon name."

"Yes but at your school you only registered under Raquel Evans. Why is that?" Breadcrumbs were caught in his pretentious little mustache. Though I know I
have seen worse things, much worse things, in my life, those crumbs hanging near those slimy lips make me want to bolt from the restaurant.

"Can you blame me? I mean, Maria Josepha Raquel Demure von Strassenberg Evans? Who wants to be responsible for all that?"

He shrugs, most likely he is the type to prefer such pretentious names. Of course he is. He is a third of a whole. Or actually two-thirds of a whole. I shake my head at my straying reason.

"Why not von Strassenberg?"

"Too long."

"Why not Maria?"

"Too *West Side Story* I guess. I don't know. That's just what Kevin decided on. He liked Raquel and he probably couldn't spell von Strassenberg. So he did what my mother asked and put that ridiculous name on my birth certificate and on a daily basis called me by what suited him best."

"And you're mother, did he tell you why she wanted you named after her?"

"No. Kevin doesn't like talking about her. Only every now and then he would tell me how much I look like her. But of course I'm going to bear some resemblance."

"Of course."

"William's very tall." *Let's get this away from me. I'm stumbling into things I would rather stay away from.* "Is that also from your father's side? You and you're father aren't short."

He finishes his roll and rubs his hands together before folding them under his chin, to better prop up his inquiring eyes. "I believe both sides had some height to them. And you? Did Kevin ever tell you your mother was tall? Or did he not want to discuss that?"

What had Kevin said about that?

Before I have time to consider it, the server arrives with our food.

Fortunately, the Second was right and the food is so good it's almost worth the creepy company. Almost, but not quite. Good food does, however, make it easier to scarf down, leaving no room for conversation. I shovel in bite after bite, probably confirming his preconceived notions of the manners of girls brought up on the wrong side of Nashville.

"I'm glad you're enjoying your dinner." I mutter my agreement and appreciation around my last few bites. He

---

lays his fork aside with a measure of finality. We have come to the point of our little dinner meeting, I believe. "Your DNA test will be back within a few days." Nodding. Yes, I know this. I didn't need to be subjected to a dinner with the creep-faced lawyer to be told this. "If it comes back positive, your life will change dramatically." It already has. I chew slowly, as to avoid choking. "What has William told you?" For William's sake I carefully plot my answer, taking time to chew each little bit, and swallow only after thorough consideration.

"Well, I asked him and he said he didn't know anything. I don't want to get him in trouble or anything," playing the dumb teenager, it's so easy. "But he really doesn't seem to know anything about my case except he was supposed to find me and bring me back." The Second searches my eyes and this time it isn't to check the color of my irises. "He won't get in trouble will he?"

There is still steak and potato on his plate as the Second removes his napkin from his lap and places it on the table beside his plate. "Not at all. It is simply what's best for you. The less you know, the less you have to hope for. If you are indeed not the young woman we have been searching for, you will not know what you came so close to having."

"I suppose that makes sense." "Well, I am glad you have enjoyed your dinner. Have a pleasant evening." And with that, he is gone with half a thirty-dollar steak still on his plate.

Belly filled and adrenaline subsiding, I hurry to the bookstore and find a new read before making a beeline to the elevator. The jittery shakes aren't gone completely but I figure a nice, hot shower will calm me down. As I am lifted up, toward the floor that houses my room, I thumb through the glossy-covered book. It's short, not as long as most books I read, but it looks like an entertaining read, vampires and zombies and unrequited love. Blood and romance, what could be better?

The elevator door rolls open and I stroll down the softly lit corridors toward my room. While the hotel doesn't bear a strong resemblance to that famous hotel scene in that horror flick from so long ago a coil of fear starts undulating in the pit of my stomach.

Not given to watching chick flicks, I am a big horror movie fan but I am beginning to think maybe they have had an adverse effect on my rational thinking. A little boy on a tricycle is not likely to peddle by and I know this. But still, I walk a little faster than necessary and check over my shoulder and around corners more tonight than I have all other times combined. It must be the residual effect of dinner with a creepy old man.

Shaking it off, I turn the last corner, forcing myself not to check that the hallway is clear, and stop dead.

He's there, waiting for me, jacket off, tie gone, and shirt collar unbuttoned. The casual gorgeousness of him has not ceased to make my feet forget how to move. My foot catches on the carpet. I stumble over my dislodged flip-flop and ungracefully right myself, trying to coolly slip the shoe back on without looking at it.

Leaning against the wall, hands shoved into his pockets, he looks up from his polished wingtips to my overtly startled expression. Those dang expensive shades hide his eyes.

William skips the formalities. "What was he doing here?"

I slide my room key out of my pocket and step passed him. "What? Do you have some rights to stalking me?" I slide the card through and the lock clicks open. "You should be warned: I'm kind of expecting grampa to show up later."

A vice-like grip on my wrist keeps me from moving into the room. Pain shoots through my hand and up my arm. I whip my head around to shout at him, nearly smacking our noses together. He is leaning in close, his face full of some revelation I have yet to be part of. "This isn't a game Raquel."

Turning my body toward him and drawing up to my full height, I plant my face directly in front of his. "And I'm not made of steel."

It takes him a second to pick up my meaning. I watch as the realization of his Superman grip dawns on him. Suddenly shaken back to reality, he loosens his hold but does not let go, keeping his grasp to pull me into the room and secure the door behind us. While he's locking us in I slip off my shoes and make for the couch. I flop down, being mindful of my somewhat short skirt. A look down at my calloused feet convinces me to tuck them underneath me instead of advertising my very unfeminine clodhoppers.

From the look on his face, though, I can tell he wouldn't notice even if I had furry hobbit feet. "What's happened?" He won't look at me but stares at the couch as though deciding whether or not it would be improper to join me. With a long, heavy sigh he sits on the far end of the couch, but only on the very edge. Elbows on knees, he removes his shades and places them on the shiny coffee table which is now littered with candy wrappers, a remote, and my two precious books. Something drastic has obviously happened since we parted company earlier.

I don't like the way he sits there, breathing slowly and rubbing the bridge of his nose, covering his heartthrob face with his basketball star hands. "What was my father doing here?" He won't look at me.

"I'm not really sure. I was getting ready to leave and he was just there, outside my door." Waiting for a response falls flat so I stumble on. "He insisted on taking me to dinner and..."

"Did you tell him I had been with you earlier?"

Shocked by the empty connotation of his question it takes me a full ten seconds to remove my head from the gutter and answer him properly. Clearing my throat, I assure him, "Yes, but you had said that they had sent

163

you."

"They hadn't."

"I know that now." He rocks forward as though to stand but decides against it. "I just don't like how this thing is playing out. They could have found you and taken the DNA sample while you were still in Nashville, let you finish out your school year and kept you comfortable in your own home."

A very unladylike snort erupts from me. Startled, he finally turns to me, those green eyes not quite sure which part I found so amusing. "It was time for me to leave anyway. The man I was living with," how should I say this? "Well, he's a drunk and he was becoming overly aware," I can't finish the statement. Blushing, I make a sweeping gesture down my body. William looks away, staring at the blank television.

"Ah."

"Yea, so it was time for me to leave."

"But my father and grandfather didn't know that when they asked us to find you and bring you back *with as much discretion as possible.*"

"Like ninjas? Ninja spies?"

"It's not funny, Raquel."

Maybe I should be ashamed of my juvenile humor, but I am a juvenile. The whole situation, when I stop to think about it, makes me wish I was back in Nashville, but that's not an option anymore. These people now know what I look like, in various disguises, and I have complete faith they would find me again. And, they're really not the problem. Kevin would find me. Who knows what kind of a mood he's in now? "Is it really that bad?"

"What did my father talk to you about?"

Eye color?

"I don't know. He just seemed to be curious about how much I know about my mom and everything. And then we got into this weird discussion about eye color and family traits and he got almost abrasive, which was weird, and then he left without finishing his dinner."

164

"Eye color?"

Embarrassing. "Well, I had mentioned that your eyes are so green and his are so gray, and I asked if you had your mother's eyes."

"I don't."

"He told me. You have your paternal great-grandfather's eyes." William won't look at me and I hope he's mulling this new intel over instead of focusing on the fact that this stupid teenager was asking his father about his green, green eyes. "I told him that I thought you only came to see me because you're worried that I'll bolt. I didn't tell them that you said they had sent you." Or that we spent hours together seeing the sights.

"Thank you."

An awkward, hanging silence descends. I swear I can hear his watch ticking. William runs his hands through his hair, inadvertently tousling the thick black strands. My feet are starting to go numb and a cramp is beginning to develop in my hip. Minding my skirt and my modesty, I unfold my legs and stretch them out to rest on the coffee table.

He speaks suddenly, not looking my way. "I did some more research after lunch." A long, slow sigh rolls from him before he continues. "I was working on cross-referencing the names Demure and von Strassenberg."

"And?"

"In 1877 Demure drew up some legal documents for Klaus von Strassenberg. The son, Viktor von Strassenberg, was apparently preparing to get married to some girl from Austria."

"And?"

"From that thread," he leans back, troubled and disappointed. "Nothing else. There was just that little blip in the newspaper archives online."

If that's all there is then I don't understand. His entire mood has shifted since this morning. "Is there something else?"

"A corporation."

"A corporation?"

William rests his cheek against the back of the couch, his eyes meeting my own and holding them. "Or something like a corporation. It took a lot of digging to find even the slightest mention of it and I'm still not sure what it is. It's some very high-security engineering corporation of some sort. I don't know. Maybe a think tank would be a more appropriate label or a research facility."

"They don't have a website?"

He snorts and I'm glad he gets that I'm just teasing. "No. No website. And I wouldn't be surprised if they were some how involved with the government."

"Why?"

"Being as low profile as they are requires knowing people who agree that you should be kept under the radar and who have the power to keep you there."

William turns away and the quietness that follows is not awkward, maybe because it isn't empty. The room is filled with the silent noise of our scrabbling logic. I'm ready to change from the dress, which demands too much thinking about modesty and posture, and so I hop up to retrieve my new jeans and t-shirt from the dresser. William continues to stare at the black screen of the television as I step into the bathroom.

A corporation or a research facility. *If* those names really even had *anything* at all to do with the Demure and von Strassenberg of their late 19th century St. Louis counterparts. They could be completely unrelated. Just because a Williams and Smith had worked together in the 1850's didn't mean that a Williams and Smith that were working together these days had anything to do with them. But, William is right. Demure and von Strassenberg are not common names.

In the bathroom, I unbutton the safari-trench coatdress and let it fall to the floor. My toned, pasty white reflection depresses me but I know I don't have the motivation to look like one of the poolside bunnies, ripped and bronzed. My efforts stop at readjusting my much-padded bra and running a hand through my short, chestnut hair. I consider reapplying eyeliner but decide that William isn't looking at me like that anyway.

But maybe he would if I put a little more effort into it. I lean in and carefully line my eyes and smooth my eyebrows. Staring at the pile of jeans and t-shirt I decide against them. The dress looks smokin' hot on me, pasty skin and all, I know that, and the commissioned sales girl had told me so. I pull the dress back on and button up, checking my hair and teeth before heading back out.

He hasn't moved. I doubt he's even blinked. His gaze remains fixed as I reclaim my end of the couch. "I think you should leave," his voice is nearly a whisper. I think of reminding him that this is my hotel room but stop myself, remembering that he is in no mood for my smart-mouthed comments. "Why? We have no way of knowing..."

"I've worked with my father on high profile cases before, Raquel. None of them ever required vaults or had documents that were so sensitive that I wasn't allowed to see them. As far as I was told this was a simple issue of finding a living heir for a deceased client. It was a bit unorthodox but we've had eccentric clients in the past."

"And this one apparently had a lot of money."

William stands abruptly, skirting the coffee table while pondering something he isn't willing to share just yet.

"Right?" I try to encourage him. "Someone with enough money to keep you guys interested all these years? Or has your family just always been so abnormally devoted to your clients?" If not for the distant, contemplative stare directed at his feet I would think he's ignoring me as he slowly makes his paces. After a moment he stops, standing still in front of me, looking down at my upturned face.

"The thing is," he squats, resting his arm on the edge of the couch. "I don't think this client is deceased."

Like ice water with a flaming chaser of molten lava, his words hit me. "What?" Intern Drexler thinks I have a surviving family member who is actively searching for me?

He takes a moment to ponder again, weighing his options. "I have to know that I can trust you." I try to think of an equally dramatic response but come up empty. Signing in blood? Swearing my life? They've all been done before, and in their lack of originality is their insincerity. All I can think of, staring into the pleading and painfully beautiful face of William Drexler, is to shrug helplessly and to speak honestly. "You're all I have William. And," I hurry on, so as not to be mistaken in my meaning. "I don't mean that in some kind of sappy, sentimental way, but I left everything – and that's not much, I know - to come here and find some hope of family, of knowing who my mother was and that she wasn't just some slut that bedded a drunken, inept guitar player from the bayou. Not saying that Kevin's my father, because he's not," I bite my lip, clamping down on my uncontrollable rambling. I look at him, into those unshaded deep pools of green, pleading with him to understand, forcing back the heat of the idiotic tears that have sprung into my eyes. "If I don't have this then I have nothing. I followed you here William Drexler, because I thought there was hope for something more than what I had, and, despite your creepy father and only somewhat less creepy grandfather, I trust you, and I'm depending on-"

His lips meet mine with such force and speed that I nearly gasp in shock.

Everything slips away. Whatever it was I talking about, I don't know anymore.

The universe is just beyond us. His lips are soft but the kiss is hard and intent, never breaking, just pressing on through my shock to my acceptance. And just as I begin to melt, he pulls away, stopping with his face just inches from mine.

"I'm sorry," he says in a very stoic kind of whisper and I want to slap him because he seems to honestly mean that he really is sorry. "I don't know why..."

I edge back and wave him off like I'm so cool and unruffled and this kind of thing happens to me all the time. "Don't worry about it. It was just one of those intense moments and it was nothing."

Nothing but my first kiss, ever. But it's fine. Let's apologize.

"It's fine," I say and wonder if I already said that. I can't remember. My thoughts have flown off into the universe that was just so close at hand, the big, wide-open universe where only William and I had existed. But it would be fine. It didn't really matter. It was just an accident. He's still staring at me, shocked, I think, by what he just did.

"I'm so sorry."

"I said it was no big deal. We're both on edge and..." He swoops in again, fast as a striking cobra, pressing his lips more fervently to mine.

Not wanting to miss the opportunity, I press back before he can change his mind again, letting him know that it is so much more than nothing, clasping my hands behind his neck, drawing him close. Whatever reserve I had is lost in the soft warmth of his lips. He tries to pull back but I am desperate for more. I kiss him ardently, fingers working into the dark feathers of his hair. His strong hands wrap around mine and pull my grasp away from him. Surrendering to the fact that he has wavered again, I sit back, my breaths coming fast and shallow.

"I'm sorry," the tip of his nose brushes against my cheek. "But..." he begins without being given the chance to complete his thought as I snap my hands out of his loose grip and shove hard at his chest, trying to topple him over. I fail to factor in the fact that in his passion he had risen from his haunches to lean over me, the better to press his lips against mine. I shove at him again but, again, he barely moves, quickly recovering his grip on my wrists. I fight against him, silent in my efforts to not cry, trying to inflict some pain against him so that he will know that I am not some soft, little thing he can break. Even though he has, in his stupid apologies and repeated apologies and repeated kisses, broken a little piece of me. A piece that I hadn't realized was so fragile. What a girl I am becoming.

"Raquel," he secures both of my wrists in his one hand, using the other to wipe away my traitor tears. "I can't." I squirm against his iron grasp, considering the value of kicking him in the shin. "It wouldn't be right. But," he whispers, his thumb brushing against my quivering lower lip. "I did mean it." The insufferable man leans in to lightly kiss my cheek before releasing me and quickly stepping away. He grabs his shades off the table and, walking toward the door, without looking back, says, "If my father comes here again, don't answer him and lock the door behind me."

The door clicks and he is gone.

forty-one

She had done this once before. This time she would not bother with the front door. Katherine had waited until even the servants had settled in for the night and then, packing a small satchel with food, a few items to sell if need be, and the silver dagger from her father's study, she had sneaked out the door and into the glow of the brightly lit moonlit night.

Hugging the stone wall, fighting her infernal skirts and the thorny undergrowth that snatched at them, she had made her way to the service gate. It had been unlocked and partially open as it had been so many weeks ago. The windows were all dark but Katherine had seen those heavy drapes drawn across the new glass panes and imagined that behind more than one darkened opening was a burning gas lamp.

Her skirts flew behind her as she ran faster than ever across the grounds, bypassing the carriage house and hurrying directly to the kitchen door. A fire burned low in the massive hearth. With a shaking hand Katherine tried the door and found it to be locked. A swear rose to her lips but she clamped down on it, afraid even the quietness of her whispered curse would be deafening in the silence of the night. The door being locked had not been part of her plan. Though, she now realized, it should have been.

A man like von Strassenberg would not risk another unexpected visit. Katherine believed he had most likely even chained the doors inside, to prevent Viktor from escaping.

Not being quick to surrender, Katherine felt her way around the perimeter of the house. She wondered if anyone would hear if she smashed one of the thickly paned windows and decided the troll-faced butler would most likely hear a feather drop.

Somewhere from behind her a door fell open. A low, muttering voice followed the loud thunk.

Sticking to the shadows, Katherine made her way back toward the kitchen and silently sighed as she found the source of the noise. The cellar door lay open, allowing flickering light to pour into the darkness of the grounds. A hulking shape was climbing back in, still muttering to himself.

The cook, she decided.

He pulled the door back over the opening, taking his endless stream of complaints with him. Katherine waited, peering through the kitchen window. Minutes, she knew not how many, passed by with excruciating slowness. She took a seat beneath the window. Her bones and muscles had begun to ache. Though she was soaked through with sweat she did not care. She knew Viktor was in love with her and wanted to be with only her. All he would care about was that she was there with him. Hearing a clatter in the kitchen, Katherine stood and peered in. The cook was stoking the fire.

Gathering all her strength and thinking of Viktor locked away in his room, Katherine slowly opened the cellar door. It was heavier than she had anticipated and took considerably more strength than what she knew herself to possess. Yet what she lacked in physical robustness she made up for with her hardy stubbornness. It took her longer than she had wished but eventually she had eased her way in and closed the door over her head. A lantern glowed in the corner of the tidy, well-stocked cellar. A small bed had been made up in one corner. From there the cook could both rest for his few hours each night and keep an eye on the abundant store of the von Strassenbergs's cellar. Curiosity began to work its way into Katherine. She wondered what a cook would keep beside his bed and what it would reveal about him as a man, but she squashed it down firmly and made her way across the stone floor to the steps leading to the kitchen.

Her heart raced uncontrollably, feeling like the pounding of a stampede trapped within her chest. She knew nothing would calm her heart, nothing except being free of this place and whatever secrets it was hiding.

Katherine took each step one at a time, placing her weight always flush with the wall, trying to avoid any creaking which might occur. At the top step she heard the faithful mutterings of the cook and prayed silently that he would remain caught up in whatever it was until she was able to hide herself. The broad back was to her, the shoulders hunched as he worked at something on the small table. She could see the entrance she took to get to Viktor the first time, but that would not do.

A loud scraping sounded across the worn wooden planks of the kitchen. The cook was pushing back, done with whatever irritation he had just been muttering over. Wild fear rising in her, Katherine looked around her but she was trapped in a corner. He would turn and see her. She flew back down the steps. The musty scent of the vegetables descended on her as she raced back into the *flickering light of the lantern. Snatching up a burlap sack that still smelled of potatoes and dirt, Katherine darted behind a row a shelves and hid herself in the darkness at the end. The burlap was rough against her face but she paid it no attention as she used her free hand to tuck her skirts under her. She should have dressed more sensibly, maybe borrowed the stable boy's trousers or something. Skirts just didn't do when one was in perilous flight.*

Heavy steps descended the stairs, accompanied not by mutterings but tired, "Oofs." Katherine hoped he was as tired as all his complaints made him out to be. If so, she would not have to wait long before sneaking back up the steps. The too little bed creaked and groaned under the cook's substantial weight. He sighed gratefully and, after a moment, blew out the lantern.

Not eager to tempt her good fortune, Katherine remained under the stinking, rough burlap until soft snores rumbled from the open mouth of the cook. Even then, she did not move. The room was pitch black save for the remaining firelight trickling down the first few steps. She used this as her guide as the cook's snores turned thunderous and seemed to make the drying onions and herbs sway from the rafters. She shed the burlap sack altogether and climbed the steps to stand alone in the cook's kitchen. Admiring his spotless workspace for just a moment, Katherine hurried across the scrubbed floors and into the darkness beyond. She hoped she could remember how to find Viktor.

Forty-two

I waited all morning for William or William the Second to descend upon me again. Neither did. After a quick lunch I decided to buy a suit and head to the pool. I've been here for an hour, reading my new book even though it's lost its appeal. Vicarious romance is no longer necessary. The pool bunnies are crowded in a bronzed cluster at the other end of the pool. Their long, sleek hair is wet and matted against their heads. The better to see their perfect faces.

In their midst is a guy I haven't seen before. He's probably my age, maybe a year older. And I can't say I blame the bunnies for their interest. He's tall and ripped and, from what I can see, he has a perfect smile and chiseled jaw. My book falls aside and I find that I am staring, enraptured as the bunnies are. He is a beautiful specimen, tall and tapered from shoulders to waist.

They don't make boys like that in Nashville, at least none that I ever saw.

"Enjoying the view?"

Drexler.

I feel my teeth instantly grind at the sound of his voice. Maybe some girls would have spent the night reliving the beautiful moment of their first kiss. Not this girl. I had been done wrong and I wasn't going to have it again. Kiss me and tell me you're sorry you did it and then kiss me again and tell me it's wrong? Oh no, I don't think so. I had been stupid long enough. It was time for that to end.

He continues to stand beside me, gazing in the direction of the girls clustered around the bronzed, living *David*.

Letting him know I have every right to stare at any man I want because he isn't mine and I am certainly not his, I answer curtly, "I certainly am."

He pulls the neighboring lounge closer and sits, his tailored suit looking a bit out of place. "I see you've been swimming."

I open my book. "Not yet. Although it's looking like a good time to hop in."

"We need to talk." There's something in his fingers. He plays with it idly, watching the other end of the pool.

I stand and drop my towel. I may not be boasting the best cleavage or even the firmest bum, but I know I look good. At six feet tall I have something these girls don't: super long, lean legs. They may be pasty, but they have great length. William looks startled by the sheer amount of naked skin running from heel to hip. His admiring eyes reach my bare abdomen before he remembers to look away, cheeks flaming. "What're you doing?"

I don't answer him. Why should I? What do I owe him? He owes me. I take the few steps to the edge of the pool and dive in. The cool water rushes around my body and holds my weight. I had forgotten how good it is to jump into the water and be held by it. I swim until my momentum and breath run out. Bright and hot, the sun greets me at the surface. I land halfway between the bunnies with their god and William, who is standing at the edge in his suit and tie, hands on hips. He motions for me to come join him. I know he's right. There are issues, outside of the kiss, that we need to discuss. He certainly doesn't look like he's in the mood for my feminine games, but I'm not quite in the place I need to be for rational discussion.

"Fine," I mutter and head back under.

When my head pops back up Drexler is waiting for me, towel in hand. It makes me feel a bit smug. He needs me to cover myself. It's a small revenge, but it's delectable. "Talk," I command him, folding my arms on the edge of the pool and studying the high polish of his shoes.

"Please get out of the pool."

"Why don't you get in?"

Hitching up his perfect pants, he squats down in front of me. "Why don't you get out?"

I push up on the ledge, forcing him back as I plant my nose in his face. "Why don't you make me?" He's tired of my mood and I'm glad for it. It's beginning to occur to me that his surprise desire followed closely by his rejection is stinging worse than I have allowed myself to admit. The more I irritate him, the more obvious the pain is. Which, of course, makes me want to irritate him even more. Backwards, but true. William looks away from me. He seems to be gauging the available audience. "I can, you know?"

He sounds like he can, but I ain't buyin'. I'm a big girl and he's in a high-dollar suit. Leaning back into his face, I taunt him, "Then why don't you, Mr. Smith?"

With a note of finality, more for himself than me, he drops the towel, "Okay," he simply states, as though it's an agreement we just reached. With those ridiculously fast movements I thought I had gotten use to, William has his hands under my arms. He has to be kidding.

He isn't.

Without so much as stumbling he easily lifts me from the pool, barely getting a drop of water on his jacket. He stands me on my feet. I'm too stunned to move. In a haze I watch him bend and pick up my towel. He offers it to me, but in my numb, rebellious state I slap his hand away.

"Let's go talk. Game time is over."

"I don't want to go anywhere with you right now," my words trip all over themselves in a completely unconvincing way. How in the world did he get me out of that pool?

He grabs for my wrist again. It's getting annoying. Sensing his movement, I jerk back, losing my balance. Still slightly befuddled by William being able to lift me so easily from the pool, my brain can't connect with my feet. I start to reel backward, unable to regain my balance. William starts forward but never makes it. Someone else beats him to the punch.

Someone else's strong arm has caught me around the waist, keeping me from plunging back into the water.

The bronze *David*.

William is not impressed. But I am.

Sea-storm eyes gaze earnestly into mine. He is not flashing his brilliant smile. He is not happy. Trying to right my stupid feet, I grip his arms.

With absurd attention to detail (maybe because it's such a strange sensation) my mind notes that even though my hands are not small, they aren't even close to wrapping around the circumference of his biceps.

"Are you all right," he asks, in a deep, sincere voice. William holds the towel out for me, the muscles in his jaw clenching quite visibly. "She's fine."

The stranger, whose biceps I have not yet released (he hasn't asked me to and I'm not done covertly admiring them), turns his piercing displeasure on William. "I wasn't asking you." He looks back at me and I'm pretty certain I would like to marry him and have his babies. It all flashes before me. "Are you all right?" His skin is so smooth and hard it's inhibiting my thought processes.

Someone else touches me, pulling my hand away from the carved beauty of the *David's* arm. "I said she's fine." I'm moving inside the circle of his arms, being pulled away from it as William tactfully tries to disengage me. With one arm the *David* pulls me close, using the other to calmly push William away from us.

"And I said I wasn't asking you." Leaving his large hand firmly in the air just inches from William's chest, he turns back to me. "Are *you* all right?"

Speak, I order myself. "Uh, yea. I'm fine. We're just," I motion to William without looking at him. Why look at William when I can look at the fine square jaw of the bunnies' god? I can hear them at the other end of the pool, beckoning him back. "We were just having a slight disagreement."

He smiles and my heart aches. "I picked up on that." I actually giggle. And in my giggle William senses danger. "There, she said she's fine, now," he takes my wrist again. He's just dying to get that towel wrapped around me.

"And *I*," the *David* swivels me away from William, stepping confrontationally forward. "Don't like how you keep putting your hands on her." His straight nose is mere inches from William's and I notice that he is actually a bit taller than the young lawyer. Taller and hotter. Well, debatable, but unworldly hot anyway.

William doesn't back away. "I don't think this is any concern of yours."

The bunnies have fallen silent. They are either bored or waiting with bated breath for a fight. Even if it isn't over them it would be exciting and romantic.

The *David* holds me tightly against his side and, with aching clarity, I note the cool, hard feel of his wet skin. "Well why don't we ask the lady if she wants to make it my concern?"

Oh, wouldn't I?

But I also wouldn't like either one of them battering their beautiful faces. Coming back to myself I squirm just enough within his grasp to let him know it's time to let go. Just because I can, I rest a hand on his nice, wide pectoral as he looks into my eyes in search of confirmation. Nodding, I step away from him, though he is reluctant to release me. I feel like the girl who has just won the biggest teddy bear at the county fair. And it feels good.

The boys still have their horns locked and I think

179

that William might just haul off and deck him, so I take the towel and wrap it around myself. "All right Drexler, let's go."

Relaxing just slightly, William backs away.

"Could you please get my book and my shoes?" I could get them myself but I want to offer my thanks in private. Without turning his back, William goes to retrieve my things. The sun glints off the water still clinging to the *David*. He is physically perfect in every aspect. I've never seen anything like him. I just want to touch him, just to touch him. I settle for resting my hand on his forearm. Eat your heart out bunnies. "Thank you, very much. It was very," the words don't want to come, his attentive gaze has stunned me. "Chivalrous. But I'm really okay. We're just under some stress."

William hangs back, satisfied that I will be following but displeased that I am lingering.

Without shifting his steady contemplation of my expression, the *David* nods in William's general direction. "Is he your boyfriend?"

"No." What is he? "We're just working on something together." I hope Drexler heard that.

"In that case," he takes my hand from his forearm and engulfs it inside his own hands. "Would you like to get some coffee later?" He notices my prolonged consideration and confidently pushes on. "You could meet me in the bookstore, they have a little café. If I bore you, you can always find a new book to read."

Oh dear. He *knows* he is charming and funny and slick without being slimy. But he looks at me with those big, sincere eyes and I can't stop the smile that tugs the corner of my mouth up. "If I finish up with him," an unenthusiastic nod toward William. "I'll meet you around four?"

He squeezes my hand gently, a smile reaches up into his eyes. "I'll be waiting."

I tuck the towel more tightly around my waist, needing somewhere to look to escape the intensity of his candor. Barely meeting his gaze as I turn to a fuming William Drexler, I grin, "I hope so."

As we leave, I hear him plunge back into the pool.

Forty-three

Katherine was never afraid of the dark, being sensible enough to know that there was nothing in the darkness that was not there in the light. But that night, in the coolness of the stone corridors, she feared the darkness very much. Had she been wandering through the corridors and up staircases for hours? She could not tell. Time seemed thick and unmoving in the blackness. Without openly admitting it to herself, Katherine knew part of her resolve had diminished. Maybe running off in the night and sneaking into the fortress of Klaus von Strassenberg was not the most well-conceived plan. There was nothing to lead her through the darkness. The doleful melody of Viktor's violin did not guide her to him.

Had she gone up too many flights? She cursed her stupidity. Last time had she climbed three flights or four? Fear and weariness were diminishing her memories of the place. Uncertain of where she was going, Katherine turned back, hoping she could remember where she had just been. There were so many turns and alcoves it was maddening. Caught up in her thoughts, Katherine gave a little start as her fingers left the cool stone and felt only the empty blackness. She carefully edged around the corner, wondering if this was the staircase she had ascended only a little while before. Certain it must be, she pressed her palms against the wall and sought the first *step with her slippered toes.*

"Crazy, stupid girl," she hissed at herself, certain there was no one to hear her. Her toes hung over the edge and Katherine slowly lowered herself into the heavy darkness. She was too fatigued to notice these steps were not carpeted as the others had been.

Forty-four

We only get halfway to the elevators before the Third gives in to his jealous curiosity.

"Are you going to meet him?"

"That's between me and," what's his name? "Him." William presses the UP button and we wait. While I am quite content to wait in silence, he persists. "I don't think it's a good idea."

I speak to the shiny doors. "Of course you don't." When the elevator finally opens an elderly couple strolls out. The old man smiles at us as though we are the picture of young love. Not wanting to burst his bubble, I smile back, but once they've cleared the way, I plant myself firmly in the corner. William presses the button for our floor, *my* floor, and shoves his hands in his pockets.

"Well you certainly have the damsel in distress role down pat."

I want to sneer at him but don't, instead I address the opposite wall. "You have only yourself to thank."

"What does that mean?"

The door slides open. I'm instantly in motion. "That until you, I had no idea it would work so well." He follows me down the corridor. With that ridiculous patience of his, he waits for me to find my key and let us into the room. The door clicks open and I stroll in, leaving him in charge of locking us in. "But honestly," I say, dropping the towel across the arm of the couch, "It takes too much plotting and thinking and..." I sigh and shrug. William locks the door and strides toward me, loosening his tie and removing his jacket. He tosses it across the back of the couch as he comes to a stop directly in front of me. He's very close and my bare skin suddenly feels very exposed.

Slowly, methodically, he reaches those long elegant fingers up to remove his shades and fold them and, leaning forward, he places them on the table. His shirt brushes against my thigh as he straightens back up. I hope he doesn't see the gooseflesh erupting where his shirt touches me. *Don't fall for it*, I tell myself, but the sensible part of me is ignoring the very fleshly other part of me. Why does he always addle my brain like this? It's those dang green eyes, so serious and searching. "I don't think you plotted anything," he nearly whispers.

Comeback! Think of a comeback! No. I've got nothing. He's too close. So I just stare like I'm really unimpressed.

Without bothering to give me a little more personal space, he unbuttons his cuffs, taking his sweet time to roll each one up to the elbow. Frozen, I wait for his ludicrous demonstration of self-control to end. "I think," he says evenly, straightening one rolled cuff. "You're too smart for games." Those green pools lock onto my gaze, which I'm sure is no longer quite so unimpressed, even though I'm trying my best to hold it. "And besides," he makes a mock gesture of being overwhelmed with all the work before us and steps closer, "I could probably keep you busy *all* night." The fabric of his shirt tickles my gooseflesh belly. He pauses a moment, his desire just a breath away. I think he's waiting to see if I will shove him again. I should. I know I should.

A long, steady finger caresses my cheek.

Shove him! But I can't hear my thoughts over the torrent in my ears. My pulse is beating so wildly and my breath coming so fast and shallow, it sounds like a hurricane in my head.

In a fluid movement, the same caressing hand cups

the back of my neck. His fingers are warm against my skin, which is still cool from my brief swim. When he speaks, his lips tickle my own with each word. "I don't want you drinking any coffee tonight." He kisses me softly and quickly. "Or tomorrow night."

The realization is loud enough to be heard over the hurricane in my head. He's only trying to keep me away from someone else who might actually want me and want me *now*. William is closing in again, his arms wrapping around me, drawing me closer. At the last second I turn my head, planting his kiss on my cheek. "I think," I say, squirming away. "That we should keep this at a professional level. I mean, it wouldn't be right."

"Raquel," he whispers in frustration.

I step away. "You just said yourself, I'm too smart to play games." Grabbing the towel I head for the bathroom. "I'm going to get dressed and then we can discuss any news you have, but we have to hurry it up. I'm having coffee at four."

Forty-five

Coming down from the last step, Katherine realized her folly. Fighting angry, frustrated tears, she pushed the damp chestnut curls away from her eyes. "Stupid, stupid girl," she cried in a desperate whisper. Her legs trembled from the overexertion and her lungs felt tight, the breaths had become increasingly more difficult to draw in. Looking back into the darkness of the winding staircase, so steep she had lost count of her steps, Katherine knew she would not be able to make it back to the corridor where she had lost her way. She would first need to rest here.

A new terror was beginning to creep into her thoughts and she could not ignore it. Her concern was no longer for Viktor and her determination was no longer simply intent on finding him and running away together. She now knew she could be lost here, unbeknownst to anyone, for days, weeks even. In her exhaustion she had allowed her feet to continue moving her despite the protests of her reason. She knew this was not the way she had come, not earlier this night or the time before, yet she had continued down the winding staircase, too weakened to stop her own descent.

With a tremulous sigh of defeat Katherine sank in a pile of skirts at the foot of the staircase.

Forty-six

Breanna had once told Char and I that men are not so unlike dogs. They may have a toy they never touch but if another dog gets anywhere near it, well suddenly it's that dog's most precious possession. He'll scoop it up and play with it like a young pup until the rival dog leaves and then the toy is forgotten again. Char and I had rolled our eyes and chalked the whole speech up to Breanna being embittered by some young man who really didn't appreciate her high-maintenance self.

Now I know the truth and I will have to make a call to Breanna at some point and thank her for her sage advice.

Maybe there is some spark between William and I. Maybe he thinks the kiss last night has somehow marked me as his. Maybe it would have if not for today's nonsense. When he had shown up on the pool deck it was strictly business, until he realized there was a significant rival to be dealt with. Only then had he cared about claiming me as his own.

I won't be his chew toy.

Ridiculous boys. Even going out for coffee is beginning to look like a waste of my time. Lucky for Captain Sexy, I have nothing better to do this afternoon. So coffee it is. In the bathroom I strip off my two-piece suit and step into a nice warm shower. William can wait while I rinse the chlorine from my hair. The water is only minimally warm but feels almost hot after the coolness of the pool. I sigh beneath the heat as it cascades over me. I love water. So far the best part of the hotel has been the long, lingering showers with no one yelling at me that my ten minutes are up.

Remembering that William is waiting I snap back from my reverie and quickly wash my hair and body with some soap I bought in the mall. The smell of peaches rises in the steam and I wonder how William feels about a sweet, citrus scent.

"Irrelevant," I say aloud and switch the water off.
No longer concerned with snapping up the young lawyer I don't bother with the hair dryer or the eyeliner and throw on the jeans and t-shirt that had been too casual yesterday. I look young and clean, edgy without trying. This is me. Not the Lauper girl and not the sassy safari coatdress girl, but this. And this, will be what Captain Sexy would see this afternoon.

The thought of seeing him again almost makes me giggle. Who needs William Drexler the Third? I throw the door open, ready to be strictly professional.

The room is empty.

Forty-seven

The insignificance she felt in the endless darkness was maddening. Katherine wondered if sunlight even reached this part of the mansion. Why had she kept following the steps? Knowing with frightening certainty that no one would hear her, she allowed herself to weep openly. The tears began slowly, as though they were testing her sincerity toward shedding them, but once she did not stop them they flowed in a great flood over her cheeks. Her sleeve was soon soaked through. "This is not how it was meant to be," she whispered to the blackness. "It was supposed to be so much simpler."

At the conclusion of her words tiny hiccups escaped her and the tears came faster. Not only was she lost in the home of the most vile man she had ever met, she had also failed Viktor. She hoped they found her corpse one day and gave him the ring she wore. Unthinkingly, Katherine stroked the jeweled circle beneath her glove. At the memory of it she gasped in pain, sobbing uncontrollably.

And then, beneath her own pain and fear, she heard something else. She almost paused to consider how quickly her own tears and wails ceased.

The soft, low moan coming from somewhere in the darkness, however, consumed all her thoughts. Sitting frozen, waiting, she longed to hear it again. Katherine wiped at her face with a handkerchief she had tucked into *her sleeve. The silence settled around her again. In her home the floorboards or rafters would have shifted giving some relief from the unsettling stillness, but here, silence was entombed within the great stone walls.*

"Aahhh."

In the space of a breath Katherine was to her feet, clutching the wall. The voice was low and deep and pained. It was an unsettling sound, which made her at once long to run to him and to flee from him. The man making that sound was in pain.

"Help me."

Had he heard her crying and cursing herself?

"Please."

It was nothing more than a whisper carried to her along the smooth, cold walls. Determined to find him, for the strained, anguished voice was surely his, Katherine forced herself along the wall, sliding her feet carefully.

It seemed forever passed while she made her way, following the sound of his tormented pleas. She wondered if he had refused the Austrian girl's hand and so Klaus had locked him away, just as she had feared.

"Please," the voice cried and she nearly joined him in his weeping. But he would need her strength. She had to be strong for him and no matter what state she found him in, he would not see her shock or grief. He would see only her resolve to save him and to take him away from this place of evil. Her fingers reached out along the stones and found an opening in the stone. He was crying now, a sound more desolate than the heartrending song of his violin.

She could hear his rasping breaths and was grateful for the darkness. If he was injured she would not see it, nor would he see her reaction. Katherine reached out, trying to find the opposite wall of this corridor and her hand struck something hard and cold and not stone. Disconcerted she pulled back as though burned and slowly, hesitantly reached out again.

Not stone, but metal, smooth and round.

"Oh my sweet Lord," she whispered without meaning to and hoped he, in his soft moaning, had not heard her. Her skirt whispered against the floor as she walked along the row of bars, hands guiding her way. Not that she needed the bars to lead her to him anymore. She could hear him clearly now.

He was close.

A voice was screaming in her head for her to run but she dismissed it. She could no more run from this place than she could fly from it. Reaching the spot she believed to be directly in front of him she stopped. From the rasping sound of his breathing she knew he was lying down, behind the bars. "Viktor," she whispered and told herself it was ridiculous to be so quiet. No one would hear her. That was why he was here, alone in the blackness. "Is that you?"

The voice croaked dryly, "Yes, is that you Katherine?"

Parting her lips to say that yes it was and she was here to help him, she snapped them shut. Her horror and shock and anger had risen fiercely and she knew the only sound she would make now would be a most unhelpful screaming cry of agony. She settled for a firm, "Mmmhhm."

He shifted, blankets rustling beneath him. "You have to help me." Swallowing her primal rage, Katherine whispered, "I will, just tell me what to do."

He coughed, it was an unhealthy, wet sound. "Just

down the corridor a little ways is a door, beside it is a key ring. Bring the key." She nodded fiercely, knowing it was pointless, and felt her way down to a wooden door. Feeling along the frame she found the iron hook in the wall. From the hook hung a single iron key. It clinked against the wall as she lifted it and she heard him shift again.

"Bring it here Katherine," he croaked.

"I'm coming."

More sure of her surroundings now, Katherine hurried back to him. She screamed, and quickly bit down on her lip, as his long, clammy fingers found her hand in the blackness. He made no apologies for frightening her but stole the key from her hand. The trembling had returned and she knew she would faint soon. There was a clanking beside her as the key struck the bars of his prison and then a click as the lock opened. "Oh Viktor," she cried, rushing toward the sound of the opening cell door.

The body she threw herself into was much taller and broader than Viktor. Her mind told her it was impossible. She knew Viktor's voice...and she now admitted she had made allowances for the slight differences because of his presumably deteriorated state.

Unsympathetic, powerful hands held her by the arms and hot breath rolled over her face. "Hello Katherine," the voice she now knew was not Viktor's whispered beside her ear. "It was my dearest hope that we could meet. And," a hand, much larger than Viktor's, lovingly stroked her face. "Here you are." An iron grip forced her against him.

The last thing she remembered hearing, besides her own futile screams, was the clank of the iron bars as the cell door swung closed.

Forty-seven

As I get close to the bookstore I've very nearly changed my mind.

This is a stupid thing to do. He might be a punk. Any young man who surrounds himself with pool bunnies can't be the sharpest or the deepest. Maybe I should just go back to my room and wait for William to bring his professional self back for our conference.

Through the glass storefront I see my new friend at a table in the rear of the café.

My breath catches at the sight of him.

"Cover me, Charlie," I whisper, not caring if the other shoppers hear me. "I'm going in."

The smell of coffee doesn't hit me until I'm nearly at the café. It brings back memories of my first real job. With my first paycheck I had bought a Starbuck's coffee. White chocolate mocha with raspberry. My taste buds could still remember the sweet, comforting goodness of it. It had been worth every penny it had cost, but I hadn't had one since. Too many pennies.

Even if the date is a bust I will at least get some good coffee out of it. He looks up from something he's reading and sees me. I think maybe I should have put on the eyeliner or messed with the hairdryer but the smile on his face says he doesn't care. I stride toward the table and as I get close he stands. My insides feel like they're melting into a pile of goo. A black t-shirt clings casually to the sexiness beneath and I just want to touch him again. He's still smiling. I hope he hasn't said anything yet, because my roving eyes didn't hear it.

"Hey there," I say, figuring that's safe even if he's already spoke.

"Hey," he motions toward me. "Glad you could make it."

I laugh a bit too readily. "Yea, well." He steps back to offer a seat to me and concern ripples across his handsome face. "You didn't have any more trouble did you?" I take the offered chair and scoot up to the table as he sits opposite from me, leaning across the table with very sincere interest. "No," I wave his fears away. "We're in the middle of something, professionally speaking, and he's just a little on edge and impatient."

He closes his magazine. "That doesn't give him license to put his hands on you the way he did."

"Well," I admit, "I kind of dared him to but I didn't think he would, or rather, I didn't think he could." Let's not point out my Amazonian build just yet. Divert. "So what's your name?"

He extends those long, beautiful fingers. "Peter." I slip my hand into his and give him a firm shake,

"Raquel."

"That's pretty."

"Thanks, I had nothing to do with it."

"Yea, I definitely understand that. So listen," he rushes on, away from the topic of his name. "What will the young lady be drinking?"

"Oh, it's all right. I'll get my own."

"Absolutely not, this one's on me." My cheeks burn fiercely, venereal thoughts flashing unbidden through my head. "So what will it be?"

"White chocolate mocha with raspberry." He winks and strolls to the counter. Trying not to but losing, I watch him go. The khaki shorts he's wearing are too complimentary.

Life was easier before I started caring about men and how their clothes cling to them. I guess I have Kevin to thank for the delay in that. His endless string of women had taught me what it is that men want. And I wanted nothing to do with that. So while other girls were writing love notes and fawning over quarterbacks I was avoiding all of it. But now, admiring the tall, tapered form of my impromptu date, I am losing my resolve. I try not to think about the truth of the situation, but I know it was William who first melted my defensive walls and gave me a glimpse of what I was missing.

Forty-nine

"You should have asked me before you did this."

A deep, gravelly voice scoffed, "Because you would have consented? You should thank me for not keeping the key."

The floor beneath her cheek was cold and hard. A light glowed amber behind her tightly-pressed eyelids. She did not want to open her eyes and see the reality of the horror beyond them. Her body was still aching from the shockwaves of it. Opening her eyes to be certain of the truth of it was unnecessary.

"She is too frail to be part of this," Klaus von Strassenberg hissed at her captor.

"As was that French maiden. You let me have her."

"And it turned out badly."

"Perhaps," there was a satisfied tone to his laugh. "For you."

Katherine jerked defensively as something crashed to the floor. She would not look, could not look and see her assailant in the light again. Without the light she knew he was a monster. She knew things would not improve with further investigation.

"We will need to dispose of her."

Clamping down on a grateful whimper, Katherine considered how good it would be to no longer be in his grasp, even if it meant no longer being anywhere. He was cruel and merciless and used her in the most abhorrent

197

ways. Even if they did release her while she still lived, Katherine was not certain her spirit would survive it. Already she felt she was part of the spirit world, hanging somewhere between the living and the dead. Every breath she took in this reality felt surreal, as though it surely could not belong to her, not in this place, not with these wounds inside her. None of this could be her life. This was not how her story went.

But there would be no such respite. "Not just yet."

Klaus von Strassenberg sighed impatiently. "Did you at least get the ring?" The monster stood, the bed creaking with relief as he lifted his considerable weight. Katherine tried to relax herself, knowing too well that fighting against him would only prove an amusement for his sick humor. Without any effort to be gentle, he reached down and jerked her arm up. A gasp of shocked pain burst from her and then she felt him sliding the ring Viktor had given her off her finger. He dropped her arm to the floor, taking the ring to the doctor.

"She will not last you long if you continue treating her with such disregard."

"Go away old man."

Though she tried, Katherine could not keep herself from cringing away from him as he approached her again. "And leave the light burning."

My coffee is down to the sunken syrup at the bottom. "So," Peter laughs and he almost sounds nervous, but I don't believe it. "My father has this fancy, boring, dinner he has to attend tonight. He insists that I go, since this is our bonding time, but," he clears his throat. "I doubt he would mind if I bring along," another charming pause. "A date." His stormy blue eyes hold mine with such intensity I have to look away.

"I wouldn't have anything to wear," I tell the syrupy remains of my coffee.

"You would have enough time to get some shopping done. I'm sure they have something for you out there," he nods toward the front of the store and the mall beyond. Curse him! Peter seems to assume that just because I'm staying in this hotel for a prolonged time that I must have come from the money side of Nashville. I don't know how to tell European boarding-school raised Captain Sexy that I spent most of my life living above grocery stores and record shops. We even spent a month in the one car Kevin ever owned. The thought of going to some ritzy medical conference shindig doesn't really sit well with the little white trash girl inside of me.

"I don't know Peter. I kind of blew off my...work earlier. Before I can give you an answer..."

"It's all right. I understand." With all the confidence in the world that I would want him to do it, he reaches across the table and takes my hand. "We'll just be here in the hotel. Dinner's at seven." His thumb strokes the inside of my wrist, sending heavenly thrills up my arm. "I really hope you'll make it."

Boys. The more I have to do with them, the more I am starting to resent them...even more than I already did. Before it was just based on objective study. Now, it's personal. And they're irritating me. Do they actually think that just because they charm me and give me little thrills I'll follow them anywhere?

Of course, that's probably what a sultry young man such as Peter is used to. If he wanted, the entire entourage of pool bunnies would most likely follow him to a boring medical conference dinner.

I stand, picking up my cup and reclaiming my hand. "Thanks, I'll have to see how things go." Noticeably thrown off, Peter hurries to follow me to the trash. "Did I say something wrong?"

"No," I assure him. "I just..." Oh, what to tell him? The truth or games? I decide to see how thick his bronzed skin is. "I've had enough of men lately, to be honest. But I had a good time, thanks for the coffee." Tossing the cup in the trash I continue through the bookstore toward the exit. He stays a pace behind me as we enter the mall.

"Raquel?"

People move around us as I turn to face him. He looks slightly bewildered. "Did I offend you?"

"No, Peter, it's hard to explain. It's just been a really rough week." He reaches down and takes my hands again, trying to comfort and coax me.

"You know, we just met like five hours ago," I slip my hands out of his and turn to start walking again. In one long, easy stride he catches up to me and stays at my side. To my surprise he doesn't try to redeem himself or persuade me. He just walks along side me, waiting. We're nearly to the hotel area before I speak. "I'm just not one of those girls, Peter. I'm not going to follow you up to your room and give you a good send off before you embark on your college journey. You'd be better off with one of the pool bunnies."

I didn't mean to say that last bit, at least not in those words, but they just fell out of me. Peter laughs loudly, startling a woman in a business suit as she rolls her luggage past us. "Pool bunnies?"

We reach the elevators, but I don't push the button. "Yep, pool bunnies. Of which, I am not one."

"Even though you were at the pool?" He mocks.

"Even though."

The elevator opens. A family piles out, completely oblivious to us. Peter steps in and pushes the button for his floor, motioning for me to please join him. I should get the next elevator, but I follow his lead anyway, pushing the button for a floor beneath mine.

"What makes you think I want a so-called pool bunny?" Tired of everything, I just look at him. He knows why. I don't need to say it. He shrugs. "I go to the pool to swim and girls circle me. That's not my fault."

I sigh, "Look, it doesn't matter."

"Maybe it does." Peter slides along the back of the elevator, smoothly edging closer to me. "Maybe I prefer the girl who gives me space and blows me off. Even if I don't understand why she's doing it."

He's getting uncomfortably, dangerously close again and this time I know why he's doing it. He's testing the thickness of my skin, the strength of my resolve to not be swayed by his rich boy good looks. The elevator door slides open. With a mockingly coquettish smile I challenge him, "Then let's see how well you prefer this." Without another look back I exit the elevator. The doors slide closed and carry him away and I turn to find the stairwell that will take me up to my floor.

Fifty-One

Katherine shoved the bowl away from her.

"Eat it," he ordered her.

She turned her head away, her petticoats piled in a pillow beneath her, offering some comfort from the stone floor she laid upon. Time had no meaning in this place of endless night. Only when the doctor came, carrying food and light, did she have the misfortune of seeing her surroundings.

The cell was larger than she had believed. There was a sizeable bed, necessary for the sizeable man who slept upon it, a tub for bathing, and a commode. Piles of books littered the floor and, to her amazement, an easel with an unfinished work was situated in the corner. She assumed the rolls of canvas at the base of the easel were the monster's earlier works, but she truly did not care.

The light from the lantern would last several hours before finally dying out, bringing untold hours of the blackness that no longer terrified her. She was grateful for it. It shielded her from the demon she shared the cell with.

He was a hulking, powerfully built titan of a man. She had never seen a man of such stature or build. It was not difficult to imagine him snapping thick trees in half. Were she able to stand beside him she would find her head *came only to his abdomen, but she could not stand beside him. She could only lie there and hope he had grown tired of her listless body.*

In the light she could see his nearly colorless eyes. But when he was horrifyingly close she could see they were not colorless but pink. He had caught her investigating this strange fact once and the resulting slap across her cheek had sent her crashing into the metal bars of their cage.

While the light still burned, if he was momentarily bored with her, he would read heavy tomes of science or literature and sometimes amuse himself with painting her unmoving form upon his canvas. She had spied his new work while he rested and had spent the next hour weeping over the stark reality the likeness had shown her. The brute had accurately portrayed her bared legs and feet, her skirts, torn and filthy, draped at her knees and her face covered by a mass of loose chestnut curls.

When the oil was gone and the darkness came, he would wake, reinvigorated and he would take her while she slipped into a world of numbness and shades of gray. In the beginning she had tried to recall better times, but the images were weak here in the dungeon beneath Fortress von Strassenberg. When happier times failed her, she tried to conjure images of her escape, but as the never-ending blackness dragged on, even those wishful thoughts gave way to the numbed, gray escape she was now coming back through.

With his foot, he pushed the bowl back to her and barked, "Eat."

Tired of being his obedient slave, Katherine rolled a lethargic eye up to behold him in the last glowing shades of the oil lamp. "Why?"

His hand stopped halfway to his mouth. She had not spoken to him, had barely even cried out since that first night.

All he said was, "Eat."

Pushing herself up on her one good arm, Katherine challenged the colossus. "Why? So you can keep me alive longer? So you can torture me longer?" Taking the bowl, she threw it against the wall behind him, the contents flying across his neatly made bed. He was unmoved.

He simply answered, "Yes."

Exhausted from the outburst, Katherine slumped back to her pillow of petticoats. "In that case, you eat it," and she slipped back into the darkness.

Fifty-three

"This is William Drexler the Third, please leave your name, number and a brief message and I will get back to you as soon as possible."

I hang up. He'll see me in his list of missed calls anyway. For two hours I have waited for William to return my call. He hasn't. It's half an hour until the convention's dinner, dinner with Daddy Moneybags.
I can't make up my mind as to whether or not I want to endure it but decide to go shopping anyway. Every girl should have the opportunity to buy an evening gown at some point in her life and my time will be now.
Tucking my plastic into my pocket I head out to find my favorite sales girl and hope that she is working today.

The mall is emptier than usual this evening. I hear there's a game or something at the stadium tonight. If the entire population of St. Louis isn't here, then they're at home situated in front of their big screen TV's.

My stroll down to the boutique is quiet, allowing for contemplation I do not want. It is seriously bothering me that William is unavailable. Maybe he's working on another case. He could even be in court right now or writing up some legal brief. He certainly has to have better things to do. A legal intern couldn't have time to give scenic tours every day of the week, even if he is working for daddy and grandpappy. He might even be following up on some of the leads for my case. There is no telling. It's not necessarily personal reasons that are keeping him away. I shouldn't be thinking about him anyway. I'm going to dinner, probably, with Peter and his father. Will there be speeches? I wonder if it's that kind of dinner. I don't care how sexy he is, nobody is worth that kind of boredom.

My sales girl, the one always quick with the adoring compliments, is working. Or, at least, she is at work. The boutique is empty. "There's my girl!" she exclaims at the sight of me. "What do we need today?"

It takes a minute to form the foreign words but I finally eek out, "An evening dress."

Her face explodes in a radiant burst of impending sales commissions. "What kind of evening? Are we going dancing? Or are we just eating?"

I shrug. "I'm not sure."

"It's all right," she reaches up and pats my shoulder encouragingly. "I know just the dress for those long legs and overactive sense of modesty you have."

Ten minutes later I am certain that Felicity must have been my bestest friend in a past life. She knows me too well. The dress she has chosen is actually perfect for both my height and my modesty *and* my fledgling sense of my own sexiness. "Felicity," I say in undisguised astonishment. "You are amazing. The gun-metal gray even appeals to my more masculine side."

"It makes you look dangerous," she laughs.

I admire myself in the continuous reflections of the three-paneled mirror. A daring slit runs up the outer length of my right leg, stopping mid-thigh. The skirt falls away from the opening in a beautiful cascade of ruched satin. "Felicity," I say, squirming to test the upper part of the dress. "I'm not too sure about the off-the-shoulder thing. What if it falls off?"

"Then it's not tight enough!" She laughs with that contagious mirth of hers and it smoothes over some of my nervous edges. "Now," she is suddenly serious. "Will you scare off this young man you're going with if you wear heels?"

"Only if I trip over myself."

"Is he tall too?"

"Exceptionally."

She claps as though this is the best news ever. "Excellent, I have just the shoes." Felicity takes another fifteen minutes to finish playing doll with me. Strapping me into a sassy pair of three-inch heels, highlighting my features with carefully chosen cosmetics, and playing with what is left of my chestnut waves, she declares me a *Venus* and ushers me out. "I'll hold on to your clothes, you smokin' hot thang, you just get yourself to that dinner!" And off I teeter toward the front desk where, I hope, someone will point me in the direction of my first date.

Fifty-three

Mrs. Demure took to her bed after a week had passed since Katherine's disappearance. They knew Katherine had left of her own volition, having discovered some of her most precious belongings missing, as well as Mr. Demure's silver dagger. Yet Mrs. Demure was certain her sickly, youngest daughter could never survive a week on her own without her mother to care for her.

Mr. Demure had left in pursuit of his daughter only hours after waking to find she was gone and had not yet returned. During his search he stopped at the office of the St. Louis Globe and asked that they run an announcement of his daughter's disappearance. He offered an unspecified amount of money for any information leading to her whereabouts. Despite his efforts, there had been no word.

On the first day, Henrietta had suspected her sister had run off with young Viktor von Strassenberg but had been relieved when he had shown up at their door that evening. He had heard the servants whispering about the disappearance of the Demure girl and, as evening fell, he sneaked out of his father's home. He had pounded heavily at the Demures's door and was overwhelmed by sickening shock when Henrietta confirmed her sister's disappearance.

She and Viktor both knew in that moment that things

were much worse than they had expected. And in his devastation she saw that his love had been for Katherine and not for her. In her own selfish rage she had nearly slammed the door in his face but Mrs. Demure had asked him in and told him everything she knew. He had left as determined to find her as her own father had been, and, in that, Mrs. Demure felt a whisper of hope.

By the time their mother took to her bed, Henrietta wished Katherine had *run off with Viktor. Her selfish ambitions had died within her and left her terrified for her only sister.*

Fifty-four

I could really use a map to this place. Not that it would really help. I'm directionally and spatially challenged. The lady at the front desk had told me where the conference dinner is being held and I think she very nearly offered to help support me to my date. The three-inch heels and I are not best friends just yet.

There are probably hundreds of people at this thing. I hope I can find him without making an idiot of myself. I'll probably trip on the carpet or on my skirt before finding Peter and his father and he'll run before he has to acknowledge that I'm with him.

Very slowly, with little bitty steps, I round the corner.

Leaning casually beside the doors is a very dapper, sexy young man and he is stunned at the sight of me. I don't blame him. No one from Nashville would believe that I am me. He meets me halfway, still looking at me as though he can't wait to usher me in and show everyone that *I* am with *him*. It's an excellent feeling.

"I knew you were a supermodel in disguise."

I roll my eyes. "Are you saying I wasn't hot earlier?" I take his proffered arm, noticing that the diagonal stripes on his tie match the color of my dress. Did Felicity know? Impossible.

"It has nothing to do with the hotness," he whispers and he's very close. The heels have nearly put us on an equal level. "It's a matter of attitude. Did that confidence come with the dress?"

"Yes, but it was on sale, so no worries."

He walks me to the door and stops abruptly. "My father was called out for an emergency procedure. So you're saved from that."

"But not from the boring dinner?"

"No, I'm sorry. You will still have to endure a boring dinner with me, but I did manage to get us a private table."

"And how is that?"

He leans closer with mock discretion. "I caught one of the servers making out with a married surgeon."

"You did not," I hiss, holding back my laughter.

"No, I didn't, but I still got us a table. So, don't worry, you won't have to make it very far in those heels." With the little clutch Felicity insisted was integral to my ensemble I whack his arm. "Not nice." Flashing that perfect, charming grin, he holds the door open and leads me in to the swankiest place I have ever been in. Our table is behind all the others, romantically private without giving us the feeling of being social lepers. We aren't outcasts, we are the ultra-privileged and it feels good. Peter stands behind my chair and pulls it out for me. I just might die. As I sit and get comfortable, I thank my lucky stars that I came here tonight. Something tells me it's going to be worth it.

Fifty-five

Katherine wiped the blood from her nose with the filthy handkerchief. If he did not cease with his abuse she would need to make tissues from her petticoat. The good doctor had just left their food. He had offered no word of the outside world, no stories of the harrowing efforts to find the missing Katherine Demure. She wondered if anyone was still bothering to look.

Klaus von Strassenberg had, however, insisted she be allowed to bathe. Her captor had snorted and said that if it would make the doctor feel better his little toy could have a nice, relaxing bath, but she had suffered for his kindness. She wiped the last remnants of blood from her face. It was a silly thing, but she didn't want to get any more blood in the water than necessary.

The monster had sat patiently while the doctor made his many trips in, carrying buckets of warm water in from the door beside the iron hook. He never left the door open, always locking them in as he went to retrieve more water for her. His generosity ended when the tub was filled only half of the way. It would be enough to wash the filth from her, perhaps.

"Leave her be while she cleans herself."

The monster laughed as the doctor disappeared. Her right arm was still healing from his abuses on that first horrible night. Struggling with her left arm, Katherine *tried desperately to free herself from her dress. Why had she dressed so inconveniently for this journey? She had wanted to look beautiful for Viktor, but what good had that proved to be?*

Her captor ignored her plight as she fought to lift the dress off. It had been days since she had cried. It seemed a pointless and tiring endeavor anymore. But now, in the flickering amber light, silent tears slipped over her cracked and trembling lips. The warm bath water waited for her, taunting her, and there was nothing she could do. Never did she think to ask for his help. Even if he would give it, she would not take it. She imagined that he would just tear the dress off her body and she wondered now why he had not done so already. Whatever his reasoning was, she was grateful for that one small thing. At least in this place of unending tortures she was allowed one simple reminder of the fashionable young lady she had been. Shaking with uncontrollable frustration Katherine threw her handkerchief down and stepped into the tub, skirts and all. She sensed him look up, startled by her decision, and knew he watched her as she leaned back in the tub.

The water wrapped around her in a warm, soothing blanket and coaxed a stream of tears from her swollen eyes. The warmth and comfort of the bath felt like home, even with the weight of her clothes floating around her. A soft sigh of relief rolled from her salty lips.

What he said next startled her from her reverie. "You will die of a chill now."

She slipped further down, feeling the strands of her hair float up around her face. "One way or another, beast, any will do." But for now, *she thought,* this is my moment of heaven before eternity claims me.

It was ten o'clock before I pleaded exhaustion and Peter walked with me to the elevator. Standing there in sweetly enclosed privacy, after the hours of talking and dancing and dancing closer, was a great lesson in self-control. But I had told him I wasn't one of those pool bunnies who would follow him back to his room and I intended to keep that promise.

It was difficult.

As I stroll down the corridor in pursuit of the lonely comfort of my bed, I consider running up the stairs and finding him, but fight back the urge. It would not go well. Actually it probably would, but I would have no respect for myself in the morning. Amazing the changes one night on the dance floor could bring. Peter had been a perfect gentleman and had introduced me with such pride, he looked as though he would burst with it. And we had danced until it felt as though my feet would need amputated, although I believe he would have held all my weight in his arms just to keep me there. Before getting off the elevator he had sweetly kissed my cheek and released me with some difficulty.

Caught up in sweet remembrances, I almost cry out at the sight of a long, lean body standing sentry outside my door. I had forgotten about him. Almost.

"What're you doing here," I snap.

He ignores my rudeness, just as obviously stunned by my get-up as Peter had been. I pull my room key out of the clutch, glaring at his roaming eyes, and letting myself in. "What...are...you...doing here?"

William clears his throat. "You called me. Five times. And didn't leave a message."

"And so?"

He has recovered and is insinuating his way into my room. "And so I was concerned."

I let him in, more from wanting to take these ridiculous shoes off than anything else. "How long have you been waiting out there?"

Bolting the door behind him, he follows me into the room. "It doesn't matter."

I flop down on the couch and undo my shoes, "Stalker." Slipping off their confinements my feet almost utter their own sighs. "So I'm safe. You can go." He's staring again and trying to look away, because it's the *right thing to do*. It hits me that the slit in my dress is on his side. I stand, knowing it only slightly minimizes his conundrum.

"Let's go for a walk," he says.

"You are insane."

But then again, maybe it's safer. Morally speaking. "Well, fine, if we're going to walk, I'm going to need to change."

"That's fine." He straightens up. It's only then that I realize I have run out of clean clothes. Today's clothes are down in the boutique, locked away until morning.

"Crap."

"What?"

"All my clothes are dirty." "

You didn't buy enough for the week?"

"No," I snap. "I was kind of taking it day-by-day."

"And you didn't send anything with the maid?"

"What? No. I didn't know you could do that."

"You could."

"Well I didn't so you're going to have to deal with me wearing the stinky, sweaty dress again. Or my swimsuit, whichever..." I stop. He's removing his jacket and loosening his tie. "What're you doing?"

He looks up from the buttons he's undoing. "You can wear my shirt."

"Why because it's cleaner than my dress?"

"Yes, I keep a fresh change of shirts at the office, just in case."

"You're neurotic."

He pulls the shirt off, leaving him standing there in his undershirt and trousers. "All to your benefit," he says bitterly, holding the shirt out for me to take.

I snatch it away from him. "It's so sweet, you changed before coming to see me."

"Don't flatter yourself," he says to my back. "I spilled coffee on the other one."

"Sure you did." I close the bathroom door behind me. Housekeeping has noticeably been here. My pile of clothes is neatly folded on the chair. I remove my jeans, the ripped up ones, from the seat and place them on the vanity. I admire myself for a long moment before reaching back to undo it all. Despite the hours of dancing and flirting, Felicity's *Cinderella* job still holds.

Grasping the zipper at the small of my back is no problem. Undoing it, however, is a much bigger obstacle. It will go only an inch before refusing to budge farther. I yank at the tightly clinging fabric, trying to swivel the dress around to where I can more efficiently deal with the zipper. It's a no-go. "Crap, crap, crap!" I swear at it. Before giving in, I take one more long look at myself, more of an introspection this time. Asking for his help in a moment like this is utterly humbling and unhelpful to the cause.

With a sigh of defeat I open the door and stand there for a moment, waiting for him to notice I'm still in the dress. His green eyes flicker over to me. "I'm having zipper issues," I state flatly so that he will know this is not a plot.

He lifts himself from the couch and I see that he is tired even though he's trying to hide it. As he gets close, I turn around so he can address the problem. In the vanity mirror I can see him reflected behind me, his head bowed down as he surveys the troublesome zipper. His fingers brush against my skin as he fights to clear the zipper of the rogue satin. Little tremors shudder through me and I hope against hope he doesn't notice. He gives the fabric a good tug that proves to be unfruitful and sighs. "Maybe you should have bought a size bigger."

I stomp on his big toe but he doesn't give me the satisfaction of a pained yelp. Instead he places his hands on my hips and meets my eyes in my reflection. Softly he whispers, "I'm teasing. You," he gently squeezes my sides with those dang long fingers. "Are absolutely beautiful. Stunning. Really," he says more loudly, slipping his hands back toward the zipper. "There aren't words for it."

He gives another tug and I feel the zipper slide down my back. "William..."

"Hush, " he looks across to my reflected eyes again. "Just because I've been a jerk doesn't mean I can't be honest. If anything," he turns me to face him. "It means that I should make a more concerted effort to tell you nothing other than the absolute truth."

I have stopped breathing again. Apparently my lungs have picked up on something my brain has been trying to ignore.

Without my permission, he has brought me back to that place where I can't breathe and I can't think. "William," I whisper breathlessly this time and I hate him for it. I can feel his hands clenching anxiously at my waist. Sensing the release of his own inhibitions, he moves his hands to my arms, squeezing and caressing them restlessly.

"Raquel," he whispers, his warm breath rolling across my neck. "I'm going to give up on doing the right thing if you don't get in there and change out of that ridiculous dress right now."

"Is it just the dress then," I whisper back, hating myself for moving in closer.

217

"Shut up," he says and kisses me hard and fast, his hands gripping my arms so desperately it almost hurts. "And go change."

With every last ounce of remaining resolve I step backward into the bathroom and close the door against his tormented gaze. I turn back to my reflection, even though I don't really want to look at myself right now. "Well isn't this just the perfect pickle we're in?" I ask the unfamiliar girl staring at me.

Fifty-seven

"Did you pay her to leave?"

"Whatever for?"

Viktor stood solidly in the doorway. "You feared I would not have Countess van Swieten, that I would run from you and so you paid Katherine to go away."

The doctor continued scribbling in his large leather volume. "You do not think highly of your young love, to believe she could be persuaded with money."

Anger coursed so fiercely through him that Viktor feared what he would do if he stepped into the room any farther. "Then you threatened her, her or her family. I cannot believe she left of her own accord. It is impossible."

Completely unimpressed with the darkening red shade of his son's countenance, Klaus von Strassenberg turned to the next page and began again.

"Tell me what you have done!" The sound of his scream echoed from the rafters and died at the scratching of his father's pen. Willing, even eager, he rushed his father's desk, and with one long sweep cleared the surface of its contents. Except for the journal. In a surprisingly limber move, Klaus had moved from his chair to stand at a safe distance from his son's tirade. "Tell me," he screamed again, furious tears rolling down his ragesplotched cheeks. "Tell me what you have done to her!"

The doctor placed his journal back on the desk and settled himself in his leather chair. "I think," he said calmly. "That it would be best for you to go lie down. The stress of her disappearance has upset you, you will make yourself ill and then what use will you be to her?"

Pushing a hair back from his glowering eyes, Viktor swore to his father, "I swear I will find what you have done with her and," he could not say the words, could not bear to think them. "If you have hurt her, caused even one scratch on her beautiful skin I will kill you."

"I did not raise you to be a man of empty promises, Viktor. Go to bed," Klaus said to his scribbled words.

In a graceful flash of movement, Viktor was back at his father's desk, leaning heavily over it, forcing his father's frigid gaze to his own.

"I know what kind of man you have attempted to mold me into, father. My words are not empty. I will kill you."

Fifty-eight

"So tell me," I say to William as we step from the elevator. The ride down had been silent, almost awkward, neither one of us sure of where we stand. Couples stroll across the ornate lobby, some more inebriated than others. He leads me over to a couch but before we can reach it, a voice calls out to me.

"Hey there!" William goes rigid with undisguised dislike. I turn but he doesn't. "Hey Peter." Dressed down in jeans and a polo he walks right up to me and folds me into a quick hug, brushing a kiss onto my flaming cheek. I step back, noting the irony of the physical triangle our positions create. Peter looks relaxed enough, if not a little curious as to what his tired date is doing in the lobby with another guy at eleven o'clock.

He motions toward William and I. "So, working?" His tone is more facetious than trusting.

"Yes, actually, Peter, we are. I could have finished up earlier, but I was at dinner—with you."

"And now you're leaving with *him*." That perfect grin is radiating from his face but his nod in William's direction is not friendly. "And I don't think it's a good idea."

I'm starting to feel like the stupid chew toy again and I'm not one of those girls who enjoy such sensations. "Well, I don't really think it's your business. And, for that matter, Peter, where are *you* going at eleven o'clock? Aren't you tired after a night of dinner and dancing?"
Eager to see the reaction to this, William turns around. I

try to ignore the smug look on his beautiful face.

Peter looks from me to William and considers his options. After a few moments of strategizing he holds his hands up in surrender. He addresses only me. "Look, I don't want to fight with you. I just, I've been burned pretty badly in the past and..."

I stop him, "Peter, we just met today. We're not engaged, we're not dating. At this point, and I'm sorry to say this, we're just summer flings. You're leaving in a few days and I probably am too, so..." I shrug.

He laughs quietly, bitterly, looking away. "I hadn't really thought about it like that Raquel." Those stormy eyes lock on mine and their words are clear. "Peter, I really," I sigh. Aren't girls supposed to be the difficult, emotional ones? "It's too fast. If you and I were going to be in the same general vicinity for awhile, I'd consider it, but you're going to Massachusetts in two months," William's head snaps back up at this, but I can't see his expression. "And I don't know where I'm going."

For a long, uncomfortable moment Peter studies me, gauging my possible reactions again. In the end, he looks to William. "Can't your business wait until morning?"

"No."

"Why?"

"That's not *your* business."

Peter takes my hand, "Raquel, if you're still not tired, come with me. I know some places nearby."

"She's busy."

"I won't make you dance," Peter tells me, sounding like a parent coaxing a child. "But we can just go, hang out." His smile is so sweet and sincere that I almost fold. William steps in closer and our staging can no longer be described as triangular. William has cut Peter out of the equation. "She's not going anywhere with you." Cool and calm, Peter shifts his gaze to William. The menace there, though checked, makes the hair stand on the back of my neck. I step directly between them, warding off any violence that might be creeping to the surface. "Look

Peter, I really need to discuss some things with him tonight. I'll meet you at the pool around ten? Tomorrow?" Sensing his defeat, Peter releases my hands and squares his shoulders.

"Is he going back to your room with you?"

I almost slap him. Instead I step up to the powerfully built young man, emanating menace of my own. "If I want him to, he will. And if that's the kind of girl you think I am, well, you have a nice life."

His eyes, several inches above my own, never flinch as he considers whether or not I'm bluffing. "All right," he says. "But you should know," he strokes my cheek gently with those enormous fingers of his. "I'm a one girl kind of guy and I expect the same loyalty from whoever I'm with."

"Fair enough," I state placidly, even though he's really irking my noodle. "But I'm not *with* you. I'll be at the pool at ten."

He glares over my shoulder at William and lowers his fingers from my face. As he turns to stride toward the exit, he says a little too fractiously, "Nice shirt."

I'm not sure if he's talking to me or William or both of us. Irrelevant. I turn back to William who has furious storm clouds gathering around him. "So what about you," I ask, ignoring what just happened. "Do you have some trendy hotspot to take me to?"

He smiles sourly. "You're standing in it."

"Ah, neat-o."

"I don't like that guy," William leads me the rest of the way to the couch.

"I know you don't. He's starting to bug me a little bit too." William sits and waits for me to get comfortable on the opposite end.

"Although I can't fault him."

"For what?"

"For wanting to keep you to himself."

My patience is wearing away to the point of extinction. "Yea well, at this point, neither one of you stalkers get the honor. Obsessive freaks that you are. Is it my poverty you both find so endearing?"

"Does he know you're from the wrong side of the tracks?"

Good point. I still haven't told Peter anything about my previous situation in life. "No."

"Then that's probably not it." I lean back, stretching my legs across his lap. "You can put the girl in a swanky hotel and buy her purdy things but that don't mean she don't stay white trash 'round the edges."

William pushes my feet off his lap. "You were never white trash."

"What do you know?"

"If you'll stop running your mouth I'll tell you."

I try not to smile at him, but it's nearly impossible. "I don't like it when my men get sassy."

"Then, Miss von Strassenberg, it's a good thing I'm not your man. And," he leans toward me. "Yes you do."

How is it he knows me so well?

Fifty-nine

Katherine woke upon a decidedly softer surface than what she had become accustomed to. She felt warm, even comfortable. Amber light flickered more brightly beneath her heavy eyelids.

Without opening her eyes she was certain it was his bed she was curled upon like a small child. She was also becoming aware of the fact that she was without her dress or her remaining underclothes. Spying from beneath the blankets she could see her dress strung along the bars of her prison. Somewhere, she realized, a fire was crackling. Edging from her cocoon in silent increments, Katherine craned her neck back. A great hearth in the corridor beyond had been uncovered. Flames danced around the shape of an enormous log. She wondered if the good doctor had demanded all these comforts. It seemed a trifling silly thing to do, when his objective was to eventually dispose of her.

Beyond the crackling pops of the fire, her ears discerned a softer sound, the quiet scratching of charcoal across canvas. Ever curious, she began to pull herself from the blankets.

"Be still," he barked.

Katherine settled back into her nest. She knew he was sketching her again. It made her ill to imagine that one day someone might find her image depicted in this horrible way. She wondered if anyone would recognize her. Had she altered so considerably on the outside as she had inside? She doubted it, though she knew that her already slender form was taking on a skeletal appearance.

It seemed an hour passed while he stood there, scratching at his canvas. When she could take the silence no longer, she offered, "Thank you for the fire."
There was no response. She had expected none. Kindness would not motivate him to speak; of this she was certain. "Why does he keep you locked away down here?"

Long, tedious moments drew past until she believed he would not answer, and then, startling her, he said evenly, "Because I allow him to."

Well, that seemed obvious enough. The monster had drawn her in and tossed the keys out on that first night. When the doctor came to deliver food and supplies, he never bothered to chain the titan to the bars. They must have a mutual understanding. Katherine could not keep herself from inquiring, "But why?" He answered more quickly this time, pausing in his sketching. "It is better this way."

A laugh, bitter and harsh, escaped her. "Is it?"
"Better one than many. Yes?"
"I do not believe you care that much."
The scratching of the charcoal began again. "In that, dear Katherine, you would be correct."
"Then why?"
"I understand his purpose."

Katherine puzzled over what purpose it could be. It certainly was not to protect innocent maidens from the monstrosity who was now absorbed in his charcoal sketch. "And what purpose is that?"

"You would not understand." He paused and added, "Were I to be discovered, captured or killed, generations of careful research and planning would be lost. Moreover, it is none of your concern."

She full-heartedly disagreed. There was little she did not believe she could comprehend, if given sufficient explanation or resources. And, being that she was joined with him in his voluntary imprisonment, she believed it was very much a concern of hers. She began to question him further, but he snapped at her, "That is enough. Speak no more or you will live to regret it." Knowing he was a man true to his word, Katherine held her tongue and curled back under the blankets.

Sixty

William considers where to begin his tale. While he decides, I watch a couple, only a few years older than William, stumble in. They are draped all over each other and considerably disheveled. They laugh and kiss and maul each other while they wait for the elevator. It is no small relief for us when they are taken away to a more private setting for their passion. William clears his throat. "I heard my grandfather on the phone today."

"Okay."

"I told you before that I thought our client was still alive?"

"Yes."

"I wasn't able to hear the entire conversation, but they were discussing the DNA results." Hope sprang to life in the pit of my stomach, joined with a sudden sense of mourning. Results might mean I have to leave. "Are they in?"

"No. They were discussing what will happen when the results do come in."

"And?"

"It was difficult to grasp exactly what they meant, but they will take you somewhere if you are who we've been looking for. I don't know Raquel, from the sound of it they're worried about something. If you are who we need you to be and they take you to where our client requested, well, my grandfather was saying he wasn't sure it was the safest course of action."

I lean back into the couch. All this cryptic nonsense. Really William has a whole lot of nothing to report. "Maybe they're just worried that my low-class self will be unappreciative of whatever is coming my way."

William shakes his head. "It sounded more serious than that."

"Well, I don't really see why we should get our panties in a bunch when we don't have a clue as to what they're talking about. Do you really think you're grandfather would cheat me or wish me harm?" He doesn't answer right away and that doesn't comfort me at all.

After actually taking time to ponder it he answers, "No, I guess not. But it doesn't explain why they should be so worried. You'd think they'd be ecstatic to be rid of this case."

I slide across the couch to sit beside him. "So really, you don't know anything new, again?"

He doesn't think it's as funny as I do. "I know that something just isn't sitting well. My grandfather waved me out of the room when he realized I was there. I'm part of the case."

"Yea but you're just the intern."

He shakes his head, rubbing his eyes with his long fingers. "No, there's something and, when it's too late, we'll figure out what it is."

I stand, stretching. "I'm tired William, take me home."

He walks me to the elevator, looking slightly crestfallen. "I'm sorry to drag you out so late and for apparently so little. But Raquel," he says, cupping my chin in his hand, "I'm just trying to keep you safe."

I push the UP button. "I am. You just worry too much." I smile but he doesn't join me in it.

"I hope so." We step in and the elevator closes behind us. "There's one more thing. I missed it at first because I thought it was the same thing." He pauses and it isn't just for the effect. "I don't know if it bears any relevance to what we're dealing with but both of the Demures's daughters disappeared. Your great-whatever-grandmother, if that is indeed who she is, disappeared in 1877. Ten months later, in 1878, Mr. Demure posted another advertisement, this one requesting information on either Katherine or her sister Henrietta."

Well, that seems a lot more substantial than being waved away from a phone call. "Maybe she went to find her sister? Maybe Mr. Demure was evil and they both ran to get away from him?"

William shakes his head. "Both girls were old enough to marry."

I shrug. "Maybe they were unfortunate in the looks department? Maybe they were just the adventurous sort?"

The doors slide open, "I'll walk you to your door and say good night."

"Worried?"

He smiles mischievously, "No, just jealous."

Sixty-One

"How long have you kept me here?"

"Do you have an appointment to keep?" He ripped the meat from the turkey leg with his long, sharp teeth. Never had she seen teeth like his, so narrow and sharp and long.

"No."

Setting the leg down he took up his goblet of wine. "Then, pray, what does it matter?" She could not possibly tell him. It would make no difference. Katherine pulled the thin blanket the doctor had given her closer. "I just have no idea how long I have been here." The goblet clashed against his plate as he went back to his turkey. "Be grateful it has not been long enough." After a long, appreciative swallow of wine he added, "To soothe your curious mind, I will tell you, the better part of two months has passed." He bit off another chunk and spoke around it, "Now eat your food."

For once, Katherine conceded and slowly began to eat.

Sixty-Two

The bunnies are at the other end of the pool, pouting because their young god is ignoring them. All of his attention is honed in on me.

"Not swimming today?"

With all of the weirdness flying around, being half-naked just doesn't feel right. "No, I'm kind of tired."

"Long night?"

He's digging and I know it and I don't like it. "No, not really. Except some guy dined me and danced me last night. More than anything else, I think it was those shoes that made me so tired." We share a laugh and it's nice; a little, infinitesimal piece of the awkwardness falls away.

Sensing my slight shift in mood, Peter takes my hand and guides me over to the lounges. He sits down across from me. He hasn't been in the water yet, his dark hair is perfectly dry. It gives a girl some hope that he's honest. At least he didn't join the bunnies while he was waiting for me. "I have a surprise for you."

"Do you?" The excitement he's feeling doesn't rub off on me. Peter has been a little too forward-thinking for my taste and I'm afraid he could potentially get down on his knee right now.

"I do. It's nothing set in stone yet, but I spoke with my father this morning." Heaven help me, he is going to propose. "He's agreed to let me buy a loft here, in the city." Well, I guess it's better than a proposal, although a little bling can never hurt when you're acting like a clingy maniac. My thoughts must be pretty clear on my face. His excitement plummets. "You're not happy."

"I'm just not sure what to say."

"It's just an opportunity for us to get to know each other better. I still have to leave for school in August, but when I have breaks, if you like, I can stay at the loft and visit you." He's serious. The shock of it isn't allowing me to think. It kind of feels like we're moving in together. That will probably be his next priority.

"I don't even know if I'll be staying in the area."

"Well, you should know within the next few days."

"She'll know today."

Peter and I have been so consumed in our conversation that we didn't even notice William's approach. Sometimes he's a little too ninja. Peter is on his feet, hopping up to stand between William and I, squaring his shoulders to face his adversary.

"Save it." William warns him. "I'm really not impressed."

"Why is it you're always showing up at just the wrong time?"

Unconcerned with Peter's dislike, William walks around the lounges and steps up to us. "Have you ever thought, that perhaps I'm always showing up at just the right time? It's all relative, isn't it?" Turning to me, he says in a tone that makes me not quite so sure that I wouldn't rather stay with Peter, "You're results came in a few hours ago."

Peter scoffs, "And you decide to bring them to her at *ten*?" I wave Peter off, hoping he'll calm down.

"There were preparations, as I told you, that needed to be made."

"And they sent you to take me there?"

"Take you where?" Peter keeps trying to claim territory in our conversation but I really don't have enough generosity left in me to pay attention to him.

"You need to go up and pack your things, you're checking out."

"Wait a second," Peter says and I'm kind of right there with him. "Now?"

"Yes now. We need to go."

William starts to pull me along, but Peter grabs my free hand. Those gray-blue eyes plead with me, "How do I call you?"

The bunnies would think I was the most stupid girl in the universe if I allowed a young man like Peter to walk away without my number.

Maybe they are right.

He's a little overzealous, a little demanding, but that doesn't mean it isn't worth a shot. And, I have to admit, the circumstances are a bit Darwinian. By looks I would imagine Peter would win the competition of the fittest, but by sheer will and stubbornness the prize would belong to William. I think. Peter is pretty relentless. I hear William's pen click open behind me as all these thoughts of locked horns and bright plumage tumble through my mind. "Here," his long arm reaches across me, offering a card to Peter. "For now, you can reach her at the number on the back." With a smile that looks more like he has just been slapped rather than handed a gift, Peter cups my face in his hands.

"Would you allow me to call you?"

I don't think either of them has considered how very awkward all of this makes me feel. "Yea, sure, just maybe not until tonight. We apparently have things to sort out. It might take some time."

"Sure. I understand." Closing the small gap that had separated us Peter presses his lips against mine in a tender, passionate kiss that speaks of things to follow. While Peter embraces me against his well-built bod, the other hand gripping mine threatens to break my fingers. "I'll be seeing you," Peter whispers in my ear, all the better to cast a challenging sneer at the man behind me.

"Yes you will," I smile encouragingly at him and squeeze the hand behind me with as much strength as I have, digging nails in where I can. The grasp of steel yanks me

---

away, pulling me from the pool deck and the mournful eyes of Peter Strauss.

"Is breaking my hand really necessary?" Stretching my fingers out in an attempt to make sure my hand actually still functions, I lean back against the elevator wall. I won't miss the elevators and hope wherever we're going doesn't require them. William simply shrugs but that dang smug little smile at the corner of his lips is being unruly. "It's not funny. It hurts."

"You're a big girl, I think you'll survive."

"You know, the way to a girl's heart is not through reminding her what a freak of nature she is." With an efficient, clinical air he snatches up my hand, inspecting it for any damage.

"One freak of nature for another," he whispers and raises my hand to his lips.

I consider asking him exactly what that is supposed to mean, but instead I ask, "Why did you give him my number?"

"How do you know I gave him *your* number?" The door rolls open and William is out and moving. I follow, a bit impressed with his devious act. "You're a schmuck."

"Well, that's a first," he rounds the corner and comes to a stop outside of my door. "Are you upset at the idea that he won't be able to call you?"

Am I? A little break from the tug-o-war is definitely welcome, but there's a bit of sadness at the idea that Captain Sexy won't be wowing me anymore.

Noticing that my answer is slow in coming, William sighs, "I gave him your number, let's go."

I unlock the door and we go in to pack my sparse belongings and bid adieu to our little love nest.

Sixty-three

Things were not progressing as Klaus von Strassenberg had hoped. They rarely ever did. Hence they found themselves in this uncivilized new land, attempting to reestablish what his family had built throughout generations in Austria. The von Strassenbergs had passed their bold, inquisitive ambition from father to son since Nicholas von Strassenberg had proudly held the title of Assistant to the Royal Surgeon to the Empress Dowager Maria Theresa of Austria. It was their reason and fearless questioning which had propelled the von Strassenberg family to the upper echelons of the Austrian court. It also had been their undoing. Fearing the loss of all his family had worked to achieve over the last century, Klaus had fled to France and then Spain and, finally accepting that they were too conspicuous, they traveled the three thousand miles to the infant nation across the sea.

Now, as he watched her sleep fitfully on the iron bed he wanted to blame her for his undoing. Yet while Klaus von Strassenberg believed he could deceive even God, he could never fool himself. This was his own doing. He had kept from his son the purpose of their lives and the proud heritage they carried within themselves. Imagining Viktor to be too naive, Klaus had never dared speak of his research or his work. When his young son had asked him *why he must be bled the doctor had simply explained that he was removing the bad blood from his system. Trusting in his father, Viktor had never questioned him.*

The bodily shock of the transfusions had weakened his son physically but the effects never seemed to reach his spirit or his intellect. Despite his naïveté, Viktor was a brilliant and inquisitive child. He faced his "condition" boldly and merely accepted it as fact. It was months ago that Viktor had come to know the truth behind the lies his life was composed of.

Brought to the laboratory hidden within the house Viktor had been joined to the crude machinery, joined to the monster through glass tubes and syringes. It was not the first time he had given his blood for the sake of the beast that was kept unbeknownst to him in the family's cellar. It was, however, their first meeting. Klaus had sedated the colossus and covered the pale, sharp-toothed face. Little comfort did this act of discretion grant Viktor. The hulking form on the table looked too large to be simply human. Viktor had asked his many questions and they had all been ignored. He could never know the truth. Klaus considered himself a failure for raising a son who would shun the work and the genius of their forefathers, forsaking it for a sense of moral integrity that could not yet comprehend the purpose of their craft.

The small, frail girl shifted on the bed now, moaning softly. She would need to be moved. "We shall need to find her more suitable accommodations."

The prisoner laughed around his food, "Why? To grant her more comfort?"

"Your reserve will only last so long. We cannot risk..."

"She stays."

"You cannot have her anymore. It is unsafe."

Dropping his food to his plate with a clatter that startled the girl who seemed leery of attack even in her sleep, the beast stood and crossed to the bars. "Try and take her from me old man."

"She cannot stay here," the doctor insisted more forcefully, hoping that this merciless man who had understood the von Strassenbergs' purpose when Viktor had failed to, would see reason.

He pressed the translucent skin of his face against the bars, displaying his sickening rows of sharpened teeth. With a loud hiss, the monster snarled, "You will not take her from me. She is mine."

"I will find you a new girl, a woman."

Looking down at the still form, the prisoner shook his head. "She is mine."

"Remaining here will kill her."

"Then you must find suitable accommodations for the pair of us."

"Do not be so ridiculous, I can more easily find you someone else." Gripping the bars of his prison so strongly that the bones of his knuckles showed prominently through his pale skin, the monster growled again, "I will have no other."

Nearing the end of his patience, Klaus demanded, "Why? Why are you being so impossible?"

Turning to the diminutive creature beneath the blanket, he smiled nastily, his light red eyes gleaming, "Because he wants her."

Sixty-Four

A no-nonsense male voice guides William toward our destination. Uncertain of where to find the address his father had given him, William had plugged it into his GPS. The voice leads us away from the hotel and from downtown altogether. We move to an area that looks both older and younger than the city of St. Louis. The houses have a more refined, dignified look here. "It's not far," he assures me, not knowing that the past ten miles have felt like a hundred. He reaches out and squeezes my hand. "It will be okay. You must be who we've been looking for or I would be driving you to the airport."

He tries to sound reassuring but I know he's still worried about what's going to happen next. I smile at him with a weak effort and we continue on in silence down an old, residential street that smells of money.

A high, stone wall pops up out nowhere. As we near the gates, William slows the car. Someone must be there waiting for us. The iron gates swing in, beckoning us to enter.

"What is this place?"

His eyes are quickly surveying the tree-lined road that stretches out before us. "I'm not sure." A manicured lawn spreads out on either side of the trees, beyond that, there is nothing to see. In the distance sunlight glistens off the surface of water, it is gone before I can take it in. "Whoever owns it," he says almost reverently. "Isn't hurting for money. A piece of property this size and in this area, that's a lot of cash ." With what little I know about real estate, I know he's right. "It must be old," he goes on, slowly turning the car to follow the paved road. "Built before the sprawl."

He sounds as though he has more to contribute, but stops short at the sight of the house at the end of the road. Though not large by today's standards, it is impressive. Built of brick with a wrap-around porch, it looks like a solid kind of house. A house that could stand for more than a century. A Mercedes is parked in the circle drive. William stops his car behind his father's and goes around to open the door for me.

"Breathe," I tell myself, certain I'm going to have the first panic attack of my life.

He opens the door and extends a hand to me. "All right?" He asks.

"I don't know. Ask me in a few hours."

Smiling, he tucks my arm under his and together we climb the steps to the porch. Everything looks freshly painted. Flower boxes along the balustrade even boast pretty little peonies. Someone must live here and whoever it is must be my relative. My daytime talk show moment has come. Minus the cameras, which I'm very grateful for.

William pulls open the screen door and lifts his fist to knock but the door swings open.

The Second is there and he seems none too happy. He ignores his son and looks only at me. "Miss von Strassenberg," he motions for me to follow him.

The inside of the house is shadowy and cool. The Second expects me to be following him but my awe at the perfection around us has stopped me dead. It is like walking onto a movie set or into a museum house. I had been in one once, when we went on a field trip in middle school. The house and some of the furnishings had been preserved but the house had an empty, tomblike quality. It isn't that way here. Everything is here, family photographs, doilies, everything. "Miss von Strassenberg?"

My voice is just a whisper. "How old is this place?"

"If you'll follow me, we'll get to that." He leads me into a study that is lined floor to ceiling with books. The First sits behind the sturdiest desk I've ever seen. He's so ancient himself it looks like his natural habitat. He winks at me but there is no joy in it. "Please have a seat, Miss von Strassenberg." I follow his gesture toward one of the high-backed leather chairs, aware of William standing sentry behind me. The Second takes his place beside his father. With an official tone I have not heard him use on me before, the First plunges in. "The results of the DNA test have arrived."

"I heard."

He goes on as though I did not speak. "As it turns out, you are indeed the Maria Josepha Raquel Demure von Strassenberg we are looking for."

I snort before I can stop myself, "Are there that many others?" William's hand clamps down on my shoulder. The Second, not at all appreciating my lack of respect for my horrendous name, states, in a withering tone, "As a matter of fact, you are the sixth Maria Josepha Raquel Demure von Strassenberg."

"What?" William and I gasp together.

"I have brought you here today with good reason. This home was constructed in 1851 for the Demure family. Mr. Demure and his wife, *Raquel*," he looks at me pointedly, "Had this home built for themselves and their two daughters, Katherine and Henrietta. Both girls disappeared within a year of each other. Henrietta resurfaced years later and obeyed her father's wishes to have the home preserved for the day when Katherine, or one of her children, in this case her," he counts off on his fingers, "great-great-great-great-great," he smiles at me with his watery eyes. "Grandchild, should return home."

It's a good thing I'm sitting. "You've got to be joking."

"I am not. I assure you. Mr. Demure and his wife were remarkably attached to their daughters, particularly Katherine who was, from what we can gather, a sickly girl. They wanted to ensure that if she ever did find her way home, home would still be waiting for her."

"But for all these years? How does that even work?"

"My grandfather was also a lawyer—"

"Go figure."

"Sorry?" He leans across the table. I'm grateful his old ears didn't pick up on my muttering even if the younger ears of his son did. "Nothing. I'm sorry, go on."

"My grandfather was a lawyer and Mr. Demure entrusted him with the preservation of the home. He was also asked to do all he could to find Katherine or her children and bring them home." The First folds his powder soft hands and looks at me earnestly. "My family has been looking for you for five generations."

"Not exactly *her*," the Second points out.

I don't like that man.

The First laughs which causes him to cough in a raspy, unhealthy way. When the fit passes, he smiles, "Not *her,* but the *possibility* of her."

The Second steps in, cutting to the chase. "With the house comes a considerable fortune, which we will gladly outline for you and give you," I can see the muscles clench in his jaw. "Give you access to and full authority over."

"What?"

It's too unreal.

All I have been expecting is a little box with the initials of my great-something-grandmother inscribed on it.

"We would like to offer to purchase the house from you. Today. If you like."

"Why?" William snaps from behind me, stepping around my chair to confront his father.

"This house has been perfectly preserved and updated by our family for more than a century."

"That doesn't give you any right to it, it belongs to

Raquel."

"She cannot possibly appreciate the unique quality of this home. Everything is here, as it was, the day Mrs. Demure died, still waiting for her daughter to come home."

"And she has come home," William seethes.

Throwing an accusatory finger in my direction, the Second booms, "*That* is not her daughter! That is a piece of trash that will ruin this house!"

"If you knew you wanted to keep it, why did you find her? Why not just keep it to yourself?" They are both leaning across the table, their pale faces flaming with rage. It is the Second who backs away, straightening his jacket. The First looks at me kindly, speaking softly, "Raquel, forgive my son and I. We know better than young William what our family has gone through to keep this house ready for you.

"Perhaps you should have clued me in," William retorts.

The First ignores him, "It has required more time and work than you could possibly imagine. Our dedication has cost some of us our families." The Second looks away, watching something beyond the warped glass of the study's windows. "We found you so suddenly and we simply weren't prepared to let go of what we have been holding on to for so long."

I forget the other two and speak only to him, the only one who seems to truly understand what's going on. "Why did you do it then? Why go through all the trouble?"

"My grandfather impressed upon my father the importance of seeing this case through to the end. And, when it was time, my father did the same for me. We have fought against thieves, developers, imminent domain, so many things, to keep this home here, for you," he points to me with decidedly more kindness than his son had. "We just want to know that you won't destroy it, in your youth and," he waffles over how to phrase it. "Lack of experience with the finer things."

I sit back. In a week's time I have gone from the ramshackle side of Nashville to hotel life to being the heiress of a considerable fortune complete with real estate. Is this what I want for myself? This old house with all its old things? This house hiding behind its high stone wall? They're all waiting for me to answer, to give them some reason why I deserve what their family has fought so hard to protect for more than a century. "Mr. Drexler, I have never had any family, not even a single picture, not even a distant cousin." The Second coughs somewhat rudely and walks away. He must know where I'm going with this. "But everything that is left of my family, even if I didn't know them, is here. And I," a large lump has developed in my throat over the course of the last few words and an unbidden tear slips over my lashes. "I need this. At least for now. Maybe after it all settles, maybe then I'll think about selling it, but...if Mr. and Mrs. Demure wanted so badly for me, or someone like me, to be here in this place, I think that's what we should go with. For now. Anyway?" I end on a question, still expecting it to all fall away.

For a long, excruciating minute, all the First does is stare at me from those intelligent hazel eyes of his. "Dear child, it is not for us to decide whether or not you may stay." At that, the Second takes an abrupt exit from the study, his heavy steps echoing down the hall. "It is only for us to give and it is an honor."

I believe the kindness of his smile as he reaches out to hand me a handkerchief for my tears.

Sixty-five

Experienced hands lift her ever-expanding form away from the blankets, handling her as though she was nothing more than a fragile leaf. "Where are you taking me?" she moans in her debilitation. There is no reply, only movement away from the bars and the mammoth bed and all the outward reminders of her torture.

Was it time then? Had he grown tired of her and conceded to be rid of her? Katherine gulped, strangled by the sudden sorrow of her own demise. She had been worthless to him for months now. The doctor had kept him from her, protecting her in his own diabolical way for unknown reasons and now he had come to dispose of her and replace her.

She had watched through one torpid eye as the doctor came in, as he ever did, to deliver their meal and had seen the doctor plunge a great needle into the back of the monster. They had wrestled for several long, violent minutes, spilling blood and breaking bones, before the sedative took effect. The beast simply slumped heavily to the stone floor then, breathing in a sleepy rhythm. It seemed forever before the doctor was able to move toward her, his face covered with blood from his broken nose. Two of the fingers on his left hand were bent at odd angles.

Despite his injuries and the pain he must be in, Klaus seemed intent on accomplishing what he had come here to do. He had also come prepared with another syringe. Katherine waited for him to plunge it into her but in a quick, expert movement he plunged it into his own thigh and emptied it. Stepping around the mass on the floor, he knelt and lifted her away from the chamber of her nightmares.

Sixty-six

"William will be available if you have any further questions. His father and I must return to our other clients." The First shakes my hand with a surprisingly firm grip. "Good luck my dear and remember, be respectful to what you have been given."

"Yes sir."

"Time for me to get some lunch," he laughs.

The Second bids me no farewell. He helps his father down the steps of the front porch and into the passenger side of the Mercedes. Without even a word to his son to tell him what to do, the Second races away. Apparently he still isn't ready to let go. The Third and I stand on the porch, side by side, and watch them disappear around the bend and into the line of trees.

"Well, that wasn't so bad, was it?"

Smiling in a slightly defeated kind of way, he shrugs. "It could have been worse. I'm sure my father would have been all right if you had cursed the house as being too old and fussy and thrown the deed in his face."

"I bet." There is so much space, my eyes can't take it all in. Amazing to think it is all mine now. "I still don't understand it."

He shrugs again, apparently at a loss for words today. "A father's love for his daughter."

"I definitely don't understand that."

"I'm sorry, I didn't---"

Taking his hand in my own I lead us back into the coolness of the house. "It's all right. I'm a big girl." The door clicks shut behind us and suddenly it feels more real. We are in *my* house. That is *my* beautiful staircase. To the left is my study and, just beyond it, is my dining room. In the hours following the announcement and my acceptance, the First informed me of all of my financial assets, stocks and bonds and the real estate (explaining that rather large portions of the assets had gone to the upkeep, security and modernization of the property). He had then given me a tour of the first floor of the house.

The kitchen, while still boasting a large hearth for cooking, had been modernized with a gas stove and running water. The Second grudgingly escorted me into the old root cellar. It was converted into a laundry room and storage area. The room off of that shocked me. They had sectioned off an area to serve as the security room. From here I could view and record the live feed from the cameras stationed throughout the property. It kind of gave me the creeps and the need for it, or the perceived need for it, actually made me feel a little less safe than I had felt at the iron gates.

Back on the main floor, they had shown me the dining room with its long, mahogany table and cushioned chairs to match. Large, ornate furniture occupied every room and most of the rooms held at least one bookcase and scores of picture frames. I am waiting until I'm alone to have a private meeting with the faces of my family.

The sitting room across from the study is lavishly yet sensibly furnished, with a chaise lounge being the first piece of furniture to be encountered. Maybe poor Katherine was a fainter and the Demures had set it there for her convenience. Above the generous mantel was a large family portrait painted on canvas. I didn't want to look at it just yet, even though it was difficult to ignore. The second floor, being the floor of bedrooms, was left for my own exploration. Maybe later.

"What now?" William smiles, the edginess fading from him as he accepts that giving this home to a genuine piece of Southern white trash was the only issue of concern for the First and Second.

What now? Indeed. I can't even begin to think of what now. "Let's do something normal," I offer.

"Okay, what's normal? After the last week of your life," he laughs, looking more like that young man in that tiny elevator.

"Exactly what does normal look like?"

"Well, do you think they stocked the fridge?"

"I suppose it's a possibility." He follows me into the spacious kitchen with its copper pots hanging above the scrubbed butcher's block. Several threadbare aprons hang beside the servants' door. It looks like they hauled the refrigerator in this week. It's one of those fancy, save-the-earth types, and it's big enough to accommodate Char and all her sisters' rather manly appetites. It suddenly occurs to me that I can invite Char over. Just as quickly I realize that Char could create a sticky situation. If Kevin were to question her again, if he has at all, I don't think she would be able to keep it from him.

William opens the refrigerator, "It's empty, but cold."

"Well hey, that's favorable."

"Want to go shopping?"

"What girl doesn't?" We both know the answer to that and we smile at each other with our common knowledge. Although, I have to give Felicity her due props, she does make shopping painless and even fun. Maybe I will buy all my clothes from her or steal her as my personal shopping assistant. I just might be able to afford one now.

Sixty-seven

Viktor slumped into the leather seat across from Mr. Demure. Weary and dirty and devoid of hope, he could barely bring himself to report on his journey. The stained glass doors of the study had been drawn together to protect the more delicate ears of the ladies, should the young man's adventures have proven unfavorable. Mr. Demure's tireless searching through his endless network of friends and colleagues had uncovered not even the slightest of clues. Katherine was simply gone.

Mrs. Demure had taken up a post outside the doors, attempting to hear over the desperate pounding of her heart.

"May I offer you a drink?" Mr. Demure asked, presumably out of a sense of hospitality. In actuality, his goal was to spur the boy on to tell his tale. Viktor shook his hanging head and rubbed his eyes with hands that were far removed from the soft, unlabored hands of so many long months ago. The boy looked harder now. Before his departure he had possessed a graceful musculature, the lean muscle of a man who had spent long hours training to fence. Now he possessed the brawny muscles of a man used to physical labor.

Mr. Demure seemed cool and collected as he waited,

but his breath struggled to find its way to his lungs and his heart nearly forgot to beat. In contrast to the young man who had left six months ago to search as far as his money would carry him for the girl they both loved so dearly, Mr. Demure's physical form had shrunken into itself. He was nearly a concave man, reflecting the near-emptiness inside him.

A man of sense and practicality William Demure was also a man of romance. He had been blessed greatly in marrying a woman whom he loved and respected with a ferocity that had not diminished in their twenty years of marriage. Never did he wish his daughters to need to marry for anything other than the strongest love. For this reason he had climbed the heights of his profession and worked his way into the most powerful circles of society. He had taught himself to invest in stocks and bonds, seeking out the advice of the richest men this side of the Mississippi. Whenever a businessman from the East made an appearance in St. Louis, which was frequently, Mr. Demure quickly gained his acquaintance and his confidence. So zealous was he in developing his social connections and acquiring the wisdom of the wealthy that he had amassed a sizeable fortune before the girls were of marrying age.

Henrietta was flighty and thirsty more for status than love, but Katherine, he knew would marry only for the greatest love. She was intelligent as any man he had ever met and made of stronger fiber than anyone he knew. Except, *he thought,* for this one here.

Viktor had taken what little money he could find in his father's study and a small fortune given to him by Mr. Demure and set out to find Katherine. He had promised not to return without her.

The young man, bronzed by the sun he had been shielded from all his life, opened his mouth to speak and quickly thought better of it. Mr. Demure saw him swallow hard and blink against impending tears. Viktor cleared his throat and attempted to speak again, "I promised not to return without your daughter. Forgive me sir, but I," he fell silent again, looking away to gather himself. "I could not." In his weariness and despair, his voice broke, "I could not find her or any word of her."

Outside the stained glass doors, Mrs. Demure stifled a cry. Josephine, aware of her mistress's eavesdropping, was quickly at her side, holding her steady and leading her slowly up the staircase.

Mr. Demure flinched at the news. He wanted to declare this report unacceptable and demand the boy leave and not return. Instead he cleared his throat and looked away from the heart wrenching sorrow on the young man's face.

Viktor rallied on, forgetting his pride and speaking through his tears, "I traveled to the mouth of the Mississippi on the west side and to New Orleans." He shrugged. "I returned on the east side of the river, stopping at every town and village, every camp. There was nothing," with a gasping sob that toppled Mr. Demure's last fragment of restraint, Viktor whispered, "There is nothing. She is gone."

The man, hardened by war and years of professional restraint, felt his composure fail as the withheld tears escaped his hazel eyes.

Viktor forced himself to press on, "I did not want to return without her and so I continued on to Chicago, assuming it would be as good a place as any for a young lady to try and establish herself. I did not wish to return, *but the money was gone by the time I reached Springfield. I had to work for my food the rest of the way, there and back." He laughed with a sour tone. "And discovered that, like everything else he has ever told me, my father either lied or was grievously incorrect concerning my illness associated with daylight. It is only my eyes that are affected. It was impossible, you see, to only travel in the darkness. Perhaps not impossible, but too slow for my liking. But I found that even the issues with my eyesight were manageable." Viktor used his sleeve to wipe the trails of wetness left by the tears. "After Chicago I was on my way East when I ran into a...well, a gang of ruffians if you will. They stole my horse and my boots and my change of clothes, everything but my trousers and shirt, and left me for dead far from any town or farm."*

Viktor lifted his head to meet William Demure's gaze. The older man started, but Viktor waved his concerns away. "They are mere scars now," he consoled the man, referring to the jagged scar at the edge of his left eye. "The hidden ones are far less fetching."

"Mr. von Strassenberg, I cannot..."

"Do not apologize, I would have gone even had you not asked." With noted abruptness, Viktor stood, his newly acquired clothes hanging unfashionably on his changed form. "Mr. Demure, as you most assuredly have surmised by this point, I am in love with Katherine and I will not rest until she is found. I came home only because I feared my own death and that you would never know what happened to either of us." Moving toward the stained glass doors, he continued, "Tonight I will return home to gather a fresh supply of my things, though I do not imagine my old things will fit," he smiled somewhat proudly at this. "And I will replenish my funds, find a

new horse, and return to our search."

"I cannot thank you enough, son," Mr. Demure rounded his desk to quickly open the door for Viktor. "We are deeply indebted to you."

"No," Viktor stepped into the foyer. "I am not doing this for you or your family, but for my own selfish reasons. I have to have her safely home."

They crossed the foyer to the front door. Placing his hand on the knob, Mr. Demure realized he had forgotten something. "What about the Austrian girl?"

"My father can marry her if he so desires." He stepped out into the darkness. "When I find your daughter, Mr. Demure, I will bring her back and make her my wife." Without waiting for approval Viktor turned toward the lane, disappearing into the cover of night.

Sixty-eight

Being that it was already after noon, William treated me to lunch at a sandwich shop not far from the house. Fully satiated, we headed out on our exciting shopping adventure.

"So," he smiles from behind the wheel of his Jag. "Where to first? And are you planning to continue buying your clothes one day at a time, or would you like to address,"

"Haha."

"That issue as well?"

"You're a funny man."

He shrugs with false humility. "I try."

Grocery shopping and clothes shopping in one day...It might kill me, but better to get it all done in one day than have to do it again tomorrow. What *will* I do tomorrow? "Let's hit a clothing store today, nothing fancy, please, and then find some food."

"Sounds like a plan."

We pull into the parking lot of yet another mall and I groan audibly. "Shush," he tells me as he climbs out, "There's an *Old Navy* in here. That should be casual enough for you." Opening my door, he adds as an encouragement, "There's also a bookstore and an electronics store, if you were wanting to get a television."

"Do I have cable, satellite?"

"Good point. We'll get you a *blu-ray* player while we're at it."

"And some movies!" This is starting to become exciting. There isn't anything in this mall that I can't afford. I can pay for anything with my own money, well, with the Drexlers's card until all of my funds are in order. They'll be deducting my personal expenses, such as televisions and clothes, from my store of treasure. We have an understanding.

The doors slide open, welcoming us in to a consumer's paradise where anything I want can be mine. It's intoxicating. The mall suddenly holds an entirely new appeal for me. Trendy, sleek-haired girls click by in their summer heels, rolling their eyes at my torn jeans and wrinkled t-shirt. *Laugh* , I think, *I have more money than your daddy.*

William winks at me, "Just because you can, doesn't mean you should."

"What?"

He turns me in the direction of the blue neon declaring, OLD NAVY. "There's more power in restraint and accumulation than in spending."

"I wasn't even..."

"Wanting to show off a little bit? I saw that smug look on your face," he laughs as I open my mouth to protest. But he's right. I've been a tightwad all my life and it would be stupid to change that now just to impress people I don't even know with things I don't even need.
"Fine," I say. "But I'd still like one of those big HDTV's."

"Who doesn't?"

William waits patiently for me to pick out an armload of shirts and jeans. "No accessories?" He teases.

I sigh, "I wouldn't know where to begin." Hearing us as she walks by, a sales assistant lunges at her chance. "I can help you with that." She's a cute little thing, probably five sizes smaller than me. I watch William to see if his eyes flicker in her direction, they don't. He must just like his women big. The assistant hooks me up with some scarves and a couple jackets, just to add pop, and leads us to the register. I wonder if she works on commission.

She rings us up and William flashes the company plastic. "Come see us again," the tiny bird chirps with a special smile just for William. Maybe she thinks he's shopping with his sister. We're both of such exaggerated stature to make siblinghood a possibility. "I think she likes you," I whisper at him as we lug our bags into the open corridor. He just shrugs, "I get that a lot."

"Oh do you?"

"Yep. Where to next?"

"So girls are always winking at you?" He stops and turns to face me. "Where do you want to go next?"

"Fine." I pout and shrug off toward the next store.

Sixty-nine

A heavy bolt fell with a thunderous boom.

Viktor had found himself unable to enter his home without notice. Every window, every door, was bolted securely.

The wizened face of the von Strassenberg's butler emerged from the darkness behind the door. If he was startled to find his young master home at long last, he did not show it. "Walter, good to see you," Viktor began. "Is my father home?"

A moment and then, "He is in his study, sir."

"Thank you, Walter." There was no acceptance of his thanks as Viktor moved past the old man. "I will be in my room Walter." Still no response. Viktor expected none. The old man had been with the family since Klaus was a boy and he made his dislike of the younger von Strassenberg evident at their every meeting.

The corridors flickered with the light of the oil lamps, guiding Viktor toward his room. He reached his turn, finding that the lamps in his wing had not been lighted. Of course, he thought, I am not expected. It made no difference to Viktor. He had spent his life in the shadows and knew his way through them. Without faltering, he made his way to the heavy oak door of his room. He almost expected to find it locked but the door opened easily, swinging open to release a wave of stale, musty air.

He would pack his things and wait for the silent hours that seem neither morning nor night. When he felt certain his father would be asleep, he would go to the study and unburden Klaus of a fair amount of the family gold. This time he would not return, with or without her. Taking the gold was an equitable trade for the forfeit of his inheritance.

Though considerably tighter, Viktor was relieved to find his clothes did indeed still fit, somewhat. Shouldering a small satchel, he shrugged uncomfortably beneath the confining threads. He would still need to purchase new clothing. This would not work. He kept waiting for the sound of ripping fabric, groaning and giving way for his new physique.

As he had packed and waited no one had come to welcome him home. No one had come to light the lamps. He did not even know if Walter had bothered to inform his father of his return. It did not matter. He was ready to be on his way again. Katherine was somewhere, he was certain of it. She was not a silly thing in crinolines who would throw herself from a bridge upon hearing her beloved was set to wed another. No, his Katherine would abandon her life of ladies' teas and gentlemen's standards for the life of adventure she always longed for. He wondered if she had gone further west. Perhaps she would even attempt to make her way to Europe. There was no telling with her. She wanted so many things of life. Her *romantic ideals could have borne her anywhere.*

Viktor considered his next destination as he walked away from the darkness and into the light of the corridor leading to his father's study. It was past three in the morning and unlikely that Klaus would still be sitting behind his massive desk, scribbling in his sacred journal. Viktor wondered how the other doctors at the University received the maniacal zeal of Klaus von Strassenberg and doubted it would be long before his welcome wore off.

He knew every man in his family, for as many generations as could be remembered, had been a surgeon. He often wondered if following in the footsteps of one's great-great-great-great grandfather could actually lead to insanity.

Steeling himself for whatever lay beyond the doors, Viktor took a deep breath and pushed his way in. The room was dark, but for a lazy fire crackling in the hearth. In the shifting shadows, he could see nothing but the shapes of Klaus' collection of their ancestors' strange instruments. No longer useful in the laboratory, Klaus kept them in his study as a constant reminder of how far they, as a family and as a profession, had progressed.

There was enough light from the fire to lead Viktor to the desk and the false-bottomed drawer with the most easily accessed capital. As a curious child who had largely been kept from the outside world, Viktor had taught himself the art of prying where he was not meant to pry. In the hours of the night, when everyone else slept, or while his father was gone for days working in the University of Vienna's laboratories, Viktor had taught himself many useful things.

Lock-picking was his personal favorite. Everything dear to Klaus von Strassenberg was always kept under heavy lock and key. It had become their own private battle once Klaus had realized that his son had managed to rifle through his most sensitive documents. The paranoid doctor had then gone from lock and key to combination safes.

The newest contraption had been bought just for this house. Viktor had yet to find or crack the largest edition, where the bulk of the family wealth was housed along with Klaus's most sensitive documents. What he had managed to find was the double combination lock hidden beneath the false-bottomed drawer of his father's desk. This is where he had found the heirloom ring he had given to Katherine. He had seen the small velvet jewel box and opened it and had been stunned by the intricate beauty of the ring.

His first thought had been of Katherine and presenting her with such a lovely token. True, it had been in the von Strassenberg family for more than a century, supposedly belonging to his great-great-something grandmother.

When he had given it to Katherine, he had intended for it to stay in the family. From that first sight of her toes peeking out from beneath the tapestry and the stubborn set of her jaw against him, he had wanted her as his own. He had known of his father's plans for him to marry Gertrude van Swieten, which he had dutifully accepted, understanding his duty to the family and having never found love on his own. But when he had seen Katherine that night, beautiful and dynamic in spite of her tumbling humiliation, he had sensed the flight of his father's well-laid plans. Viktor craved her plucky insolence, her disregard for the senseless confines most well-bred young ladies accepted as a matter of fact. He *had wanted her fiercely since that day, to hold her in the gentle hours of the night and hear every dream and notion that stewed inside that passionate brain of hers. He yearned to take her away to all the places she had been told she would never see.*

He would protect her and strengthen her and allow her to be whoever was hiding beneath the proprieties and petticoats. All he wanted was Katherine and her cheeky courage. He would die before he surrendered his search for her.

Viktor slid the drawer open. The sound of it seemed dangerously amplified in the silence of the darkest hours of the night. Random books and papers hid the panel beneath. He lifted these out in a pile and set them aside before popping the panel up. It occurred to him then that Klaus may have removed anything valuable from this drawer. He tried the combination he had last used, listening to the gears whir and click. Offering up a silent prayer, Viktor pulled on the heavy lid of the safe.

With a faint click of submission the lid opened. Viktor pulled it back until it rested against the side of the drawer and then he reached in to feel out the contents of the drawer. Papers, many, many papers. A leather pouch that jingled with a very satisfying sound. Viktor pocketed this. A wooden box, perhaps five inches thick. He opened this and, finding stacks of American currency, slipped those into his satchel. This was considerably more than he had discovered six months prior. Of course, with all the doors and windows locked tightly and his thieving son gone for half the year, Klaus had little to worry about within the fortress of his home. Viktor was about to finish his search when his finger struck something small and square.

Lifting the velvet jewel box from the safe, an awareness began to snake through him. As he pulled back the lid, numbness trickled into him. Moonlight filtered through the windows, sparkling off the blue diamond he had last seen on her perfect, delicate hand. Something moved in the flickering shadows near the fire. Caught, as he had been, in a trance of dawning terror, Viktor had not noticed the old man move from the safety of the shadows beyond the light of the fire. His ears, now well-trained to the sound, registered the click of a pistol's hammer as it was drawn back, prepared to fire.

"Take what you will and leave this house."

Viktor drew himself to his full height, a powerful figure silhouetted in the moonlight. "So many lies, Father."

"Lies," his father spat, stepping into the full light of the fire. "It was your weakness, your lack of appreciation for what we have fought for generations to preserve, that required them." Klaus von Strassenberg, calm and steady, held the revolver in front of him, aiming at his son.

Undeterred, Viktor stepped forward, the numbness in him giving way to starling alertness. "And what is it you have fought to preserve? Generations of thieves? Of madmen and power mongers?!"

Klaus laughed coldly. "You cannot begin to understand. You have no loyalty. No sense of pride in belonging to something greater than yourself."

"I belonged to something greater than myself!" Viktor screamed, overwhelmed by the rage and sorrow which had propelled him for more than six months. "And you took her!" Reaching into the satchel, Viktor drew the Colt .45 given to him by Mr. Demure. "Where is she?" Closing the distance, so that their drawn weapons nearly

263

touched, Viktor pulled back his own hammer. "Where is Katherine?"

"Why should I know," Klaus shrugged casually, no flicker of remorse belying his innocence.

Viktor held out the opened box, displaying the ring. "The last night I saw her, she still wore this on her finger. How did you get it?"

Another unimpressed shrug. "She left it for her father when she ran away, asking him to return it to me. Apparently she believed she had no right to it, as you would soon be wed. She wanted no reminder of you on her journey."

A breath hissed through Viktor's clenched teeth, "He would have told me so."

"Would he?"

"Yes."

"I suggest you determine the validity of that statement before doing anything rash." Klaus lowered his gun, as though tired with the childish games. Viktor did not. "What have you done with her?"

Nothing. Klaus simply stared at his son as though he were a crazed lunatic. "Where is she?" Viktor rushed forward, pressing the gun into his father's chest. "When I find her, and I will, I will come back and kill you."

With all the arrogance of his station, Klaus challenged, "Then why not do it now?"

Leaning in close, whispering in a vengeful hiss, Viktor promised, "So that before you die you will know you have failed." Lowering his pistol, he added, "But for now, this shall suffice." The blow caught Klaus unaware and sent him reeling and bleeding to the Persian rug. A fountain gushed from his broken nose, staining the artfully woven threads. Satisfied with the damage he had *caused, Viktor did not turn his back as he departed from the room.*

Seventy

It has taken William and I the better part of two hours to mount my new television. He had respectfully removed the family portrait over the mantel and set it in the study. While he had placed a stepladder in front of the fireplace and worked at carefully removing the portrait, I had inadvertently stolen several glances.

They had been a handsome family. Mr. Demure was a proud looking, broad-shouldered man with straw-colored waves. Mrs. Demure, Raquel, looked to be a wisp of a woman, with delicate bones and bright green eyes and hair that could either be auburn or a rich brown with flaming highlights. What I wouldn't give for a color photo and not just a colored likeness.

The girls in the portrait look so close in age it's difficult to tell who's older. One girl, with a haughty grin and mischievous eyes that were either light brown or hazel like her father's, had beautifully set flaxen blonde waves. She was chestier than the other girl and more substantially built otherwise. The smaller one, pale and even more delicate than her mother, would be Katherine, I thought. Even through the artist's hand I could see a sadness and tiredness that set her apart from her sister. A chestnut curl lay against her slender neck and I found myself reaching up to touch the remnants of my own curls. *So you're responsible for my frizzled mane*, I think to her. *Thanks for that.* And then William had carried her away and hidden her green eyes, so like her mother's, behind the stained glass of the study doors.

I'm trying not to think about her and what must have happened to her, such a small, delicate thing, after she had disappeared. Giving a face to the mystery and seeing what could be my own hair whispering across her porcelain neck, has thrown me off balance a bit. In my mind, I had imagined her to be more like me. She was strongly built and confident in her size. But, in reality, she was nothing like me, aside from the hair color. I must have gotten my size from my father.

"Just have to plug this in," William practically growls, trying to get the *blu-ray* player hooked to the television. "And figure out the settings and all that."

I'm beginning to think it might be midnight before we're ready to pop the movie in. That's actually not unfavorable in my view. I would be quite happy to not spend the night alone here.

I have never believed in the supernatural but this seems a likely place for ghosts to hang out. "If you want to go up and shower, or whatever, while I'm finishing up, I don't mind."

"What are you trying to say," I smile.

"That you stink."

"Such a charmer. Fine." I turn to go, but my heart isn't in it. I haven't been upstairs yet. It has kind of been my plan to just avoid the upstairs for as long as possible. For some reason, the idea of going up there gives me the willies. My bags of clothes and towels and toiletries are still waiting at the foot of the staircase. Eventually I know I'm going to need to go upstairs. And it would be best, I reason with myself, to go while William is here with me. That way, if the ghosts attack, he might hear me scream and have time to rescue me. Maybe. As I haul the bags up the stairs I wonder how long it might take a ghost to kill a flesh and blood girl.

At the top of the staircase a long, patterned rug covers the dark wooden floors. To my left is a closed door. I set the bags down and push the door open, letting it fall away from my hand. The hazy light of evening fills the sizeable room. Two four-poster, canopy beds, complete with lace curtains, sit opposite each other. Hand-stitched quilts cover both beds, at the end of one an extra quilt is neatly folded. I assume this was Katherine's bed. Being sickly, she might have needed extra covers. There is a vanity and a writing desk, an armoire and a lace-covered window. I back out of the room. There is no way I'm sleeping in the room of the two missing girls. At the other end of the balcony is another door. I observe this room the same way: by not going in but by just standing outside the door and looking in. This is obviously the master suite. There is a large, four-poster bed with velvet curtains tied to the posts. This room has all the same furniture—the writing desk, the armoire, the vanity—but every thing in here is larger, grander, the fabrics richer and plusher. Across from where I stand is a set of French doors. They must lead to a balcony but I'm not even about to have a look-see. I close this door too, silently begging that Door Number 3 is a guest room.

The third door swings in. This room is small and has a fittingly smaller four-poster bed. There is an armoire and a small vanity but no writing desk. It is a pretty room, but without the frills of the girls' room or the plush richness of the master suite. Green wallpaper with a gold peacock pattern covers the walls and a green and gold patterned rug covers the floor. *Ah,* I think, *this is the green room.* I like green. I can deal with this.

To the right is another door. Even though the setting sun still offers enough help, I flip on the overhead light before entering and crossing to the other door. A modern bathroom has been added here. Everything is new, without any signs of age or use, but was chosen to fit the era. There is a separate shower and a large, claw-foot tub. It must have taken a considerable amount of the family fortune to create this space, but I don't mind. It's lovely and it's mine.

I go back into the hall to retrieve my bags and William's voice calls out to me, "Did you find something?"

"Yep! Guest room! With it's own bathroom!"

"Nice!"

"I know, right?" I loop the bags over my arms. "How's it goin' down there?"

"You're having more fun than I am."

"Don't be so sure." I head back in and dump the bags of clothes and toiletries on the green rug. At first, I go to close and lock the door, but think better of it. If a ghost really does try to kill me I don't want William to have to work too hard to save me. Besides, I don't really feel a need to lock the door against him. He knows I'm in here and he's a gentleman. It's fine unlocked. I also think about storing away the clothes in the armoire, but decide against that as well. They can wait. There is a tub awaiting me.

As I unload bottles of shampoo and conditioner and body soap and rolls of toilet paper, it begins to sink in. *This* is home. This is where I can stay, forever. There is no landlord. I have done nothing to deserve it, besides being born, but it is mine. It fell out of the sky and landed on my head and it's mine to keep. No more moving. No more scraping by.

Looking at *my* shampoo on *my* shelf in *my* shower is too much. A great, shaking sob rolls through me, taking my breath and sending tears flowing over my cheeks. Moved by the revelation, I sink in a pile of boneless gratitude, weeping onto the clean tile floor. Somewhere in Nashville Kevin is most likely shacked up at a lady friend's house, just a place to stay for free for a night. He'll need to establish a line of conquests to keep a free roof over his head now that I'm not there to pay his rent and his electric bill and buy his booze. Because I am *here*, in this place, in my grandmother's house, however far removed she may be. All those years, he told me, screamed at me to be grateful because he was all I had and he didn't have to keep me, I was no blood of his. So be grateful, you snot-nosed brat, you should be thanking me. And I played the grateful bit, so I wouldn't get in bigger trouble.

But I *am* grateful now.

A well, so deep and hidden I didn't even know it existed, erupts inside of me, the force of it racking my body with repressed sorrow and anger. Gasping and spluttering like a newly sprung geyser, I press my face to the cold floor, with no will left in me to stop this violent release of my long-controlled despair—despair for my mother and for never knowing anything about her, despair for the drunken, whoring slob she left me to, despair for all those hungry nights and days that stretched into weeks and all the laughing and humiliation from my peers. And, in the middle of all the misery and rage, is a golden warmth. A gratefulness, a relief, and a desperate need to thank whoever had orchestrated it all and saved me.

"Raquel?"

And a gratefulness for the voice which calls to me now, for the man who has shown me that not all men are Kevin and that not everything in me is cold and callous. He swoops down beside me, taking me and all my tears and mess and wipes at my face gently with his fancy embroidered hanky.

Between hiccupping sobs, I goad him, desperate to pull us away from the sob fit I have just embarked on, "Who—even—uses these anymore anyway?" William gently wipes the newly sprung tears from my lashes. "Shut up," he whispers.

And then he just holds me, drawing me into his lap as he cradles me on the tile floor. He doesn't ask what's wrong and offers no words of comfort. Just over a week ago he had found me, shapeless and faceless among the working poor on the wrong side of Nashville. He had met the emotionless, embittered me and watched her break and fade away. He doesn't need to ask. He just needs to hold me.

And that's exactly what he does.

Seventy-one

The corridor beyond the study had been plunged into darkness. "Thank you, Walter," Viktor called, not knowing whether or not the man was actually close by. Undeterred, he walked into the blackness.

On his journey to find Katherine he had discovered that his weak eyes were both a blessing and a curse. For while they could not bear the intensity of the sun, or even strong light filtered through a cloud-covered sky, he could see clearly at night. While others stumbled and groped, he remained surefooted. He had hidden himself from the sun for weeks before daring to step into the light. Fears embedded in him since childhood gripped him with a ferocity that made him feel much younger than his twenty years. He had fought visions of his body plagued with boils, of sudden, pitch-black blindness, of death, and then he had stepped into the light. Trembling, chest heaving, he had waited.

And nothing had come, except for brightly stinging pain in his eyes. Viktor had retreated to the shadows and waited for the glow of overexposure to fade from his vision. He had checked his skin for lesions or burns. None. And as the outer glow had faded from his sight, he knew he had been lied to. For whatever reason, his father had kept him prisoner all these years. Bitter anger had swelled inside him, choking his well-mannered acceptance of his supposed illness, of the years he had spent alone in the dark.

The hatred for his father was quelled, however, by a gratitude for his condition and his life of shadows. They enabled him to search day and night for her, unceasingly. He was not hindered by the setting of the sun as others were.

His stop in New Orleans had proven useful. A man there had fashioned a pair of darkened glasses for him, to shield his eyes from the sun. Between a wide-brimmed hat pulled down low over his eyes and the darkened glasses, he was able to continue during the day. It was a small, personal victory in the ocean of his unending defeat.

Viktor strode down the corridors of his home, his feet never hesitating. Where they were taking him, he did not know. If his father had done something to Katherine, if he had taken her prisoner, she would be here, in this great maze of a house. Of that much, he was certain. But where? Viktor had not been involved in the design of the house; a strategic move by his father, he was sure. There were twists and turns and rooms only entered through other rooms. It could take him weeks to search the entire house and even then he may never find his way back out.

He forced his feet to relent in their unguided quest. Thinking of the twisted and devious man that was his father, Viktor considered where in the house he would keep a prisoner. A dungeon, perhaps, but Viktor had found none in his midnight strolls through the house. Away from windows, so that she could not alert the outside world. Wherever she was, Klaus was obviously confident Viktor could not find her, or he would not have allowed his son to leave the study.

"He wanted me to leave the study," he whispered without meaning to. Turning abruptly on his heel, Viktor started back toward the bloody mess he had left behind. He was moving faster than before, now certain of his destination. Nearly at a jog, Viktor hurried around the final turn and was stopped by the sheer brute force of an overzealous butler.

"You should be leaving now, young master."

Viktor, having been knocked to the ground by the boney old man, gathered his feet beneath him. As a child, he had always been frightened by the peculiar man who was more wraithlike than human, but now that had all passed away. He had been beaten and stabbed and shot and left for dead in a place far from home. No longer did this ghost of a man hold any threat great enough to frighten him.

Calmly, he asked, "Do you know what my father has done with her, Walter?"

The wizened butler stood solidly, arms folded behind his back, "I only know that it is time for you to leave, young master."

Viktor stepped forward, making it clear to the stubborn fool that he would not be leaving. "Tell me where she is, Walter."

The strangest sound began to bubble up from the cracked and wrinkled mouth of the butler. Viktor realized it was a laugh, a guttural, unsettling, madman's laugh. "You are a fool," the old man continued through his maniacal cackling, "And you are no von Strassenberg to me." Within the same breath, the laughter turned into a growl, and Walter sprang to life with startling speed and agility. From behind his back, in his white-gloved hand, a dagger sliced through the shadows. The old man cried again, planting the dagger in Viktor's side, screaming all the while, "No von Strassenberg to me!" Too late, a shot echoed through the corridors and the seemingly immortal butler slumped against his young master, blood running from the base of his throat and soaking his neatly pressed shirt.

Stumbling back, allowing the body to fall to the cold stones of the corridor, Viktor grabbed at the dagger. Another inch to the left and it would have missed him altogether; he had underestimated Walter. It was a small blade, though, and had not gone through the other side. He dropped it to the floor beside the body of the butler and removed his handkerchief from his pocket, pressing it against the wound.

Two more doors and he was at the study again. Without entering, he swung the door open, listening and waiting.

Nothing but the lethargic pops of the dying fire. "Father?" he called into the fading glow. Stepping into the silence, gun drawn before him, Viktor crossed to the sofa. Blood stains on the carpet, on the cushions of the sofa, but no Klaus and no further trail.

Viktor looked around him, considering the possibilities.

The west wall was the exterior wall, complete with soaring windows. The east wall ran along the corridor. To the north, the staircase circled down. Viktor turned his attention to the south wall, hidden in the shadows. There was, he knew, a windowless room just beyond the study. His father had said it was for storage, family artifacts that were too unpleasant to be displayed and whatnot. He had been in the room to see those monstrosities and had agreed with his father's assessment. Not all Austrian art was worth beholding. He had also not seen another door. Quickly now, sensing she was near, Viktor raced to the westward end of the back wall. He wondered if it could be something as silly as a hidden staircase behind the shelves of books. Was his father so trite?

Viktor searched for a crevice or a notch that would deceive the sturdiness of the built-in bookcases, but there were none. There was nothing to even hint at a secret passage hidden on the other side. "Of course," he whispered. "That would be the point." Viktor stepped back to more carefully consider the bookcases. They were oak, heavy and solid, and reached from the floor to the ceiling. And they were divided into three sections. He removed the books along the first break, ran his hand along the smooth, vertical surface between each section and found nothing. Not bothering to replace the books, he moved on to next section. The volumes on this side were thicker and heavier, massive treasures of scientific inquiry as opposed to the novels on the other shelves. Reaching up to grab the first book, he groaned with the pain that shot through him. It radiated out from his side, flashing across his vision in a lightening bolt of anguish. The massive tome dropped with an echoing thud, catching his smallest toe as it landed. With a disgruntled kick, he smashed the book against the shelves, and watched as it fell open. The cover had disappeared beneath the bookcase. He looked at the open pages and the binding straining against their weight, stunned.

Dropping to the floor, less quickly now, minding his wound, Viktor peered at the line of darkness beneath the bottom shelf. Excitement surged through him along with *an increasing sense of desperation. He unsheathed his rapier, forgetting the pain and the blood, and shoved it beneath the shelf. Again and again he tried to find a latch or a lever or some hint at how this confounded contraption worked, and just as he began to accept that it was not the door to a secret passage merely poor construction, he heard the sound of metal hitting metal. He tapped it again. There was something at the back of the bookcase. He angled himself around, trying and trying, until he felt and heard his rapier slide through something metal. All the pushing and levering in the world would not budge the object. He needed something to hook onto the metal piece. It would have to be strong and thin and crooked.*

He stood and sheathed his rapier. Instinctively, his eyes flashed to the fire. In the iron stand, with the poker and bellows, was another object. It was a thin, folded object with a shepherd's hook on one end. He must have seen it a million times in his life and never given it a second thought. In a few enormous strides it was in his hands. Viktor unfolded the tool so that it hung at a right angle and placed the iron sliver of a shepherd's hook onto the floor. Offering a silent prayer for help, he slid the arm and the hook beneath the shelf and latched it onto the metal object. With a strong tug that sent another shockwave of pain through him, the latch gave way and the bookcase slowly swung out. Viktor dropped the tool and stepped into the blackness of the passageway.

Seventy-two

Why don't you stay? Please?"

We're standing on the porch, my hand gripping his so tightly he could dangle me from a cliff and I would be safe. I don't want to be alone here. He gently pulls away from my grasp and cups my cheek in his hand. "You're safe here, you'll be fine."

"Is that why all the security is necessary?"

"Raquel, that was just a precaution. The house was always empty. That invites trouble." He smoothes my hair and allows his hand to fall to the small of my back. "I wouldn't let you stay here if I thought you would be in danger."

"Your father could kill me out here. He knows the security system. He doesn't want me to have the house." The excuses, all but the real one, roll endlessly from me. William shakes his head pityingly and pulls me close. He smells of the night air and of dried sweat and beneath it all there are still traces of his cologne, the scent of it has become as comforting as a mother's lullaby. His long, gentle fingers stroke the back of my neck.

"You have her hair, did you notice?"

"I did." But I don't want to discuss it. "Stop trying to change the subject. Stay with me." I cling to him even as he gently pushes me away and looks down his fine, aristocratic nose at me.

"I can't."

"Why? Because it wouldn't be right?" I say it mockingly, as though I'm joking that he would actually be concerned with moral obligations now that everything is tied up with a pretty little bow, but he steps away and moves around me. It's not so funny to him. Grabbing his hand, I stall him from stepping off the porch. "I don't understand. The case is over. I'll be eighteen next week."

He brushes those ridiculously sculpted lips across the back of my hand and disentangles himself. "It was never about those things, Raquel." He begins to walk away. The Jag shines beneath the light of the moon. And beyond that, the rustling grasses and distant lake shimmer with the moonlight. It startles me for a moment, the sheer beauty of it, and stops me in pursuit of him. He notices my distraction and glances out over the grounds. "It's beautiful, isn't it? I can see why my father would hate giving it to you." William, tall and graceful in his tailored trousers and rolled up shirtsleeves looks as much a part of the landscape as the swaying branches of the large oaks.

Using this diversion, I swing around in front of him again. "Then why? There are two other bedrooms and a couch."

His smile is sweet but not condescending. "And a lot of temptation besides."

"Temptation?" Just the sound of the word offends me. "What're you? Some kind of altar boy?" I intend it as a slap even though I'm still not quite certain he meant temptation in any kind of religious way. He could have just been joking.

"No. I'm not an altar boy."

"Then what?" He's trying to open his car door, but I slam it shut for him. With a long look at the moon, he sighs and gauges my readiness for the next bit.

"I am a good, little church boy, Raquel. At least, I try to be."

Stunned, my hand falls away from the door. He takes advantage of my shock and opens the door again. It isn't possible that he's serious.

"Sorry to disappoint you," he slips into the car and is smart enough to snap the locks down as soon as the door is closed. The engine turns over and the window rolls down.

"But, are you serious?"

"Why wouldn't I be?"

"Because, you go to law school. You're smarter than..."

"Raquel," he cuts me off, but it seems he has nothing to follow that. Neither do I. I just shrug dumbly and offer no resistance as he shifts the car into drive. I have never been to church and Char and I always made fun of the Jesus crowd, labeling them as backward morons. It is beyond me to imagine the Second taking little William, all dressed up in his Sunday best, to church. "But your father is so..." What's the word? Slightly evil? Creepy?

He flips the headlights on. "My father doesn't go to church."

"Well at least that makes sense. So God thinks that I need to be here, alone when I'm scared?"

"We're not going to get into a theological argument tonight, Raquel."

"Why not?" I am so ready for a fight. This is completely ridiculous, that he would leave me here frightened and alone for the sake of some fairy tale purity he's supposed to be chasing. Whatever.

"You have my number. Call me if there's any trouble, which," he stresses, "there won't be."

"You're ridiculous, you know that?"

Everything seems to bounce off him, like he's heard it a million times over and is nearly immune to it. Nearly, except for a trace of sadness in his parting smile.

"Goodnight Raquel." Without waiting for my response he rolls away. I watch the red glow of his taillights disappear down the lane and into the row of trees. A night breeze dances across the grounds, warm and gentle. Pouting, I go back to the steps and sink down. I am alone out here in this near-wilderness. It is the most alone I have ever been and there is nothing in it that I find comfort in. Being locked away in my tiny bedroom, with Kevin just beyond the door or the neighbors out on their slanted and crumbling porches drinking beer and assuming that everyone on the street wants to hear their favorite songs, or in a hotel with hidden people moving all around me, I had been alone, but not like this. There is no one nearby. The nearest neighbor is just a twinkling light, no more than a candle flame in the distance.

I am completely alone. He has left me out here. Alone. "I should get a dog," I whisper to the darkness. "Tomorrow, tomorrow would be a great day to get a dog. I'll get up in the morning and go on a search for a great big, old guard dog. Maybe two." I'm considering how early the local shelters might open when it occurs to me. "I don't have a car. I can't go anywhere." Several expletives push against my lips, but I refuse to let them loose even on the vast and empty darkness. But not out of some religious fervor, like William. It's just one of those things I had decided when all the other girls started swearing like sailors. I didn't want to be like them. I didn't want to be like Kevin. Instead, to show my superiority, I would use big words they couldn't understand. This actually backfired, and they made even more fun of me than they had prior to the show of my personal lexicon. But I brushed this off as a sign of their own ignorance and continued on in my erudite ways. It was fun for me at least, but then, I have always been easily amused.

Shattering the silence and the depths of my ponderings, the cell phone in my pocket screams in an obnoxious, throwback ring-tone. I leap to my feet, grateful that this place is deserted and no one sees me freak out. The number on the screen is unfamiliar, but aren't they all?

"Hello?" My voice is shakier than I imagine it would be.

"Raquel? Are you all right?"

"Ah," I sigh, so relieved it isn't someone on the other end saying, *"Do you think it's safe to sit on the porch all alone, late at night with no one to save you? I like that blue shirt you're wearing."* I swallow hard, trying to even out my breathing. "Peter, yea, I'm fine, just a little on edge." I bet Peter doesn't go to church. Maybe he'll come stay with me.

"Sorry to call so late. My dad flew back in and wanted to have dinner and then I wasn't going to call you, because it's so late. So I kept waiting and..."

"Now it's later."

He laughs in a cute, embarrassed kind of way and I find him completely charming again. "Yea and now it's later. But I had to know that you were all right, that everything panned out all right for you today." My insides melt a little bit at the sincere kindness in his words.

"It did." Do I want to tell him the rest? Charming as he is, he's a little overbearing. Should I tell him where I now live? Give him the address? Invite him over to be my guard dog since William is unwilling? Why can't I just morph the two of them into one? Life would be so much easier.

"Okay, good." He says and I realize he's waiting through all my silent ruminations.

"Sorry, I'm a little batty tonight. Long day and all."

"I bet." He clears his throat. "So, were you the one?"

"The one?"

"The one they were looking for?"

I'll have to tell him something. "Yes. As it turns out, I am a genuine von Strassenberg, the last in a long line."

He sounds impressed and it puffs me up a bit, "Really? That's great, Raquel."

"Well," I deflate. "That I know of anyway. The last of this line at least."

"Well, that's great. So did you inherit all the family gold?" Even though he's laughing at the absurdity of it, there's something about it that makes my skin uncomfortable.

"Well, not gold exactly."

Silence. His tone changes from playful to curiosity to something I don't quite understand. I like to think it's some kind of veiled relief in his, "That's great, Raquel," but that's not exactly it. Whatever it is, I can't grasp it. "What is it then?"

"Um," what to say? "Enough to knock me out of the running for federal assistance for my college education," I say lightly and am glad when he laughs. "Well, welcome to the club. And while there are the obvious drawbacks, having a sizeable fortune also comes with a lot of positives."

"Oh I'm sure."

"I want to see you, Raquel," he turns on me abruptly. "I haven't been able to stop thinking about you all day."
I realize now that being alone isn't all that bad. I would rather be alone than have him here in the darkness with me. Sometimes there are scarier things than being alone. Being alone with someone you barely know in the darkness, in the near-wilderness where no one can here you scream, that's more unsettling than being here alone with my security system. I'm so conflicted. He's so gorgeous and so charming and dashing and yet, so stalkerish. What's a girl to do?

"Can I see you, Raquel?"

Well, yes, in public, surrounded by potential witnesses. "Sure, yea, um," where to meet? "How about I meet you in the lobby tomorrow morning? Around eleven? Maybe we could find somewhere to get lunch?"

A pause and I know he's disappointed. This guy is used to being invited over. He isn't used to needing to ask. "Tomorrow? Okay." I think he actually thought I would invite him over tonight. "Sure that will work. Are you sure you don't need me to pick you up?"

"No, it's okay." I might need to focus on getting a car before I worry about getting those dogs. "I can get there."

"With your personal chauffeur?"

I don't like my men to be pushy, and he's getting there again. "Peter, I'll be there at eleven, if you have a problem with how I get there, don't show up. Good night."

I click off in the middle of his, "Sleep-..." This relationship might just be a little too volatile for me. The paranoid prince and the paranoid pauper, and both of us paranoid for very different reasons. I turn my back on the grasses still dancing in the light of the nearly-full moon and go back into the house, my house. Closing and bolting the door, I pause to activate the alarm and hope that I'm doing it right.

Seventy-three

Even his eyes, so used to the shadows of the night, could not see through the blackness of the ascending staircase. Away from the dying glow of the fire he spiraled up and up until he imagined his father had created some trick of the mind with this narrow passage. His feet were much too large for the steps and several times he caught himself against the cold stone walls, nearly tumbling back into the unending darkness. Viktor trailed his finger along the wall, feeling it curve now. At the end of this final turn, a light seeped out beneath a substantial wooden door. Reaching forward, he felt his stomach clench and his hands go cold and begin to tremble. She could be just on the other side of this door. What would he find? Would she too be feeding her blood to the monster his father kept? Was that the true reason she had been taken? A convenience in more ways than one for Klaus von Strassenberg, the shunned scientist of Austria?

The door was bolted. Several locks barred his way. Viktor reached into his satchel for the tools he had been acquiring since his youth. Had he not been of such considerable moral fiber, a trait he was certain he must have acquired from his dear, departed mother, Viktor knew he could be an independently wealthy man. He didn't need his father's gold, he could find his own. There was no lock he could not best. While he worked at the lock, he tried to strategize their escape. His thoughts, however, would not be tamed. He found himself back in that room, with that thing stretched out on the table beside him. It had been chained down twice over. Its face had been covered but he had seen the fine white-gold hairs sprouting from the translucent skin. The thing had reminded Viktor of a dead fish, so pale that he could clearly see the veins beneath the sickly skin.

Klaus had placed them side-by-side for the procedure. The monster was easily a head taller than Viktor and considerably larger otherwise. He was a massive creature, with thighs the size of tree trunks and the hands of some great beast. Working furiously at the lock, Viktor tried desperately to push away the unbidden images of those hands on Katherine, of that pallid, sickly skin touching the delicate porcelain. What had his father done?

The locks clicked, one after another.

He slipped the tools back into the satchel and drew out his revolver, checking to be certain it was fully loaded. Satisfied, he pressed his back against the stones, pushed the door in, and waited.

Light poured out as though grateful for the relief from its confines, spilling down into the darkness of the passageway.

No sound came.

Steeling his nerves, Viktor repositioned himself, peering into the room without exposing too much of his body. He had learned that it is profitable to keep one's body from the path of bullets. With the experience of his months of living among the lawless, Viktor warily entered the chamber.

It was not the room he had been taken to so many months ago when his father's precious beast had become ill.

From the time he was a small child, his father had drawn Viktor's blood, telling him it was necessary to let the bad blood out. His methods, however, had changed through the years and Viktor had come to suspect his illness had turned him into one of his father's many experiments. He knew now that it had all been lies. There had been no bad blood to let. His years of illness had been caused by his father's obsessive scientific inquiry. The only two weaknesses Viktor had suffered from were sensitive eyes and naiveté. He had cured himself of the latter and found ways to manage the former.

This room was a private study and laboratory. There were books and instruments that Viktor had never seen. Portraits of unfamiliar men and women adorned the walls. Unfamiliar except for one. It was situated behind his father's desk. He had seen the likeness only once as a miniature in his father's watch. It was, he knew, his mother. She had died giving birth to him. He had grown up knowing nothing of his mother until his eighth birthday when he had found the courage to ask his father about her. "Her body was weak," was Klaus' insensitive response. "It could not bear the burden of childbearing." Understanding the topic to be closed, Viktor pushed for just one last clue as to the woman his who was his mother, "What was her name, Father?"

Klaus had sighed and begun to retreat toward the door. "Her name was Maria. Maria Josepha. She was a beautiful, intriguing woman, but weak."

And then he had left, disappearing into his university laboratory for weeks, leaving Viktor to the care of Walter and the other servants.

Staring at the life-sized portrait he had never seen, Viktor was startled by the sight of his own stormy eyes and fine, straight nose. He saw in his mother's likeness his own resolve and kindness.

Lost in his reverie, Viktor nearly released a round at a sudden moaning coming from behind a partition. It looked like the kind of thing he had seen in hospitals, separating the patients while surgeons moved in to do their work. Klaus had dragged his unwilling son with him countless times, believing exposure to such things would harden his tender child and thus prepare him to be a great surgeon. It had only resulted in a decided revulsion for current medical practices. The sound came again, a low, pained moan.

The area around the fireplace had been screened off with two partitions. Viktor skirted them, trying to discern the shapes revealed by the firelight. There appeared to be a bed and a shifting, restless form upon it. With the next moan, Viktor heard the sweet traces of Katherine's voice hidden in the pain. Throwing the partition back he cried aloud at what was revealed.

Katherine lay chained like his father's beast had been. She was soaked with the sweat of illness, her eyes were closed against the nightmare around her. At the crashing of the partitions, she jerked violently against her chains, throwing herself onto her side and writhing as though in expectation of unwanted attention. "Leave me be," she screamed and then more softly, begging and pleading, "Just leave me be."

Stashing the revolver away, Viktor dashed to her side, pulling at the chains that had left marks and scrapes along her delicate arms. She fought more violently at his

287

touch. *"Shush, Katherine,"* he offered. *With a final jerk, she lay still. A slow, wary eye opened in his direction. "I am here Katherine."*

In astonishment, the other eye flew open. The pair stared at him with aching joy. A great, wrenching sob of relief wracked her with such force she pulled against the chains again, drawing fresh blood from the healing wounds. "Have I died?" She managed through the choking tears. "Have I died at last? Are you a figment? Have I finally gone mad?"

Pushing down his own tears, focusing all his efforts on freeing her, he shook his head. "No my love, I have come to save you." She moaned all the louder, shaking her head, the sudden light which had burst so brightly in her eyes fading as quickly as it had arisen, stealing all the spark from the deep green pools. Her fleeting hope was strangled by the reality that grew within her. "You cannot. It is too late, Viktor. I cannot be saved."

Taking just a moment to reassure her, Viktor smoothed the chestnut curls away from the wetness of her brow. She was clammy with fever. "It is not too late, my love. I am here and I will take you from this place." She cried silently now, the agony too much for her tired body to bear. Viktor worked at the locks that held the chains. With the first freed he moved ever more quickly to the other side, wishing to free her of this place and these nightmares. But she called to him.

"Viktor, Viktor."

"Soon Katherine, you will be free." He continued his efforts on the second lock and felt her trembling hand touch his down-turned face. "Viktor," she wept.

"Katherine, I must," he began but stopped at her insistent efforts to gain his attention. "What is it

Katherine," he asked, with what little patience he could manage in his frenzy to take her away from her prison. Looking into her eyes, so green and wide with terror, he saw then the desperation in her request. She was so pale, even more than she ever had been, and her face was so thin. "What is it my love," he whispered more softly.

She said nothing, only rolled onto her back, removing the bundle of blankets that covered her as she did. At first, he did not understand and thought she only wished to be free from the heat of the blankets or to be a step closer to freedom.

When her anguished eyes, once so mocking and vibrant with laughter, shifted down toward her stomach, he followed her gaze.

And Viktor understood.

Or he imagined he understood the torture she had endured all these months. Though he had known his father was lacking in upstanding moral character, he had never imagined him to be completely base and obscene. And yet, here was the proof.

Katherine's lip trembled with shame and a new kind of terror as Viktor stood, mesmerized by the swelling of life beneath her nightdress. No words came to him, only the sickening realization of her suffering.

She wept at his silence, feeling more humiliation at the look on his countenance than she had felt these many months past. Shaking himself from his own shock, Viktor bent down to her, kissing her sweat-cooled cheeks and stroking her hair with his shaking hands. "I will free you of this, Katherine, and take you far from here." Setting back to his work, Viktor tried not to hear as she moaned again and pleaded, "You cannot. I cannot be saved, Viktor. I cannot." He freed the second lock, setting both of her arms free. "It is no good," she swore.

Desperate and frenzied, he stood and chastised her, "You will be safe Katherine. I am here! You will be safe!" With much effort, she sat up, "It will kill me Viktor. If you try to move me, it will kill me. The babe is coming soon."

Gathering his calm, Viktor looked more objectively at her swollen belly. He had never seen a woman with child and was shocked at the size of the life that grew beneath her skin. It seemed no wonder that she was so ill and weakened. Lowering his hands, he asked quietly, "Did my father do this to you?"

She looked away, gulping against another torrent of tears, and shook her head.

"Who then?"

"I do not know who he is."

"Where did you meet this man?" She met his eye then, nearly challenging him, as though she suspected he might have some knowledge of her assailant. "Beneath this home, in a cage." He looked away from the accusation in her eyes, but found it followed him into the images that assailed him, images of the great, hulking form attacking her. "The monster?" he asked.

She stifled a sob, "You knew?"

Setting back to his work, for it was better to work at freeing her than to be still in this hell, he nodded, "Only this year I learned of him. He has something to do with my father's work."

"Why didn't you warn me," she slumped back, the weight of the life within her too great for her unused muscles.

"I did not know," he shouted. "There was no need for it!"

"Stop it, Viktor!" She cried as her right foot was freed from its chains. "Stop it! If you take me I shall die!" She continued to rant as he began work on the remaining lock. On and on she screamed, until, without considering it, he returned, "Shut up Katherine!"

Shocked, she fell silent. Grateful for the relief from her tirade, he quickly finished his task.

He dropped the chain, which clattered loudly against the stones, and moved to lift her from the bed. She pushed against him. "Will you listen, now," she asked calmly though the terror had not gone from her eyes. Though he paused, arms scooped beneath her knees and shoulders, he would not release her.

"Tell me then," he whispered in a tone that assured her that whatever she would say would not convince him to leave her.

With feeble, trembling fingers, she touched his cheek. "If you take me away from here, away from your father, the life inside me will kill me." Viktor opened his mouth to protest and she pressed her fingers to his lips. "I have heard him, muttering at his desk, scratching at his infernal diary. 'Too large,' he says. 'It will not do.' He has said that I shall die, like your mother, if he does not take the child himself."

"How could he possibly?"

Katherine dropped her arm, tired from the use of it. "It has been done before. He will need to perform a surgery and lift the child from me."

Aghast, he continued in his protests, "He cannot."

"He must," she pleaded. "I feel the truth in what he says. The child is too large and I am too small. If he does not try, it will surely kill me."

Viktor looked at her unchained limbs, at the bruises

and sores. *"I cannot leave you here."*

"You must. It won't be long. He knows he must take it soon, before it comes on its own." The tears would not be stayed and when she gazed at him with such strength in those tormented green eyes, the tears came faster, falling from his cheeks to splash against her skin. He wiped the wetness from her arm. *"You must replace the chains and leave me."*

"Do not ask it of me."

"You can hide in this ridiculous maze of a house and come for me when it is time."

"How will I know when it is time?"

"The child will have come."

"And you will be even more weak than you are now."

Katherine shrugged in a defeated sort of way, though it showed no pity for herself. *"It is a risk we must take."*

Viktor hesitated before asking, *"And the child?"*

She had not considered this before. Her hopes had always been pinned to her death. Now, however, it appeared that she might be saved. *"We shall take the child with us. Whoever his father may be,"* her eyes turned away from Viktor, closing tightly against the image of the beast. *"We cannot leave him here."*

Lowering himself to whisper in her ear, and nuzzle against her cheek, Viktor swore, *"I promise you Katherine, there will be nothing here to leave him to."*

Overcome by his words, the tears slipped silently from her, soaking her pillow. *"Chain me again Viktor and go."*

Quickly, he did as she bade him do, being careful to not lay the chains on her tender wounds. *"I will take you away,"* he whispered into her neck. *"You and the child,* and I will make you my wife." Katherine sobbed gently, pressing her cheek against him. "No one will ever hurt you again."

Fighting against his anguish, Viktor stepped away from her, righting the partitions. "Viktor?" she called as the scene was set to its former state. Hoping she had changed her stubborn mind, Viktor was at her side again, resting his hand against her chestnut curls. "Viktor, promise me one thing."

"Anything, my love."

"If I should not live..."

"You will," he began, but she silenced his protests. "Shsh. Should I not, take the child and leave this place. Hide him from your father. Do not let him become one of his experiments locked away in the dungeon."

"Of course."

"And if it is a girl," she smiled weakly. "Name her after my mother. I always wanted to name my daughter for my mother. Promise me you will do it."

"Of course, Katherine."

"You must go now. Your father inquires after my state frequently now."

"Katherine," he nearly cried, taking her chained hand. "I love you with everything that is in me." She nodded, keeping herself from looking away from the searing passion of his storm-tossed eyes. "And I love you, Viktor. You will come for me soon."

Viktor stepped back. "Yes, I swear it." Unable to bear it any longer, Katherine turned away from him, giving him leave to slip away, back into the shadows from whence he came.

Seventy-Four

The morning came at last, bringing with it a terrible catch in my neck that no amount of painkillers would fix. Maybe if I had dared to actually sleep in the bed instead of on the antique sofa I wouldn't be in pain now. But I gave in to the chicken-wuss inside of me and slept in the brightly lit living room with the same movie looping over and over through the night.

Sunlight filters in through the lace curtains, casting patterns across the wooden floors. Still in my t-shirt and jeans, I sit up and stretch, popping and cracking as I do. They weren't much for comfortable furniture back in the day. We've come such a long way. Flipping off the TV and *blu-ray* player it occurs to me that I might need to have one modern room in this museum of a house. One room with a couch I can kick my feet up on. Of course, I guess the girls didn't do that back then. I wonder if their clothes are still hanging, waiting for them, in the armoires. The temptation to verify this curiosity does absolutely not seize me. It's just too creepy. None of it would fit me, not even Henrietta's buxom self could compare to my gargantuan form. Mr. Demure, maybe. Although, I suspect even his trousers would fall a bit short.

In the kitchen I look in one cupboard after another until I finally find the china carefully stashed away in its own tiny closet. It does look delicate and highly breakable with its pretty little vines and flowers. The pattern's a little gaudy, a bit overdone, but there's something about it I like. "Dogs and dishes," I say to the small bowl that will have to do for my cereal. The silverware is easier to find, actually being in a drawer and not in the silverware closet. A small kitchen table sits by the window, morning light streaming across its worn surface. It seems a better place to eat than in the grand dining room. Katherine must have eaten breakfast in there every morning, her servants delivering toast and eggs on silver trays.

This is what I come from. Not trash. Not people who never made anything of themselves. My grandfather, however many greats he may be, was a hard-working, intelligent man. Then what, I wonder, happened to his daughters? Why would they leave this place of comfort and elegance?

Maybe there would be some answers in Mr. Demure's study. Certainly a man like that kept a journal or diary or some other record. Perhaps Mrs. Demure kept a diary. It's even possible that Katherine herself kept a diary. I'll bet it's tucked under her mattress or a loose floorboard. Girls haven't changed so much in the fundamentals over the last century and a half. At least, I'm willing to bet they haven't.

I crunch my cereal, uneasy in the solitude of my new life. The lack of noise, even city noise, makes me certain that getting a couple dogs will be just the thing. Maybe they can't talk, but they will make noise. I will teach them to cuddle me and sleep on my feet and be ferocious. Finishing up, I wash and dry my lonely china bowl and return it to its friends in their cozy closet. Just as I'm beginning to wonder if William is at work my phone begins its annoying ring from my back pocket.

"Hello?"

"I see you survived the night."

"No thanks to you." I scoot my chair back under the table and use the servants' steps to make the trip to my room, the green room.

***

295

"But don't you feel like an independent woman now?"

"I would," I try to keep the stupid grin from starting but it spreads across my face anyway. "If I didn't need you to come pick me up so I can go get my own wheels and maybe a couple dogs."

He sighs in mock disappointment. "I thought you were stronger than this."

"Shut up and come get me."

"Yes ma'am." He clicks off without saying goodbye. It's fine because I don't have time to talk while I go through my new wardrobe. Getting dressed has become a lot more exciting than it use to be. With an armoire full of new clothes, there is actually thinking that needs to be done. Do I want to wear this today or that? Will he think I look sexier in this or that? I'm almost ashamed of my self but stash it. It matters now, that's all I know. Today will be a day for khaki cargos and a camp shirt. It seems sensible for dog shopping. Although maybe I should show a little more skin for the car dealer. Maybe he'll cut me a better deal. And then it occurs to me, I don't need him to. I will keep my modesty and spend my money. Leaving a couple buttons undone to show my white tank beneath, I nearly skip into the bathroom to fix my face and hair. Being a girl of sophistication is starting to grow on me.

It's nearly half an hour later when the buzzer sounds, practically making me spill my orange juice all over my new threads. From the little security monitor in the study I see that my white knight has come riding in on his Jaguar.

"Secret password?" I demand through the intercom.

"Shut up and let me in?"

"Fine."

As I press the button, the iron gates swing open. Why I feel giddy, I don't know. But I do. Having him come here, to my house to pick me up is exciting. His car doesn't even have time to stop before I snatch up my keys and swanky new purse and skip out the door. Almost forgetting, I skip back in and activate the alarm, closing and locking the door behind me. He rolls down the window. "Speed it up would ya?"

"Shut up, yuppy."

It was just a week ago when he had rolled his Jag up to me outside the mall. Mind staggering. So much has happened since then. I pop open the door and jump in. "Have an energy drink for breakfast?"

"No," I pull the seatbelt across me. "I'm just really," what's the word? "Happy today."

His only response is to smile. Religious nut or not, it's enough to make my heart flutter.

Car shopping takes longer than I had figured. While I feel no need to haggle, William is decidedly against purchasing a vehicle without putting up a stunning fight. He wants me to get a Jag but I like the bling of the Audi. Only after moping for a while does he finally motion to a salesman and the pricing battle ensues.

Being too adorable for words, he whips out his phone and snaps a quick picture as Bob, our sales guy, hands me my keys. He snaps a few more pictures as I approach *my* car, get in *my* car, yell at him to stop taking pictures of me as I sit in my car and as I lock my seatbelt across me, threatening to leave immediately if he doesn't put his stupid phone away.

"You'll appreciate it later," he smiles and leans down, blocking out the sun. "Where to next?"

"Don't you have a job?"

"It's Saturday."

"So it is. Don't lawyers work on Saturday?"

He's still smiling but a hint of suspicion creeps in. "Are you trying to get rid of me?"

"I kind of made an appointment."

Immediately the hands go into the pockets and he

backs away, leaving the sun to glare angrily at me. "Do you know how to get there?"

"No, but I have a GPS."

"All right, have fun. Be safe."

Before I can even think of a snide retort he turns and strides away with those quick, purposeful steps of his. Maybe I should just go pick up the dogs and forget the men.

Seventy-five

"*I see my son has paid you a visit, my dear.*" *Klaus von Strassenberg said quite calmly as he tightened the chains around her ankles.* "*Did he abandon you upon seeing your condition?*"

Though she wanted only to ignore him, she could not allow him to speak of Viktor so degradingly. Katherine shook her head, never meeting the doctor's eyes. "*Ah, then why is it he left his love chained with the madman?*" *Klaus smiled as though the thought of him being a madman was really quite comical and leaned in over her. His breath smelled of peppermint and tobacco.* "*Or are you really more intelligent than I have given you credit for? You understand then? That you must not leave?*"

Again she nodded, not turning to look at him. He stopped in his task of tightening the chains at her wrists. "*Then perhaps we can leave these as they are.*" *Katherine listened as he left the partitioned area and clattered about behind the screens.*

She had wanted more than anything in this world for Viktor to take her away, but it would be a short-lived victory. The child would come soon and she knew the doctor was right, it would be the death of her. If she could only wait, they could escape together, the three of them, and share a long and cherished life away from this hell.

299

She thought of him now, of his skin so bronzed and his size considerably greater than when she had last seen him. What stories he must have to tell! She envied him and wondered if she would ever hear of the adventures that had wrought such changes in him.

Klaus placed a stool beside her and turned her head to face him. His nose was a swollen, rainbow of angry colors. Viktor, she thought, and caught herself before she smiled. "Yes," Klaus whispered, peering into her eyes and feeling about her throat for something she did not understand. "It was him, take your satisfaction." The probing continued down to her belly. The child inside her kicked fiercely against the invasive nudges. She only wished the doctor could feel the sharp stings the child's protests sent through her body. Could her insides be bruised? She was certain her insides must be a whole array of colors from the constant violence within her. Boy or girl, she carried a tempestuous child.

"You should be quite glad he was sensible enough to promise to kill me only after he has seen you safely away." Klaus chuckled in a disturbing, cooing way as the child kicked at him again. "You will not live without the surgery and even then," he shrugged. "You are weak, a small-boned, wisp of a woman, it will not do." Pushing the stool away Klaus threw off her blankets altogether. "But what's done is done. Now don't fight. We must see how close we are."

Katherine closed her eyes against his inquiries, focusing only on Viktor coming to save her again. In her mind she saw him holding her in his strong arms, carrying her and the child away as the castle blazed to its foundations behind them.

Seventy-six

Peter is waiting for me in the lobby.

Walking over to him, I watch as other girls and even women walk by, their eyes stuck to him beyond their control. Part of me wants to feel catty but I really can't blame them and he isn't mine to be catty about anyway. None of them seem to interest him. He just stands there in his khaki shorts and slouchy t-shirt looking perfect without trying. I don't know if my self-confidence could handle having to compete with that on a daily basis. Turning away from an unsolicited smile from a tiny blonde thing, Peter sees me striding toward him. He breaks into a grin and jogs to me, sending the blonde off in a little huff as he scoops me up in a big hug.

"You found your way!" He sounds so proud, but I have to be honest. "My new car found you." Putting his arm around my shoulders, he guides me back to the exit. "New wheels, huh? That's exciting."

Out in the daylight, even more people stare at Peter. His height and beauty are a magnet for anyone walking by, men or women. He's like a freak of nature. Inevitably the younger women's eyes always fall on me with a rudely appraising kind of look. Most of them seem to disagree with his choice and believe they would be more suitable for such an awesome display of the male form. They're probably right but I revel in their dirty looks anyway, soaking it in while they assume the tall, lanky girl with the chopped hair belongs to the demigod. Peter seems immune to all of it. Of course, he's spent his life dealing with it. It's only been minutes for me.

"How tall are you anyway?" I ask as a man, not at all short himself, looks at Peter with astonishment. "I think that guy was about to ask for your autograph!"

He shrugs. "It's happened before. I look a lot like this guy who use to play for Duke. They were in the Final Four a few years back and all these people kept coming up and asking for my autograph."

"Did you sign them?"

"No. I asked them if I was supposed to be playing in Michigan, what was I doing in Colorado."

"What were you doing in Colorado?" He smiles charmingly, dang him. "Skiing."

"Of course." I dig out my keys and unlock my car. MY car. My Audi with its very shiny bling. He laughs. "An Audi? I had you figured as more of an old, beat up Ford truck girl." Does he know then? How could he? "Nope," I laugh instead of interrogating. "They were all out of rusty, heaps o'junk. I had to settle for this."

"That's unfortunate."

"I so know." Before even trying to squeeze into the passenger seat, Peter rolls it back, nearly into the rear seat. I pull my seatbelt across, asking, "So, how tall are you?"

"I didn't answer you, did I?"

"No." We wait while the GPS turns on and greets us, telling us where to go. "I'm six-eight and a half."

"Is the half really so important when you get up that high?"

"I'm competitive."

I pull into the one-way traffic, not certain if I can handle the conversation and the driving. "No kidding." Ignoring my comment and running his hand along the dash, Peter whistles appreciatively. "This is a nice ride. I guess everything went well?"

"Uh yea. Turns out I do have family. Well, they're all dead."

"Dead and generous, that's the best kind." I don't know that I necessarily agree with him, but his family experiences have embittered him even more than mine have embittered me. "It's really kind of tragic." He listens as I tell him what I know of the Demures and their missing daughters.

"Wow," is all he has to say.

"I know."

"So what now? You going to show me the new digs?"

Am I? Part of me is still hesitant, even if he's being normal right now. Of course there isn't any competition right now, so this normal doesn't count.

"Well, first," I divert the question. "I have a couple things to take care of."

He grins at me, catching me in my attempt to change the subject. "All right," he says. "I'll play. What chores do we need to accomplish?"

I tell him my issues with being alone in the house, the quietness and loneliness of it, and that dogs seem a likely remedy. As we pull into the parking lot of the closest department store, he looks at me with his brows furrowed. "Most people get their dogs from a humane society or pet store."

"No," I laugh, getting out. "I need to pick up some dishes that don't terrify me."

"So you need the dogs to protect you from your grandmother's scary china?"

"Ha, not funny." His stride matches my own as we cross the lot. I've nearly forgotten what it was like to always have to shorten my stride for Char's little legs. The brief thought of her makes my chest ache a bit and I push it away. "I just don't think it's necessary to eat cereal out of antique china."

We stroll through the store, taking more time than needed to find our way to the dishes. There's a dark, square set that calls to me. We reach for it at the same time. "Really?" he asks. "It's kind of masculine."

"So," I pick up a four-piece set. "I like it. It looks solid."

Slipping a hand onto my waist he leans over and whispers into my ear, "You look solid."

Heat creeps up my neck and into my cheeks. Would it really be so bad inviting him over? We could get some take out and eat it on the back porch.

Seventy-seven

Viktor had not been idle during his wait. Upon leaving his father's study he had found the body of the family's butler had been removed, though the pool of blood remained. Instead of returning to his room he had begun his quest to find where Klaus had hidden the vault that contained the von Strassenberg's treasures. It had been cumbersome, carrying the gold and various other artifacts across the European continent and the Atlantic and up the great Mississippi River, but Klaus was a stubborn man and adored his earthly wealth. He had chartered their own ship to carry them across the ocean and snake their way up the river to Missouri. Nothing could be left behind, he had told Viktor, as von Strassenbergs they had a legacy to preserve.

Somewhere in this nonsensical maze of a house there would be a vault, filled with gold and jewels and various other priceless bits of lore. He would find it and remove it, load by load, to a place where it would wait for the day he could carry Katherine away from this prison. Together, with the child, they would make their way into the wilderness of the West and hide from the possessive reach of his father.

If he didn't kill his father first.

On the second day of his wait, Viktor had left the

house to find a team of horses. He knew Katherine would not be able to ride after the surgery she had said would be necessary. So he bought a sturdy coach and filled it with blankets and provisions. On a whim, he had even purchased a woven basket for the child to sleep in. Only when he could imagine nothing else they might require had he returned home, hiding the coach and the team in a clearing not far from the stone wall.

That night, he felt his way along an unfamiliar corridor. As far as he could tell, he had searched all that the upper stories had to offer. There was nothing new to be found. He was wondering how many more days Katherine would need to suffer before he could go to her when a beastly roar rumbled from somewhere beneath him. A tapestry was suddenly thrown back and his father emerged, lantern in hand. Angry and distracted, Klaus never bothered to check the shadows at the end of the corridor.

Viktor's heart thundered within his chest. He had found the beast.

Hurrying to the tapestry Viktor tore it down and found a solid door, bolted and blocking his way. Hands trembling in rage, he fought with the lock again and again. Sweat dripped from him, soaking his shirt, stinging his eyes. Endless minutes dragged by as his uncontrolled shaking caused him to drop his tools time after time. He cursed himself and tried again.

With a satisfied click, the lock released its hold. Viktor breathed the breath he had been holding and swung the door open. A deep, cold blackness greeted him. Stopping himself from blindly rushing down to kill the beast, he reached into his satchel and once again made certain the revolver was still loaded and ready.

Step by step, he followed the path that had lead to Katherine's nightmare. He imagined her, lost and stumbling in the dark. Had she come to find him again, to run away with him as he had promised? He cursed himself, of course she had. She had done it before, but her second attempt had not been so successful. Instead she had found herself in this black spiral. Down and down he went, the cold becoming colder.

Toward the end, however, the blackness gave way to a soft, flickering light. "Did you come back, you coward?" A deep voice, thick with an Austrian accent, taunted. "Did you bring her back to me?" Something smashed against one of the walls and the thing screamed again, "Did you bring her back to me?"

Viktor stepped into the lighted prison. He considered being shocked for a moment but quickly decided it all made sense and was really quite civil compared to the scene in his father's secret laboratory. The monster, skin pallid and glowing with sweat, stood just behind the bars, clad in ratty black trousers and nothing more. On his feet, he appeared even more hulking and formidable. Had he not been so hideous he would resemble one of the Greek statues portraying muscular and powerfully built gods. The pink eyes leered at Viktor even as the thin, colorless lips parted in a cruel smile. Viktor stepped closer, stemming the flood of rage that washed over him at the sight of Katherine's skirts tacked to the walls like some mounted trophy. The beast followed his gaze and bared his sharp teeth. "Oh yes, she was here."

"I will kill you for what you have done to her."

"Tsk, tsk," the waxen lips mocked him. "We mustn't be so violent. It isn't fitting for a gentleman." As he was speaking, the monster retreated farther into his cage, coming back with a canvas in his murderous hands. "Do you think this is very much like her?" Before his brain could tell him not to, Viktor rushed forward, wrenching at the cell door. Dropping the canvas, the monster threw himself at the bars, locking his massive arm around Viktor's neck. The smell of sandalwood and talcum powder invaded Viktor's senses and for a moment he was caught in the absurdity of it. He realized his windpipe was being crushed and came back to, fighting against the oak tree arm. "She was mine for many months," the monster snarled. "And she will never live to be yours. The child in her," he pulled Viktor back to his feet as he nearly escaped. "My child, will kill her."

Released, Viktor stumbled back, gasping and spluttering for air.

Quite at ease, the monstrous man continued, "He used you to keep me alive all these years, did you know?"

"I know it."

"Do you?" Done with words and answers he knew he did not want, Viktor withdrew the revolver. The beast remained unimpressed. "Will you kill me then, dear Viktor?" He pulled back on the hammer. "Let me help you." The beast pressed his face against the bars and pointed his long, pasty finger at his forehead. "Right here." Holding the weapon steady, Viktor took aim at the suggested spot and breathed. "I am waiting," the beast whispered. "You had better hurry, Viktor, he takes the child tonight. The man actually came to tell me. He has already administered the sedative. He seems a little nervous about it." Grabbing the bars in front of him, the monster looked at Viktor with something akin to longing. "It is my child and he says I shall never see it. Do you think that fair, Viktor?"

"You will never live to see it. That is just."

"Then shoot me already Viktor, I am tired of waiting." Having made his decision, Viktor placed the revolver in his waistband and lowered his satchel to the floor. The beast stuck out his lips in a pout. "What is this? Poor, refined Viktor cannot avenge his lady's," he paused theatrically, as though searching for a kinder word. "Ravishment?"

Viktor worked at unbuttoning his shirt, "Not at all."

"What then? Shall we fight man to man?"

Viktor removed his shirt and rolled and knotted it. "You are no man." Removing the glass from the oil lamp and taking the lamp from the table, he saw the revelation light in the monster's eyes. The flames licked at his knotted shirt, crawling up it and devouring it. Without releasing the flaming fabric, he flung it once in the monster's face, forcing him back. The beast howled, whether in rage or pain, Viktor did not know or care. As the animal stumbled back, Viktor stuck his arm through the bars, flinging the torch toward the pile of canvas on the floor. In a sudden burst, the paintings ignited, sending out flames to devour the monster's store of oil paints. Sensing the danger he was in, the beast, ever calm and collected, approached Viktor as a wall of flame grew behind him, tasting the hems of Katherine's skirts.

"Viktor," he said quite calmly. "Look at me Viktor."

Still holding the oil lamp, Viktor said, "If you mean to appeal to my outstanding moral character, I'm afraid I have none left at the moment. I feel no pity in killing any beast." As he pulled back his arm, ready to release the lamp, the monster attempted one last time. The flames had grown high behind him, having consumed Katherine's *clothing. "Would you kill your own brother?"*

Without hesitating or even questioning, Viktor simply said, "Yes," and let the oil lamp fly. It smashed against the bars, soaking the beast. Viktor watched as the flames leapt across the space and caught on the bare, wet skin of the thing that claimed to be his brother. Turning his back on the wild screams of the beast, Viktor turned to the corridor in search of Katherine and the child.

Seventy-eight

"I can't believe you put those dogs in your Audi."
Ripping off another leather wipe, I have to admit, there
has been some misguided planning in my day. "It could
have been worse," I try. "They didn't rip the leather. It's
just drool and a little puppy spit up."

Peter backs out of the rear seat again, filling his
lungs with fresh, humid Missouri air. "It's vomit, Raquel,
whatever size of dog she is, it's vomit."

"Some doctor you'll be." I crawl out of my side and
roll the front seat back. "See? Good as new." Peter is
already at the porch steps, little Athena tumbling over
his moving feet. "She's apologizing."

Scooping the fluff ball up in his big hands, he speaks
directly to her, "Not accepted. Ares is my friend." At the
sound of his name, the big dog lifts his enormous head,
waiting for Peter's command. "No I'm not talking to you,"
Peter tells him and sets Athena back on the porch. "Only
about you."

"You're such a girl," I shout after him as the screen
door slams shut behind him. Ares, a pure bred Rottweiler
settles back into his bed. He is clearly bored with our
bantering. "You're a good boy, aren't you?" I give his
steel skull a pat and follow Peter into the house, all the
while trying not to trip over the frenzied antics of
Athena. The lady at the St. Louis Humane Society had
assured me that buying an older and wiser dog and a
puppy would be the best way to go. Ares had been her
first suggestion. His owner, an elderly, ex-military man,

had recently died and there had been no one to take the dog. I had been a little reluctant about trying to control such a colossus but she had told me he was well-trained to be a family guard dog. Looking at his brokenhearted mug it's a little difficult to imagine poor Ares being vicious, but at least he looks like he could cause serious damage.

Athena, named to match her titan mentor, is a mutt with much to learn. Even as a puppy it's obvious she'll be no small potato.

Peter approved of my sentries but not of riding home with them breathing down his neck. The spoiled little rich boy in him came out a bit and it was too unbecoming to be humorous.

I guess not everyone can be perfect. William has shown me that. William and his wavering church boy morals. Standing in my house, alone with Peter, I don't want to think about William. It just makes me angry. Although, I guess he isn't exactly alone in the hypocrite category. No more than a week ago I had laughed at girls who wore heels casually and I had used colorful names for selfish hustlers who couldn't keep themselves to one man. Now look at me. I am a casual heel-wearer and a wanton hustler.

Actually no. I am a young woman with more than one available option and important decisions such as this must not be rushed. And just because I wear heels doesn't mean I'm flashing my goods, just displaying them in a more marketable manner.

I find Peter in the study, surveying Mr. Demure's extensive library. "Your grandfather was a well-read man."

"I haven't really looked yet."

He turns to me, a question furrowing his perfect brow. "You haven't snooped?" I snap a book out of his hand and return it to the shelf. "It's not snooping, it's my house. And I just," not quite sure what my reasoning is, I shrug a bit helplessly. "I think I just don't want to disturb their things."

Peter takes a seat on the edge of my grandfather's desk and reaches for me. "If they didn't want you to snoop," he whispers and even though he's sitting, I'm only an inch or so taller than him. "They would have let it all burn." Uncertain as to whether or not he wants me to reply or just stand here, I opt to just stand. There are sounds outside of the sphere that encapsulates us, the birds chattering beyond the windows, Athena scratching at the door, the relentless ticking of the clock on Mr. Demure's mantle. It all seems a cacophony compared to the silence that spans between us. "I would stay here if you wanted me to Raquel," his hands slide from my hips and link behind me. "I would keep you safe until you know that you have nothing to be afraid of here."

I know I've gotten myself in too deep. Spending the day with him and bringing him here has only cemented his faith in us being together. "I don't know Peter," I protest so weakly that I may as well not have even wasted my breath on it.

Seventy-nine

Viktor had not gone to Katherine after turning on the screams of the caged beast. Knowing the surgery could take considerable time he had set himself to the task of finding the remaining vault. It was only when he had made his way back to the upper corridor that he had realized his folly. At the end of the row of cells had been a door. Without a glance at the inferno behind the bars, he had dashed down to the heavily bolted door. Briefly he considered just shooting the lock. Ammunition, however, should not be wasted. He took the few extra moments to spring the lock.

His inquiry did not prove to be in vain. Here, beneath the house, in this hellish prison, Klaus had hidden the family's wealth. Viktor cracked open a trunk and filled his satchel and pockets to overflowing. The room was much larger than he could tell, it continued beyond the thrashing light of the blaze, but Viktor felt not the slightest curiosity at what lay in the darkness of the shadows. He had taken his fill and then climbed the spiral stairs two and three at a time. The screams died before he reached the top. He knew that soon the flames would die as well, being starved of fuel. He would have to think of something.

And so he had busied himself with stores of lamp oil

314

from the root cellar. After an hour's work, he was satisfied. Knowing Katherine would be unconscious after the surgery, he raced across the grounds, through the groundskeeper's gate, and through the forest to the clearing. Driving the team more harshly than they deserved, he drove the coach to the front gates and tied them there. And then he ran to her, no longer able to keep himself from returning to her.

He had found his father's study door thrown open but the room was empty. Klaus was either frantic or had conceded his defeat altogether for not only was the study open and unguarded, but the secret passage as well. Not quite ready to accept his father's surrender, Viktor drew his revolver.

Light trickled down the steps. The door at the top was open as well. The partitions that had shielded her from view were gone. Panic rose in him at the sight of her blood on the sheets, but this, he told himself firmly, must be from the surgery. "Katherine," he whispered uncertainly.

"She is fine, for now." A tired voice cracked from the shadows. Viktor looked to his father, who was behind his desk, a glass of scotch in front of him. He looked old and exhausted and beaten in his bloody smock. "The child is there in the basket. You may take them and go."

At his father's words, Viktor noticed the small, woven basket on the floor. A squirming bundle, much bigger than he had imagined, breathed lightly beneath its blankets.

"It is a girl, if you must know." Klaus gulped his scotch. "A girl. Take the worthless things away from here."

"Whatever is wrong, father? Did your experiments

315

require a boy child?" The only reply was the slurping of the last bits of liquid from the tumbler. "Unfortunately father, you seem to have forgotten."

Klaus' eyes flickered up toward his son, the stormy gray eyes flashing with promised malice. "Will you kill me and not the one responsible for her current state? I did not capture your beloved."

"No. That would be the monster you keep."

"So you know."

Viktor raised the revolver.

"But do you know everything?"

He pulled the hammer back. "I know that he is dead, that he died slowly. And that is enough." Surprise and something Viktor registered as disappointment flitted across the watchful eyes. "Your games have come to an end, Father."

"I was never playing a game and you are still an ignorant and impulsive boy."

Holding the gun steady at level with his father's stony heart, Viktor inquired, "And what is it, pray tell, that I am so ignorant of?"

"The man you killed—"

"The thing *I killed—" Viktor roared.*

"He was your brother."

Without meaning to be, Viktor was moving forward, "From one of your whores!" Klaus, quite unmoved, poured another tumbler full of scotch. "He was your twin, Viktor. A fraternal twin, but a twin nonetheless. Together the two of you killed your mother." This caught Viktor by surprise and in his rage he squeezed his hand into a fist, his long finger curling unconsciously around the trigger. Caught off guard by the unintended shot, he stumbled back, tripping over a table carrying sharp and shiny instruments. *They crashed to the ground, taking Viktor with them. When he looked up, Klaus was slumped over the arm of his great, leather chair.*

Wasting not a minute more, believing more beasts could creep from the darkness of this cursed house, or that his father's now lifeless form might spring back to life, Viktor leapt to his feet and shoved the revolver into his waistband and rushed to Katherine and the child. Gently, he lifted the babe from her basket and placed her on her mother's chest. She squirmed and stretched but did not cry. With slow, careful movements, he placed his arms beneath Katherine, lifting her gently. Though he knew she was most likely under the influence of a heavy dose of laudanum or morphine, he tried to cause her as little additional pain as possible.

The weight of her limp body with the added weight of the child was greater than he had imagined. Steeling himself and focusing on nothing more than placing one foot surely in front of the other, they very slowly made their way down to Klaus's study. The child rested against his chest, wedged between her mother and him. She made no sound, only opened her eyes as though to investigate the meaning behind their movement. Viktor offered her soothing murmurs she did not require. They were more for himself.

Down the corridor and the final staircase they went. His arms began to tremble, begging him to release his burden. It was only his will that held them when he planted his feet on the main floor of the home. His arms screamed with pain and threatened to quit him altogether. The front door still hung open. He had never been so grateful to forget something. Leaning back with the weight, they crossed into the cool breeze of the night. At the threshold, he paused and considered how he would manage the next feat. He hadn't really anticipated the logistical problems that accompany carrying two limp bodies. Silently asking her forgiveness, Viktor positioned himself facing the wall and, lifting his knee and placing it against the stones for support, he ever so slowly withdrew his arm from beneath her knees. The muscles in his arm responded with sharp, stinging pains and threatened a numbness that would make it impossible to use his arm or hand properly for a time. Ignoring the pain in his side and the trickle of blood he felt snaking down his abdomen, Viktor clenched his fist in and out, circulating the blood back through the muscles. This he did several times, supporting Katherine's weight against his raised thigh, until he felt confident to reach in his pocket. Fingers still somewhat uncooperative, he withdrew a match and offered a prayer over it, "Please burn, please burn." Flicking it against the stone wall, the match crackled to life. Without hesitation or impending remorse, he tossed the burning stick to the ground just inside the door. It seemed the flame rose up to meet it.

Not wasting time in admiring his work, Viktor slipped his arm beneath Katherine's knees and carried her and the child into the darkness of the manicured grounds. He heard the roaring inferno growing behind him but never turned. The coach was nearer, a more substantial shape in the shadows. The horses stomped anxiously as the light from the fire grew brighter and brighter. Slowly, fighting the trembling of his legs and the desperation of the muscles therein to quit entirely, he lowered Katherine and the child to the ground. Throwing back the door of the coach, he grabbed the basket he had bought for the babe and gently placed her inside. Viktor tucked the blankets around her and nestled her into the coach, beneath one of the seats. He then knelt down to the new mother and stopped.

A dark, red line was spreading across the sheet she had been wrapped in. Her unfocused eyes fluttered open. "Viktor?" she asked in a voice beneath a whisper. "Viktor?"

"You are safe Katherine." Yet he knew it was a lie. There was nothing else for her now but lies and his love. "You are safe. I have killed them both." Her hand in his was cold and trembling. The line had become an abstract shape soaked across the white sheet. Viktor looked away, swallowing his own sorrow, trying to comfort her. "They are both dead, Katherine."

"His name," she whispered, a tremor gripping her. Viktor spoke softly against her ear, pressing his tear-streaked cheek against hers. "It is a girl, Katherine, a girl. I will name her for both our mothers. I will do all that you asked."

She feebly managed to move her head in the slightest movement, side-to-side in disagreement. "His name..."

"The beast," he asked and he believed he saw the faintest nod of agreement as her eyelids became too heavy for her failing strength.

"...is Peter."

Eight

"I will stay if you want me to." Peter tells me again. The evening passed quickly. It's getting so late it's almost tomorrow and I'm not quite sure what to do. Athena and Ares have calmed down for the night, giving their infernal baying a rest. It was more Athena than Ares, but every so often he gave in to the pressure and howled good and loud at whatever small sound had possessed Athena. Music blares from the television's speakers as the credits roll endlessly down the screen.

Peter had been a complete gentleman through the entire night. He had helped make our dinner and wash our dishes. It was all very nice and domestic. Not once during the carefully chosen action flick had he tried to cuddle up or even put his arm across the back of the couch. That isn't saying that the thought of a good cuddle hadn't crossed my mind. I just didn't give in to it.

Cuddles could lead to kisses and kisses could eventually lead to my guilt complex swelling to five times its current size and then me immediately joining a nunnery. Peter might be playing the saint now but I can feel the blood run hot beneath that tight, bronzed skin. No good can come from me being alone here with him. It was a mistake. I have to send him home before it becomes an even bigger blunder.

"I think," I begin, standing so as to move away from the heat that's oozing off him. "That I'll be all right tonight." At my beckoning, the *blu-ray* player spits out my disc and I take my sweet time in placing it in the proper case and putting the case back on the shelf in a very tidy, precise way.

Peter stands, following me and bringing his hot blood with him.

I pretend to be focused on finding another movie to watch, sorting through the cases I just stacked so neatly. "I don't think," he says softly, matter-of-factly. "That was what I asked." His big, strong hands slide down my arms. I'm trembling nervously. Does a girl ever get use to this stuff? He takes the case from my hands and places it back on top of the mantel. "I believe I said, I'll stay if you *want* me to."

Instinctively, I start to turn and face him, but realize that would put me directly in the line of those dangerous, perfect lips of his. What have I gotten myself into? "I've told you, I'm not one of those girls, Peter," my voice sounds decided but my body continues to betray me, quivering and going wobbly at the knees. There's something else I should say, but I can't remember what it is. Under the hot breath rolling across the back of my neck my brain has apparently turned to goo as well.

Stupid, incapacitating boys.

Those long, tender fingers trail back up my arms, slowly drawing gooseflesh in their wake.

"I don't want you to be one of those girls."

Then I am completely confused.

"I just want to be near you," his arms snake beneath mine, pulling me against him. There is no doubt he can feel me quavering, both physically and emotionally, and I hate him for it. "I don't know Peter. It just doesn't seem like a good idea."

"Would you let the suit stay?"

"What?" As though it's a switch, the trembling stops and I turn in the tight circle of his arms to face him, nose-to-nose. He's still looking at me with hooded eyes, like he's ready to dive in and take his fill of me, but my knees are solid now. I don't like being questioned like he

321

has some right to my reasoning.

"Your lawyer friend, would you let him stay here and guard you?"

"I said I don't need guarded anymore. I'm fine."

"That's what I love about you Raquel. You blow hot and cold all at once. So mercurial." As though my temper is the most tantalizing thing in the world, he bows his head, brushing his lips across my neck. I wonder if he feels the blood pulsing angrily through my jugular. "You'll have to deal with me on your own tonight, Raquel. He's not coming to interrupt us." His words plunge through me like ice. I shove hard against his chest, pushing away his advancing lips. There's a poker in a stand beside the fireplace. I step back as though just trying to put some space between us, but it puts me closer to my weapon.

"What is that even supposed to mean?"

"Calm down," he steps away, sensing that I've gone feral.

"You just plan to take what you want then?" He doesn't look offended or even surprised, just a little impatient. "That is not what I meant."

The stand is just a step behind me, one more and I can reach for the sharp, iron poker. "It sure sounded like it, Peter."

He turns and goes back to the sofa, lowering himself down carefully so as not to break the dainty thing with his substantial form. "I just meant that you wouldn't be able to hide behind him tonight, that you'd have to deal with me on your own and make your own choices. That's all."

That statement might actually make me angrier. "I'm sorry, what? Hide behind him?"

"You know you have been."

"I think you're being ridiculous. Do you remember that we only just met?" Abruptly, in a movement I'm not sure how to decipher...possibly angry, maybe just impatient...he's on his feet and coming toward me. "I

322

don't see how that's relevant. I've met a lot of girls from all around the world Raquel and not one of them has ever been quite like you. Would you fault a man," he reaches up and smoothes back my hair. "For knowing something is worthwhile when he sees it?" He's suave and charming and I'm trying to remind myself that I know these things, but it's slipping through my brain like sand. In the morning I'll be able to sweep up a whole pile of wisdom that slid through my head and out my ear and fell, unheeded, to my polished floor. "Would you fault a man, Raquel," he whispers my name as though he's blessed just to say it. "For not wanting to share, for not wanting to risk losing the most intriguing girl he has ever had the privilege of meeting?"

I try to think of William and his church boy disapproval, but that's his schtick, not mine. I'm nearly eighteen, an independent woman of means. William's approval is not what drives me. But the thought of his self-inflicted morality makes Peter's arms around me and his breath on my neck feel so much dirtier. Stupid William and his stupid morals for making me feel guilty. I'm nearly eighteen and this is normal. My knees go to jelly at the feel of the strength in Peter's arms around me. He's so very solid. It's so very nice. His lips on my neck, testing their way toward my mouth, send thrills through me and I grip his shoulders, trying to hold myself up against the bombarding waves of this sweet pleasure.

Oh sigh.

I am most certainly done for.

Eighty-one

The house had become an inferno behind them. The horses stomped impatiently at the ground, waiting to be driven away from the danger. Viktor ignored them and brushed the curls away from Katherine's pale, clammy cheek. "Katherine," he tried not to sound pleading, to not alarm her or cause her more pain, but he could not contain his grief. Her delicate hand curled slightly in his grasp, giving him some hope. The night air was a cool, shifting blanket around them and he so wanted to believe this was the reason the feverish heat of her beautiful skin was rapidly cooling. The once white sheet, however, and he turned his eyes to avoid the sight of it, was proof against his hope.

"Viktor?" Her voice, softer than the night breeze, was nearly lost beneath the roar of the fire. Lowering his ear to her mouth, he waited, praying those sweet lips would part once more and call his name again and again for years to come. Moments passed like a century between them. Tenderly, he slipped his arm beneath her neck, cradling the body she no longer had the strength to hold. "Tell me, my love, anything and I will do it." Tears spilled freely over his lashes and slipped onto her cheek.
A breath, like a sigh, rolled over her parted lips. "Take them away from here, Viktor. Far away from here."

Losing himself, he gripped the slackening form fiercely as the final breath that would ever cross those sweet lips escaped into the cool night air. "Katherine," he cried, knowing it was futile. Those challenging green eyes stared without seeing the twinkling of the last stars before morning and he watched as the light faded from her and escaped back into the heavens he knew she had been born of. An agony, unlike any he had ever known, ripped at his chest, at the very core of his soul, wrenching a cry of anguish from him that exhausted the strength of his lungs. Sobbing and clinging, he held her, whispering things to her she would never know, telling her of his love and his faithfulness to all she had asked of him.

Eighty-two

With the morning sun comes the realization that I have done something very stupid and that I can't take it back. Drunk with my own feminine power and the sheer gorgeousness of Peter (not to mention a little bit of rebellion against William the Chaste), I had gotten a little bit more...entangled...last night than I had intended.

The light burns behind my eyelids but I'm just not ready to face reality yet. The bed is soft beneath me but it might as well be a mattress of nails for the self-torture that is to come. Steeling my resolve, I stretch an arm out behind me, searching for the taught, bare skin of the young man I should've kicked out the door last night.
He isn't there.

Maybe he has spared me the humiliation and run off in the middle of the night.

Except I drove...so that's probably not it. That's unfortunate.

I throw the blankets back and plant my feet on the bare wooden floor. Do I really want to get up and go searching for him? I have no clue what I'll say to him or what he'll expect of me. Would it be completely nasty of me to ask him to leave, if he's even still here? Maybe he called a cab.

In the midst of my ponderings a sharp rap sounds against the door downstairs.

Oh crap.

The door creaks as someone, and I hope that

someone is fully clothed, opens the front door. Like a shot, I'm out the bedroom door, hurling myself down the stairs. My stomach drops to my feet like an anvil at the sight beneath me. Peter stands in the open doorway wearing nothing more than his khaki shorts and he looks gloriously sultry with his mussed bed hair. William, with more clothes on than Peter but dressed more casually than I have ever seen him, stands across from Peter, and he isn't happy. Fury broiling just beneath his surface, flickering across his features, William tries to step inside but Peter blocks his way. They're growling at each other but I can't hear their words. Neither one of them pays any attention to the dogs sniffing at their feet. I pound down the stairs and suddenly they are all aware of my disheveled-self flying toward them, horrified.

Athena and Ares rush me, nearly sending me to an early grave. I stumble around them and run smack dab into Peter's back as he positions himself fully between William and I. "It isn't what it looks like!" I blurt and feel Peter's muscles tighten across his back. It's probably not what a guy wants to hear after he wakes up in your bed but I have to recover what I can of my reputation.

Whatever William is thinking is hidden behind those dang dark shades, but the muscles clenching in his jaw give me a good idea. But he says nothing, only turns on his heel and walks off the porch. Peter starts to close the door as he tries to slip an arm possessively around my waist. Not willing to let William drive away thinking what he must be thinking, I shove Peter aside and race across the porch, jumping off the steps as William opens the door of his Jag. He pauses at the sight of me taking flight in my tank-top and very tiny gym shorts but continues in his effort to leave.

"William wait!"

What I'm going to say to him and how I plan to plead innocence when I'm wearing little more than a swimsuit I don't know, but I have to try. Keeping himself strategically placed in the "v" of the car and its door, he waits. He stands rigidly, like some warrior waiting patiently for his enemy to creep up close enough behind him so that he can turn and strike. Being the idiot I am, I ignore the warning signs of impending danger and dive headlong into the tempest. "It isn't what you think," I plead with him again, gripping the frame of the door. He doesn't turn to respond. "It doesn't matter what I think, Raquel. I just drove by to check on you. The gate was open, but I guess," the muscles roll in his jaw again. "You were too preoccupied."

I look back over my shoulder. Peter leans casually against the porch but I'm not buying it. He's poised. Lowering my voice I continue my defense, "William please look at me."

He scoffs but after a deep breath, turns and I hurry around the car door to stand directly in front of him. The intensity of his glare bores through his shades, stinging what self-respect I might potentially still have left. I wish he would take them off so I can see exactly what is going through his head. As it is, I will have to blunder on blindly. "We didn't," I begin.

"It's none of my business."

"Even if it isn't," I step forward and he reflexively steps back, now fully trapped between me and the car. "I want you to know the truth." His head turns toward Peter, who in all his glory, makes my version of the truth look like a lie.

Taking what seems like minutes but must be only seconds, William deliberates and finally tilts his face toward me, keeping Peter in the periphery of his sight. "Honestly Raquel, I'm just very disappointed."

My defense mechanism flares brightly, burying my guilt long enough for me to snipe, "You're only disappointed that it wasn't you." He won't give me what I want. His expression never changes. There is no hurt there, no more anger, just a calmly clenched jaw. In a low, even whisper he assures me, "If I had wanted it to be me, I would have stayed the other night."

My hands flies across the short distance to his face before I can tell it to stop. Not that I necessarily would tell it to stop. My brain's instant interpretation is: you're a cheap slut. So I'm glad it's a good, hard slap and I hope it stings his face as much as it stings my hand. The ridiculous shades launch through the air, skittering across the pavement. A flaming red imprint of my fingers and palm blossoms across his pale skin.

Ignoring me, William pushes past me and strides over to his sunglasses. Quite nonplussed, in the most infuriating display of self-control yet, he bends down and retrieves his glasses, wiping them off before placing them back across his eyes. I think this enrages me even more than his comment. Maybe it isn't anger, but I'm trying to ignore the deep hurt swelling in me. Before he can get between the door and the car again, I spin to face him, barring his way, planting my face in his. "Listen to me," I hiss. He tries to step around me, ignoring how close he is to me, and I block his way. "I'm just asking you to listen."

I won't let him have his way. He just wants to run away and not listen to my reasoning. Even though there's a rational part of my brain trying to be heard over the noise of my anger and embarrassment and guilt and desperation, I ignore it completely as it tries to tell me that he has every right to be disgusted by me. Tired of my antics, William grabs my arm and tries to pull me out of his way.

In a leaping bound Peter is off the porch. He doesn't bother with words or threats, only jerks William away from me, raising his fist back as he does. But William beats him to it. Quite literally.

In a movement so fast that Peter doesn't have a fighting chance to register it until he's landing on the ground, William smashes his fist into Peter's jaw. Impressive as it is, it isn't enough to render Peter unconscious. He's back on his feet in a flash. Battle, not quite unlike a clashing of two gods, or demigods at the very least, ensues. I throw myself into midst of them, trying to block their attempts to kill each other. Fists fly around me anyway and Peter finds himself flat on his back again, blood streaming from a cut on his lip. William draws his fist back for a deciding blow and I throw myself against him. In a confusion of arms and legs we tumbled to the grass. Sprawled on top of him, I open my mouth to curse him and his stupidity, but snap it shut. The shades are gone. His naked green eyes bore into mine. Beneath the wild frenzy of violence and self-preservation is a clearly evident anguish.

Caught in this brief spell of silent honesty neither one of us can think of anything nasty to spew. I'm aware of his hands at my waist, ready either to fling me from him or pull me closer, I don't know. I can hear Peter struggling to his feet somewhere behind us.

Never looking away, William whispers, "I expected more from you Raquel."

"Sorry I'm not one your perfect little church girls," I whisper back angrily, but tears push against my rage, threatening to reveal my hurt.

"I never expected you to be perfect, just smart." I try to lift myself off him but his hands hold me there, his gaze demands I meet his eyes. "I thought you were more intelligent than this." He releases me and rolls to his side. Gaining my feet beneath me, I back away toward Peter, letting my anger take hold. "What kind of whack job church do you go to," I shout at his back.

With one foot in the car, he pauses and looks over at me, "I said I was a Christian. I didn't say I was perfect."

"Oh!" I'm rushing him again, becoming completely irrational in my attempts to defend what little face I still have left, if there is any left. "So that excuses you to beat the crap out of Peter and to judge me when really you've been no better than me!? You started this! *You* kissed *me*!" My handprint is still visible on his face. His hair is mussed and a bruise is developing beneath the fire in his green eyes and he looks more powerful than Peter ever has.

"A mistake I won't make again."

"What?" I think my blood may actually have begun to boil and the pressure of it pushes the tears from my eyes. William slips into the car, rolling the window down. "Since you can't seem to choose, I'll make the decision for both of us." And with that, the window goes back up and William disappears down the road.

I spin around but Peter is gone.

Eighty-three

The blue-gray of dawn reached across the sky as Viktor began his final journey to the Demure home. For hours he had worked at digging a proper grave for her beneath the oak at the edge of Klaus's property. He had considered carrying her lifeless body home to her parents to offer them the consolation of knowing what had become of their daughter, but in the end, he decided sometimes not knowing is better. During his search for a shovel he had also managed to find a bottle of fresh milk in the cellar, the fire having not reached that section of the house just yet, if it ever would. He doubted very much that it would burn to its foundation, as he would like it to, but mostly destroyed would be acceptable.

It wasn't long before the babe began to cry and he had held her in his dirty, sweaty arms and fed her as best he could with the things he had bought for her care. He soaked a clean handkerchief in the milk and let her suck it dry between her perfect little lips, again and again until she drifted off into untroubled sleep. "We'll make it through somehow, my lovely little girl," he whispered. "And I will tell you all about your mother and how," he breathed deeply against a sob, "And how utterly remarkable she was."

Then he had tucked her into the basket.

Burying her mother was nearly enough to break him

fully. He wanted nothing more than to join her and pull the earth over on top of both of them, but he had made a promise to her and he would not fail her. Before lowering Katherine as gently as he could, he wrapped her in the sheet, kissing her cold mouth one last time before covering her beautiful face.

With the first shovel of dirt falling upon the sheet he turned, dropping to his knees, sick and retching. Even at the end, he was not well, ill at the reality of his love beneath the fresh mound of earth.

Taking the time to make his way around the grounds, he collected a bounty of roses and daisies and mums, covering the grave completely with their beauty and sweet scent.

She deserved so much more.

He whispered a silent prayer even as his heart screamed against it and then led the coach away from the oak tree.

As he pulled the team to a stop some distance from the Demure home, hiding them in the line of trees that canopied the lane, he thought of those not so long ago nights, when she had come to him. He could feel her arms pressing around him as they raced through the night, the storm chasing hard at their heels. A wave of despair so thick he could not keep himself from being engulfed by it swallowed him, filling his lungs and choking him with the salt of his own unending tears.

Pale, rosy light began creeping into the sky and he knew he must gain control of himself and complete this next step or he should never survive. Climbing down from the seat, Viktor skirted the remaining shadows of morning until he was at the house. As he went, he gathered stones in his pockets, hoping it would only take one.

At the side of the house he backed away from the wall and tossed a stone against her bedroom window. Nothing came after long moments of holding his breath. He tried again, risking breaking the window. A dark shadow appeared in the glass. Viktor waited for her to realize it was him and when she did, she did not bother with throwing the window up. She was gone from the pane in a flash.

Moments later, the front door flew open with Henrietta in nothing more than her nightdress and bare feet. "Have you found her then," she clutched his arm. Feeling the dirt and the sweat on his arms and looking closer to see the streaks of tears that had washed lines through the grime on his face, she knew. Henrietta began to swoon but Viktor shook her hard, "No," he commanded her. "We have no time for that." She began to tremble in his grasp, tears of realization flowing over her sleep-flushed cheeks. "She is gone, but...there is much to tell you. But we must hurry. Gather your things, just enough. And then we must go."

"Where," she cried. "Why? I don't understand, Viktor. She is gone?"

"Yes, but she had a child."

At this, Henrietta's sense snapped back. "A child?"

"Yes," he said impatiently. "And if you want to save the child we must go now." She stared at him, not quite comprehending. "The child needs a mother and you are her aunt." With resolve that wasn't quite in his heart, he promised, "I will take you as my wife if you will leave with me now and be mother to your niece. But you will have to leave your life as you know it behind. No one can know where we go."

Never an insensible girl, Henrietta dashed into the

house and was back out, fully dressed and packed, within fifteen minutes. Viktor carried her bags down the lane in silence as the sun crept into the horizon.

Eighty-four

I go back into the house. Peter is waiting for me, sitting on the bottom step of the staircase. I can't think of anything to say as I stand there in my bare essentials, so I settle for, "Looks like you've clotted." The blood from his mouth and nose has stopped leaking out and is beginning to dry. "Wanna go to the kitchen, clean that off?"

He sighs and reluctantly accepts, "Yea, I guess." He sits in a kitchen chair while I wipe the blood away with a wet paper towel. As I clean the last of it from his chin, he takes my hand and presses it against his cheek, closing his eyes as though this is the most comforting thing in the world. "I'm sorry," he whispers, looking up at me with those stormy blue eyes. Shocked by someone apologizing to me after all of my stupidity, I don't know how to respond. He doesn't need me to. "All of this is my fault. If I would just leave you alone and go back to my own life, your life would be so much simpler."

"But less exciting." I smile.

He kisses my hand. "And the suit's right. It was wrong for me to stay here and," he looks away. "Take advantage of you."

"You didn't take advantage of me. Things didn't get *completely* out of hand. I mean, we refrained."

"Barely. Thing is, and I'm kind of embarrassed to say it, but I don't really know what else to do in a relationship." That certainly makes a girl feel special. I slip my hand out of his and step back without really meaning to. "I know, it's a bit revolting. I never really thought about it until I met you and then last night," he shrugs letting the sentence fall into the silence. "I just think you're going through a lot of changes right now and I'm just making things more difficult for you."

At this point I am certain I have managed to lose both of them in one day and part of me isn't sad for it. Juggling them has taken up a lot of my time and energy lately.

Peter scoops me into his lap and I feel completely gargantuan and ridiculous even if he is bigger than the average bear.

"I know we don't have much time, just a couple months before I leave, but," he kisses me lightly and the irresponsible, and very loud, part of me begs for more. "I want to take my time with you. I want to take a very long time with you." And then he kisses me like he had just lied about his intentions. Sensing the rising danger, he stands abruptly and leaves the kitchen in search of his belongings.

The ride back to the hotel is quiet, our thoughts overriding the need for any radio. With a swift kiss he nearly jumps from the car and, winking, disappears into the lobby.

"William please call me back or at least answer your stupid phone next time I call."

Fifteen.

In the last forty-five minutes I have called him fifteen times. Mathematically that would work out to be once every three minutes, but I don't know if I've been that accurate.

I put the phone down on Mr. Demure's desk and wonder what I should do next. My mind is too busy for a movie or a book. It's already dark outside. And then I hear Peter in my thoughts and I agree with him, it would be a good time to snoop. The box with my grandmother's initials engraved on it sits on the desk in front of me. As

337

does the key to the box with my grandmother's initials engraved on it. I slide the key toward me, pick it up between two fingers and test its weight. They made keys heavier back in the day.

I scoot the box across the polished surface and, with the tiniest guilty hesitation, insert the key into the lock and twist. An audible click tells me this will be a successful snooping expedition. I lift the heavy little lid. There isn't much in the box. Oddly enough, there is another smaller velvet box. This proves to be more annoying than its container. I can't figure out how to the open the stupid thing and then after almost ten minutes my finger finds a little latch on the bottom and the top springs back.

It was ten minutes well spent.

Inside the itty bitty puzzle box is a ring, gold and tiny and sparkling with a big, blue diamond. My great-grandmother must've been a delicate thing. I try it on my pinky finger and it barely slides over my knuckle. It must've been Grampa who injected the Amazon genes into me. Or maybe my father. I place the ring back in its strange box and pick through the remaining contents.

Tortoise shell combs. Pretty classy. A locket with a picture of Grandmother Raquel. A smooth skipping stone and some dried flowers and, beneath it all, a crumpled and stained envelope. Gingerly, I slide this out from beneath the flowers. The envelope, brown with age, is stained with even darker brown splotches. Someone with an unsteady hand had written "Viktor" across the front. The seal is unbroken. This letter has never been opened.

For a long while I just stare at it, feeling this would be way too intrusive. But maybe it was supposed to be opened a long time ago. Maybe if someone had thought to open this little envelope Katherine would have been saved. Taking up Grandpa Demure's letter opener, I slide the blade along the seal. "All right Katherine," I whisper to the envelope and the empty house. "Tell me your secrets."

338

Careful not to damage it, I slide the letter from its sheath.

Eighty-five

"Have you changed her?"

Viktor looked at Henrietta, not quite grasping her meaning. "Her cloth," with a chiding tsk, she lifted her niece from the basket. "Oh yes, darling," she cooed to the crying babe. "You are wet." She unwrapped the blanket and gently set Maria on the coach's seat. "You have to change babies, you silly man, they wet themselves, you know." Viktor had never in his life held or otherwise encountered a baby, not that he could remember, anyway. That was why he had enlisted the help of Katherine's flighty sister. He could think of no one else who would be as invested in the child as he was himself.

Henrietta set diligently to finding the clean linens and removing the soiled ones. She stuck the pins into her hair while she tucked and folded the rectangular shapes to fit her niece's tiny bottom. "There we are," she said with noticeable satisfaction. "But she will require a new blanket, this," she held up the wetted blanket to demonstrate, "is soaked through." As she shook it for emphasis, the folds separated. A small envelope fluttered out, landing beside Viktor's foot. Henrietta did not notice, too preoccupied with her new charge. Dark red stains decorated the heavy white paper. "Viktor," was scrolled in a haphazard line across the front. He turned it, ready to *break the seal, but Henrietta was done with her diapering and changing and he hastily shoved it into his pocket.*

Eighty-six

The paper inside the envelope is stained with dark splotches. It occurs to me, this is blood. Trying not to touch the stains, even though I know they're dry and harmless, I unfold the little paper.

> *My love, if you are able.*
> *Take them far from here.*
> *Name her for my mother,*
> *as you promised.*
> *Name him Peter for his father.*
> *Peter Viktor. For you both came*
> *from your mother's womb,*
> *and you are not a devil*
> *like your brother.*
> *It is not the blood but the heart*
> *that determines who we are.*
> *Tell him that for me.*
> *Yours,*
> > *Katherine*

My phone rings, startling me so that I cry out in the silence of the study. William's name glows on my little screen. "Hello?"

"Raquel, are you alone?" He just wants to make me angry right out of the blocks.

"Yes."

"Good," he says, but he only sounds slightly relieved. There is still an edge to his voice that he has yet to explain. "What did you say Peter's last name was?"

"Um," I thought maybe he had called to apologize, but apparently he's been doing research. Or spying. Spying. Prying.

What's the difference besides a few letters?

"Strauss. Peter Strauss."

"I just checked with the hotel, there's no Peter Strauss or Charles Strauss registered there. There was however," he pauses, this won't be pretty.

I look at the note in my hand. "Wait, don't tell me." There is a very sick, nastiness starting to churn in my belly. "Let me guess. There *is* a Peter von Strassenberg."

Silence. "How did you know?"

I touch the dark stain and know the blood is hers and wish I could tell her how wrong she was about bad blood, about how everything filters down. The good and the bad. The storm-tossed blue eyes.

"Raquel," he asks again, this time more urgently. "How did you know?"

"My grandmother just told me."

NOW AVAILABLE!

--BOOK TWO—

The Blue Stocking girl

THE VON STRASSENBERG SAGA

by

Gwenn Wright

© 2011

ONE

Portland, Maine
1896

"You smell of fish."
My mother is fussing over me again.
There is no end to her torments.
"And salt."
She gives my hair another tug with the ivory comb and I dream silently of thwacking her own finely set curls with it. For some reason, I am given to violence. Father says I must master my temper. Mother makes it most difficult. No one vexes me quite like my mother.
"It is called the ocean, mother. Look out the window there and you shall see it."
Another tug and a yank at my raven black curls and she snarls at me, "You are so much like her."
This is something my mother often says and never explains. Though it is a great mystery to me it is also a blessing, for she always hurries from the room after saying it. "You are a big girl," she slams the comb down upon my vanity. "Tidy your own disheveled nest!" And then, as ever, in a flurry of skirts and curls she is gone. Sometimes I wonder how I ever sprang forth from that woman's womb.

TWO

Saint Louis, Missouri
2010

The book lies open on my desk. It stared at me all week as I pored over files and scanned web pages, trying to dig up anything I could to figure out this mystery. There is so little to be found it is impossible to believe there isn't an intentional lack of information. I close my Macbook and consider flipping on the desk lamp to read but walk away instead. I'm not in the mood for reading, especially not for reading anything that would remind me of the complete failure I have been all week.

I have failed her.

In so many ways I have failed her.

I didn't protect her from Peter "Strauss" von Strassenberg. Jealousy had overcome me and in my jealousy I became careless and focused on the wrong things. One phone call to the hotel could have cleared everything up before it got out of hand the way it did.

I didn't protect her from me. She's young and away from home and I allowed the excitement of the week and the sheer beauty of her to distract me.

And, most of all, I had failed Him and so I walk away from the book and go into the kitchen and pour myself a bowl of Cap'n Crunch even though it is eleven o'clock at night.

My loft is silent, insulated from the noise of the city below. I don't feel like watching television or playing music. My thoughts are tangled and the cacophony is too great to be overcome. We will spend a long night together, my regrets and I, sorting all this out.

THREE

Daddy sits on the veranda, a book lays open and forgotten upon his lap. He often sits like this, staring off into the distance, his eyes unfocused, his mind locked on something he will never reveal. I let the screen door slam behind me, snapping him out of his reverie. Sometimes I think I am doing him a favor when I bring him back, especially in those times when unnoticed tears slip beneath the frames of his funny, darkened glasses.

"Ah, Maria," he sighs, his long fingers reflexively snapping the book shut. He hadn't been reading it anyway.

Unlike my mother, Daddy is always glad to see me, even if I smell of salt and fish and sweat. He loves my independent, adventurous ways and never tries to stop me from doing anything. Mother says he spoils me. Most of the town says he loves me more than any daddy ever loved his little girl. I would agree with them on that.

"What are you into today, darling?"

"Trouble mostly, if you asked mother."

He laughs at this and pats the empty seat on the bench. "You've been to the beach again today?" Daddy phrases it as a question even though he knows the answer. My hair is a lopsided tangle, having only been partially detangled by my harpy of a mother. Truly I do not know what attracted my father to her in the first place. "I am sure your mother was pleased to see it."

"I think she was more pleased to smell it." We laugh wickedly together, my father and I. "I am a great disappoint to her you know, Daddy. She will never forgive me for demanding a college education." Mother had spent nearly a year setting up a perfect match between myself and young Daniel Forrester, the

son of a prominent banker in Portland. He is sure to inherit vast amounts of land and wealth when his rickety old man breathes his last. I was dragged to teas and plays and picnics and cinched into corsets and done up with the ridiculous bustle my mother refuses to give up, even though they are quite on their way out again.

Mother believes herself to be Cupid's handmaid. In reality she could not have made a more unsuitable match. Daniel Forrester, while not entirely unattractive, possesses not even the tiniest smidgeon of wit. He speaks of ledgers and stocks and bonds and the price of gold. To Mother and her insatiable lust for jewels and fashion, this is tantalizing talk. It smacks of money and power. For me, it is insufferably dull. Mr. Forrester once recounted to me his trip to Switzerland. Zurich to be exact. When asked of the countryside and the customs of the people he had little to offer. He could not even be bothered to share architectural details of the Swiss bank. He spoke of imports and exports and the shape of the European economy and the security of money stashed away in a Swiss account, but nothing more. The man lives and breathes money. For Mother this means my union with him would be most advantageous. She was aghast when I revealed to Mr. Forrester that I would not marry until I had earned a degree of my own. It seemed to me that Mr. Forrester would approve a woman who could follow him in conversation and not be baffled by ledgers and currency conversions. I had grossly overestimated him.

Mr. Forrester requires nothing more in a wife than she be easy on the eyes, a gracious hostess, and the mother of strapping young lads who would one day surely follow in his footsteps.

It had been a horrid scene that fine spring day. Gulls had soared overhead in a sky so blue it looked unreal. A soft, warm breeze had rustled the grasses on the cliff. Mother had gone early with Ruby, our maid, and set up the picnic for us. It had

349

been truly ideal, with a pretty umbrella and finely set table.

The basket had overflowed with cold meats and sweet fruits and even sweeter little fairy cakes. In my mother's mind a well-fed man would always be endeared to his wife. This, unfortunately, does not apply to my father and his wife. I suppose he loves her but I would not say he is endeared to her or cherishes her, as one imagines a man should cherish his wife, even though she makes certain his table is always suitably prepared.

Mr. Forrester had arrived five minutes early, as was his custom. Being too early made it appear that a man had nothing more important to do than sit around and wait. Being late or even right on time showed that he was not planning ahead and did not give serious thought to his business. Or yours. So that fine spring day he was five minutes early.

I was intentionally five minutes late.

And another twenty minutes unintentionally late.

George, my father's man, was supposed to drive me to the picnic but I had waved him off, insisting it was just a trifling little bike ride away. Donning a new pair of beige pantaloons that had been secretly obtained, I had straddled the bicycle Daddy had bought me and peddled away. George had called after me until I could no longer hear his protestations. He feared Mother's wrath and this was certainly an episode that might bring the fires of Hades down upon his shiny, baldhead.

It was unfortunate that George would be caught in the crossfire of my unwanted romance but it had to be done.

Everything was perfectly on schedule until I spotted Mr. McDougal's old cow ambling down the road again. Daisy was a notorious escapee and had even made it all the way to Exchange Street one time. Not wanting poor, old Daisy upsetting traffic again, I had climbed off my bike and laid it beside the road.

Kind and a bit addled in the brain, Daisy had allowed me to coax her back to her field where Mr. McDougal was already aware of her disappearance. Crossing the field with his big, loping strides, he met me halfway, thanking me profusely and inviting me back to the farm for a cold glass of Mrs. McDougal's fresh lemonade.

And maybe a piece of pie.

I had been dying of thirst.

And everyone knows Mrs. McDougal's pies are blue ribbon, secret recipe miracles.

I had wanted to accept but there was an important matter to attend to.

"Thank you so very much Mr. McDougal, that would be lovely, but I must hurry. I am already late to meet my mother and..."

My words fell away and he gently filled the blank for me, "And Mr. Forrester." A bead of sweat had rolled down his ruddy cheek, dripping from his strong jaw to water the earth below. In that moment I had felt the wetness of my own back and touched a hand to the cotton there. Even though the day was not unpleasant, the layers of corset and cotton had caused the most unladylike sweating. Mr. McDougal had smiled that wise, gentle smile of his and I wondered if it was a smile every Scots possessed. "Don't fret Miss Maria, you look verra pretty." Comforting and firm all at once, his Scottish burr lulled me. I had smiled and, without thinking of it, kissed his salty cheek.

"Thank you again, Mr. McDougal." I had turned to leave and he had called after me. "Miss Maria, I kin no other woman who could be wearing men's trousers and be dripping such as ye are and look quite so lovely. It's a right shame your mother is marrying you off to that great sot!"

I had turned to call back to him, "I doubt very much we will have to worry about that after today!"

A motor wagon, going much too fast for this narrow country lane with all its curves and bends, zoomed around the great oak. I heard Mr. McDougal shouting frantically and saw him bounding through the grasses toward me. Diving into a bramble of thorns, I was narrowly missed as the driver swerved at the last possible second. "Miss Maria!" Mr. McDougal slid down the slope toward the road, yanking me from the snarls of thorns and holding my trembling form upright as a wave of unconsciousness threatened to grip me. He shouted violently at the careless driver and excused himself for his language and then shouted some more. The driver, I saw after regaining myself, was none other than Mr. Charles Forrester. He paid no mind to Mr. McDougal's shouts but instead busied himself with trying to free his precious motor wagon from the clutches of my bicycle. Once free of the contraption he had then turned to us, and what a sight we must have been!

COMING 2012

THE VON STRASSENBERG SAGA
BOOK THREE

LIPSTICK AND BOLSHEVIKS

By

Gwenn Wright
© 2012

Thanks

To my **Father in Heaven**, who makes sense out of my stupidest mistakes and always sets me straight. To my husband, thanks for having me back and being so wonderful, I know that you are the love of my life. To my three wonderful boys, **Alex, Bruce and Collin**, thank you for sharing me with my MacBook. To my parents on Earth, **Dan and Brenda**, my heart is overwhelmed with gratitude for all you have done for us, I pray this will be a blessing in return. And yes Dad, maybe you were right about me being a writer. We'll see.

To **Abbie Leslie**, who demanded the next chapters even when they were raw and ugly and who wouldn't let me quit.

Amy Wrinkle, thank you for buying it first and being so wonderfully supportive through all these years, it's one thing to be supportive when we're all silly and in high school, it's really something else to be so encouraging when we're all grown up and forced to be realists.

To **Sarah Seigel** for arguing with me about a certain vampire love story...and getting me back into the reading of teen lit which eventually led to me writing teen lit again!

Special thanks to my big, bad brother **Dan McNeely** who actually read Filter in spite of it being an angsty teen novel, it meant more than you know.

To **Amy Joslin** for her great support in high school and now.

To **Ricky Janzen** for fixing all my technical problems and **Aaron Chastain** for allowing me to ramble about my teen love story while we were filming in the Lou and for going above and beyond to help me with editing. And to his mama, **Tynetta**, you have been such an incredible blessing.

To **Zach Ruble of Zach Ruble Productions** for saving me from my self-designed cover art. You have wicked awesome skillz. And **Jessica "Jellyka" Nerevan** of **Cuttyfruty.com** you are amazingly skilled and your fonts are stellar, I just like looking at your website because it's so cool.

To **Libbe McGlasson**, my little cousin, for saving the day. Thanks to my sisters, **Erin** and **Alden** and all my nieces and nephews. Special thanks to my nephew **Conor McNeely**. I love talking shop with you! And to my Grandparents, **Nolan and Lois**, **Bruce and Nerene** because I know you believed in me even when I was eight, scribbling stories at your coffee tables on scrap paper. You are all such a blessing to me.

Check out The von Strassenberg Saga on Goodreads!
Follow my blog at http://hereventuality.blogspot.com for updates on Book 3!
Meet other fans and join the group on Facebook at Filter: The Von Strassenberg Saga
I'm on Twitter too! @gwennwright

11843345R00189

Made in the USA
Charleston, SC
24 March 2012